LABORED RELATIONS

LABORED RELATIONS

For Tim,

Enjoy!

[signature]

Lee D. Rorman

To order additional copies of this book, contact:
Xlibris Corporation
1-888-795-4274
www.Xlibris.com
Orders@Xlibris.com
125070

Dedication

To David and Olivia. You live on in my heart.

Acknowledgments

I am grateful to those people that read through my first drafts and risked bruising my ego with their critical comments. These generous beta readers include my sons, Mike and Joe as well as my two cohorts, Jim Townsend and Paul Nitzel.

Special thanks go out to Fabio Solis and the entire publishing team who managed to allay my fears on the technical aspects of getting my book published.

I want to extend a sincere apology to the legal, law enforcement, and medical institutions for any specific mistakes in procedures and processes depicted in this work.

A shout out goes to the wonderful people of Fargo, North Dakota who make this the best small city in America.

I am mostly grateful to my wife, Marlene. Her love and support makes me the luckiest man alive.

After God had finished the rattlesnake, the toad, and the vampire, he had some awful substance left with which he made a scab. A scab is a two-legged animal with a corkscrew soul, a water brain, a combination backbone of jelly and glue.

Where others have hearts, he carries a tumor of rotten principles.

When a scab comes down the street, men turn their backs and angels weep in heaven, and the devil shuts the gates of hell to keep him out.

No man (or woman) has a right to scab so long as there is a pool of water to drown his carcass in, or a rope long enough to hang his body with.

Judas was a gentleman compared with a scab.

For betraying his master, he had character enough to hang himself. A scab has not.

Esau sold his birthright for a mess of pottage.

Judas sold his Savior for thirty pieces of silver.

Benedict Arnold sold his country for a promise of a commission in the British army.

The scab sells his birthright, country, his wife, his children and his fellow men for an unfulfilled promise from his employer.

Esau was a traitor to himself; Judas was a traitor to his God; Benedict Arnold was a traitor to his country.

—The Scab, Jack London

A Knavish speech sleeps in a foolish ear.

—Hamlet, William Shakespeare

CHAPTER 1

Clyde Gray Eagle was a cabinet maker/philosopher who lived in a log cabin slightly off the path on Toivo's paper route that had an artistic clutter about it. Not the trailer park clutter of old chairs and bald tires, but rather an unassigned collective of wood artifacts and tarp-covered power equipment. The cabin wore the husky smell of fireplace smoke, which now puffed out in an uncertain path around the roof. A long pile of crusty firewood was neatly stacked along the right side of the cabin, where nearby a long handle axe was sunk firmly in an old stump.

On Toivo's first day as a deliverer of the North Shore Roundup, he discovered that Clyde's cabin didn't have an apparent location to which he could place the newspaper. The front door looked as if it had retired from its purpose long ago. The high cedar fence prohibited a noninvasive view of an alternate entrance, but Toivo did notice that the gate was fitted with a neatly hung door with a cluster of small black bells affixed to its top.

Not sure what he should do, he tried knocking on the gate. He waited for a short spell but didn't hear any acknowledgment of his presence. This time he knocked much harder, but again without result. He looked up at the bells and decided they had a purpose that went beyond decoration. He lifted the bells gingerly and shook them. They jingled louder than he thought they were capable. He called out, "Hello."

Sure enough, he heard movement and someone approaching the gate. He stepped back with some trepidation as the door was pulled open. Standing before him was a large-framed man with jet-black hair underneath a plain black baseball cap. He immediately noticed that his hair on the back of his head was gathered into a ponytail. The man appraised the nervous young man standing before him, held his arm up in a motionless wave, and thundered, "How!" A smile opened up on the Indian's wide face as he reached his hand out for the newspaper.

Toivo was uncertain how to take in this large man, but he noticed that he didn't feel threatened by him. He had seen Indians before, but usually they were a sad fixture in town, shuffling along aimlessly with no apparent destination. Their faces wore the resignation of a history filled with persecution, stereotyping, and liquor. But not this Indian. He had a strong aura about him that told anybody who was interested that his life had a hidden purpose that would suit him fine while in return he'd stayed out of everybody's way.

The Indian stood holding the newspaper, looking with curiosity at Toivo. Toivo realized that he was the reason the Indian was standing fixed to his spot, because he discovered he was unable to turn and leave. He stood transfixed before the Indian, not sure what to make of him but knew that he needed to know. The Indian finally spoke.

"What?" Clyde asked.

"What?" Toivo returned.

"I said it first," the Indian said with a hint of a smile. "Now it's your turn."

"I . . . ah . . . ," Toivo stammered and stopped.

"Clyde Gray Eagle," the Indian said as he transferred the newspaper to his left hand and offered the other to Toivo. The Indian's hand engulfed his small Finnish hand, and he felt the strength and calluses of hard work.

"I'm Toivo, ah, Jurva," Toivo said. Clyde nodded his head patiently.

"Toivo you claim. Well, Toivo, it seems our paths have finally crossed." Clyde stepped aside and gestured inward with his arms. "Come in, tell me what you know about this world." Toivo was hesitant for sure. This was before pedophilia became a popular and well-documented perversion. But he considered that this was the last drop on his route, and his curiosity was redlining. Still, he held back. "Paths have finally crossed" skittered in the back of his mind, which countered his quest for information. Clyde was reading his thoughts.

"Have you ever built anything out of wood, Toivo?"

"No. Well, yes." Toivo had not moved and was relieved that the focus was taken off his hesitation.

"No and yes? Toivo, you are standing in front of the best woodworker in the world. Well, Two Harbors anyway." He chuckled. "So tell me about your woodworking skills."

"I, ah, once made a birdhouse in Cub Scouts before I got kicked out." Toivo looked down at his boots with a ring of snow crowning its edges.

"Yah. I would have been kicked out too if I was in it. I don't like uniforms."

He looked downward at the shivering Toivo. "You should come in and see my woodshop, or you should go home and get warm."

"I better go home." With that Toivo slowly turned and walked away. He heard the gate close behind him. He glanced back and saw the smoke trailing straight up now in the still air. The sunlight was slowly dimming as the night was checking in.

Chapter 2

Travis Tee's fascination with the idea of holding a picket sign began along a road that was under construction one smoldering August day when he was eight years old. His dad had just picked him up from school, and they were creeping slowly between bulky smoke-belching machinery and dusty sun-darkened road workers when Travis's eyes focused on a heavy-bellied man holding a sign. At the time, he wasn't aware of the man's role in this mayhem, but he knew that somehow he could make the machines and cars do what he desired with that sign. He assumed that the man was the one in charge.

His eyes stayed riveted on the sign holder as their car slowly crawled by. He made a tentative wave at the man, who winked at him. Later at home, he asked his dad why the man was holding the sign. His dad, already a six-pack into his nightly ritual, grumbled that he didn't know what the hell he was talking about.

To Travis Tee, his dad was a god. He didn't have to work because he was wounded on the job and "the damn company owed him." To Travis Tee, his dad was right up there with war heroes. He couldn't imagine how a person could go through what he did. He never knew what happened to cause his dad's disability, but it had to be bad for him to have to stay home every day.

"Why was that man holding that sign where they were fixing the road?" Travis asked.

"Jesus, what the hell are you talking about? What fucking sign?" His dad barely took his eyes off the scratchy TV picture showing a disembodied hand modeling a sparkling ring. He took another long gulp of his beer, some of which dribbled wastefully down onto his dingy T-shirt.

"Wh-when we were driving today, there was a man holding a sign and some cars stopped when he did it." His dad burped, so he continued. "They were working on the road there."

Dad was motionless in his chair. Young Travis waited, gathering up words for his next attempt. Then he noticed his dad tilt slowly to the side and stop.

"Dad?" Travis's hand reluctantly reached out toward his dad when suddenly a thunderous explosion rumbled throughout the room. Travis jumped up and screeched. Dad's shoulder silently twitched, and his body returned to his upright slouch. He wheezed out breathy chuckles.

"Fire in the hole!" Dad bellowed between his laughing and coughing fits.

A rank odor slowly filled the room, leaving Travis with the urge to table his inquiry for a more opportune time. But the desire to satisfy his need for this important piece of information kept him frozen in the stifling stink. So he waited for the atmosphere and his dad to find some equilibrium. After a time, Travis focused again on his dad.

"That man was wearing a yellow vest on him. A-and he had a big stomach—"

"Flagger." Dad's expression didn't change when he spoke.

"Flag? No, this man had, like, a stop sign. Not a fl—"

His father's eyes were now shut, and he quietly snored—gone to the world. His grip on his beer bottle was easing. Travis carefully took the bottle out of his dad's hand and placed it on the sagging table next to his chair. A flagger. That's what his father had said. Years later, he would discover that that prestigious job went to girls who wanted to get paid while working on their tans. They would never understand the power they had over the lazy river of cars and trucks wanting expedient access to their destinations. Girls didn't care about such things.

*   *   *

The next day, young Travis was determined to establish control over the cars driving on a busy road near his home. He set about finding a square piece of cardboard and a stick. He located both items in an abandoned lot about a block away. He took a ballpoint pen from a kitchen drawer filled with odd treasures only a kid would value. He spelled the words stop on one side and go on the other. He found a couple of small tacks in the same drawer and joined the cardboard to the stick. He had his "flag."

He quickly ran to the busy street and held the sign up with the "stop" side facing the street. Nobody stopped. He tried waving it back and forth as cars passed, but the drivers would only stare at him and his sign in perplexed curiosity. At one point the cardboard came loose and sailed into the street. Only two cars ran over it before he was able to come to its rescue. The sign now included a couple of dirty wheel impressions on one side and a texture of sharp road grit on the other.

Miraculously, Travis managed to retrieve the scattered tacks and knelt down on the ground to begin the task of restoring his sign. So intent upon his task was he that he didn't notice someone peering over his shoulder.

"What does it say?" The voice startled Travis, who hopped up, almost causing the other boy to fall over.

"What?"

"I can't read your sign. You should use a Magic Marker or something," the boy offered.

Travis peered down at his sign and realized that the boy was probably right. But he just gave the boy an empty look, which he took as a signal that his help was no longer needed. The boy shuffled off without another thought to the budding activist.

The following day, Travis was on the side of the street with his greatly enhanced sign. The letters on the sign were now visible for at least half a block. But the cars still didn't stop as his sign instructed them to. In fact, they didn't even slow down. They did, however, honk their horns, which gave him a warm and heady sense of recognition. Except for one car full of teenagers who chucked a beer can that struck his leg, most people smiled at him when they drove by.

Young Travis spent each of his days standing by the street with his sign. As time went by, he noticed drivers stopped noticing him by the side of the street. He guessed, and correctly so, that they were getting used to his sign and didn't care anymore. But his desire to communicate never abated. So his young mind came to the realization that he needed something different on his sign. What, he wondered.

One night as he lay in his bed while his dad snored loudly in his chair in front of the TV, it came to him. He recalled noticing while standing by the street that most of the cars were dirty. His youthful mind reasoned that it was because the drivers didn't notice their cars needed a washing. The next morning, he leaped out of bed with a renewed purpose. He found a new, or at least different, slab of cardboard and marked it with two words: Cleen Car.

Early next morning, he was at his post again and quickly noticed that the drivers were suddenly interested in his presence again. They started honking their horns at him. And as the week wore on, he noticed the passing cars were cleaner! He told them to clean their cars and they did! This achievement was more than he anticipated.

His next sign was made with his dad in mind. It commanded: No Beer. This wasn't as well received because people started yelling bad words at him when they passed by. He heard various suggestions such as "fuck off" and "eat shit, you little worm." This frightened him to the point that he was shaking in fear and left his post unmanned. He was afraid people would find out where he lived and tell his dad, and that would unleash even more trouble on him. But his dad remained in his chair drinking and farting. The world didn't end.

The street side picketing did, though. Travis knew that it's one thing to have people delight in your endeavors, but quite another to create vexation and new enemies. So Travis returned to his mundane lifestyle as an inconsequential child with a drunken dad and no friends.

As Travis grew older, his dad became sicker and angrier. Travis's vocabulary increased naturally, and when he was around thirteen years old, he began to more fully understand what angered his dad.

His dad, he knew from listening to him talk, was a hapless victim of an indifferent system. His wife, Travis's mother, had left him to raise a child alone for another man. His job left him physically damaged and unable to live a life of dignified independence.

The list of injustices foisted upon his dad was endless. A greater degree of concern for young Travis was the feeling he had that he was the greatest disappointment for his dad. Travis was nowhere near being on track for scholastic or athletic greatness. Travis believed that he was part of the world that let his dad down.

At an age when a son wants—needs—love and recognition from his father, Travis was invisible to this important person. Long simmering sorrow and regret slowly coalesced into a heavy anger. This anger calcified and became a natural, almost genetic, attribute acquired through an unholy inheritance from so many betrayed souls. The fruit borne from his developing persona found form and expression in antisocial pursuits. He grew a short-temper that led him too often into physical confrontations and the principal's office. Spray painting the side of buildings with colorful expressions in rough artistic depictions of the human form made him a frequent visitor to an idealistic juvenile officer.

In another year, Travis became an orphan when he found his dad sitting in his chair, a half-drank bottle of beer held by rigor mortis. It took more than a day to realize his dad wasn't just snoozing in front of the TV. Two clues served as confirmation of his dad's demise: one, his dad's frequent and awkward trips to the refrigerator for a replacement beer stopped and two, the white noise produced by his dad's snoring was replaced by a deafening silence.

*   *   *

His dad's equally drunk and angry brother made the funeral arrangements, complaining the whole time about his selfish brother always trying to get special attention, as if his dad deviously planned his own death to piss off his uncle. The funeral was a lonely affair presided over by a harried clergyman, who could have easily found a successful career as an auctioneer. Somewhere in the speedy intonations Travis heard the words, *loving father, commit, and good and full life*. God's spokesman barely acknowledged Travis and his uncle as he snapped his Bible shut and scurried off. The coffin sat suspended over the burial hole with no one around to lower it in.

"Hey, who the fuck is going to bury him?" Travis's uncle yelled. God's auctioneer, now quite a distance away, waved without turning around, got into his car, and drove away in a cloud of dust.

"Well, I have to go," his uncle said. "Someone will come by soon I'm sure." He glanced at the coffin then at Travis. "I'll give you a ride home. I guess you'll stay with me."

Travis nodded and gave a long look at the coffin.

"Okay." He knew he should say something to his dead dad, but all he could do was croak out a "Good-bye, Dad."

And that was that.

They got into his uncle's car and drove away. Travis didn't return to the cemetery until years later but couldn't find his dad's gravesite on that visit. For all he knew, they recycled his coffin and threw his body into the city dump. On the drive home, Travis witnessed a mob of shouting people holding bobbing signs in front of a factory. He heard indistinct shouts blaring from a bullhorn. His heart started beating in some primal excitement.

CHAPTER 3

He had long outgrown his paper route when at age sixteen Toivo became Clyde Gray Eagle's willing apprentice. Toivo would go straight to the shop every day after school, tossing his textbook-laden backpack onto the old, faded blue upholstered chair that caused the usual burst of blond sawdust to explode into the air before settling back down, some of it covering Toivo's backpack. He pulled off his stocking cap, allowing loose snow to flutter through the sawdust cloud.

"You got homework?" Clyde asked without looking up from whatever he was busy doing at the moment. Toivo couldn't completely see Clyde; but from the electric hum and scraping sound, he knew he was working at the lathe, forming wood into another one of his works of art.

"Just a little reading. I did the other stuff during study hall." Toivo long ago learned that he couldn't get away with lying to his mentor. Nor did he want to.

His respect had grown to the point that the old Indian became something more than his adopted father. His real father, along with his mother, died in an auto accident coming back from his uncle's home in Lacrosse, Wisconsin. He was taken in by his gentle grandmother, who possessed a strength honed by a lifetime of working in the logging camps as a cook for rough, hard living lumberjacks in the North Country of Minnesota. Although she was a God-fearing Lutheran, his grandmother was inured to the profane language and behavior of her customers. She had a gentle way of letting these hulking men know her boundaries and expectations. The ones that couldn't stay within those boundaries were "corrected" by the other lumberjacks.

His grandmother emigrated from Finland when she was eight years old and for the rest of her life spoke what his mother called Finglish, a cross between Finnish and English. Her Finglish leaned closer to Finnish than English. Toivo always remembered her warm smile and relaxed attitude concerning the troubles of life. But she was capable of expressing anger that came out in a machine gun flurry of pure Finnish.

After Toivo's grandmother died one summer, Clyde quickly filled out the required adoption papers and took custody of Toivo, and together they lived in the log cabin that became to Toivo both a home and a school in the art of life. He immediately learned that strength of character was a graduation requirement in this school.

His first lesson was individual thinking and responsibility. At his age, that meant doing his homework and doing it well. It also meant not letting peer pressure lead him to unsavory behavior. "Make your own decisions about your unsavory behavior," Clyde would say with a chuckle.

"Still reading about Huckleberry Finn?"

"Yeah. And I'm almost done with it," Toivo answered, knowing what would come next.

"Good. Grab a chair and get to reading then." The whole conversation took place without Clyde ever looking up from his work.

"Can't I work a little first? I was hopin' I could get the runners put on the dresser drawers tonight."

"Tell me about Huck first." This time Clyde took a quick glance at Toivo, a cigarette dangling from his mouth.

"Okay. What can I tell you?" Toivo shifted his weight from one leg to the other.

"Gimme his resume. Who is he? What's he like? Would you want him for a friend?"

"Wow. Okay. He's, ah, Tom Sawyer's friend and . . ." Toivo paused to think of what else to say.

"Aaaand . . . ," Clyde prompted with a slight smile on his face.

"Ah, well, he was a troubled kid. I mean, he got into trouble all the time. And I think he lied a lot."

"So he wasn't a good person then?" Clyde asked.

"I think he probably was a good person underneath it all. He just wasn't liked by many people because he was like, ah, trailer trash?" He said the last two words in the form of a question.

"Trailer trash . . . hmmm. Okay. And what else?"

"He liked to fuck with people." Toivo winced at his own profanity even though Clyde wasn't shy about his own use of colorful terms.

"So he might make it as a politician, eh?" Clyde tugged on the bill of his dusty cap and smiled. "Anything else? So far he doesn't sound like a hero who should have a book written about him."

Toivo felt a curious need to defend this fictional river rat. He had chosen this book to read out of a group of three choices; the others being Moby Dick, which was way too thick, and Wuthering Heights. He thought the latter book sounded too much like a girl's book or British, which was pretty much the same in Toivo's mind. Plus, he wondered if Huckleberry Finn was a Finlander. He thought having Finn as a name was an omen that he should pick that book. So he did.

At first he thought it was hard to read because of the language, which sounded almost foreign. But soon Toivo found himself moving through the novel with relative ease. He began identifying with both Huck and slave Jim because they couldn't fit into the larger society, nor could they understand why they should. In time, Toivo came to realize how much the book influenced how he behaved in a world fraught with rules and rigid mores.

"Earth to Toivo. Come in, Toivo," Clyde said, making scratchy radio noises with his mouth.

"Huh? What?"

"I lost you there for a second. You were ejumacating me about Huckleberry Finn."

"I think Huckleberry was true to himself but didn't like the world he lived in," Toivo said with some pride mixed with relief that he could make even a little bit of analysis.

"Do tell," Clyde replied. "Crap!" Clyde yelled while holding his thumb. Toivo hopped up out of the chair and was quickly standing next to Clyde with a look of genuine concern.

"What's wrong?" Toivo asked.

"Ah shoot, I just cut myself with this goddamn chisel," Clyde said, sucking on his thumb. Grab me a Band-Aid. Stat."

Toivo found the white metal box and popped the clips opening the kit. He fished out a large Band-Aid and started removing the paper wrapping as he walked back toward Clyde.

"Here, let me put it on your thumb."

"Thanks, Doc. Will I live?" Clyde said as he regained his composure.

"Yeah. I think you'll pull through today." Toivo hoped this episode put an end to the seminar on Huckleberry Finn.

"Anyway, you were saying something about Huck not liking the world he lived in. Go on. Explain," Clyde said as he examined his bandaged thumb.

"Well, his dad was a drunk and Huckleberry wasn't close to him at all. I guess you could say that he was all alone in the world. I think Tom Sawyer admired him because of this."

Clyde didn't respond as he returned to his work, so Toivo continued talking.

"Tom Sawyer actually lived in a nice house with people that took care of him. Tom had to go to school. Huck did too, but he always skipped out. He just got to do what he wanted. Hey, do you want me to finish that?" Toivo said, indicating the unfinished stretch of wood fixed in the lathe.

Clyde looked at Toivo. "What?"

"The table leg. You want me to finish it?" Toivo said.

"Nah. Let's call it a day. Besides, you need to keep reading. I want to hear more about this Huckleberry guy." He put his arm around Toivo, and together they walked out of the shop. Clyde flipped the light switch by the door, filling the shop with darkness. The two walked toward the cabin wordless in the cool winter night; the stars glittered in the night sky, the snow crunching under their boots.

CHAPTER 4

The yellow mass of strikers undulated like a field of dandelions, with picket signs poking out in weed-like intervals. The faces tilted upward, with gaped mouths chanting a mantra of protest against some unspecified joint grievance. Facing the protesters was Travis Tee, a large behemoth of a man with a huge shaved skull. His eyes were dark slits that complemented his defiant scowl. His massive arms folded across his chest as he stood planted with legs straddled solidly on the platform. In the next moment, his clenched fists shot out and upward over his hunched shoulders. The crowd went crazy. Soon he heard a new chant. "Travis Tee, Travis Tee, Travis Tee."

Travis!

Travis Tee jumped out of his reverie as if someone had jabbed him with a hot barbeque fork. "Egregious!" he yelped. His wife stood before him, with her hands resting on her wide hips. Her huge watermelon breasts languished braless atop her generous belly. All this was thankfully covered with a ratty T-shirt that honored the past king of NASCAR: Dale Earnhardt. Cigarette smoke puffed out from between her yellowed teeth.

"Did you even hear what I said?"

"Yeah, I heard," he said, avoiding her accusatory glare.

"What did I say?" she challenged. She fell into a nearby chair, causing clouds of stuffing to shoot out. "Well? What did I say?" she repeated.

Travis Tee glared defiantly at her for what seemed an eternity when his cell phone came alive with a scratchy version of "Take This Job and Shove It." Saved by the bell—or song in this case. "Yeah," he growled into the mouthpiece.

His wife let out with an audible oof as she hoisted herself out of the chair and stomped into the small kitchen area, causing the mobile home to issue plaintive creaks. The home they lived in was a 1968 Rollo Home that probably didn't provide decent shelter when it was first built. It was even much less now. It offered very little warmth against the harsh North Dakota winters.

If you dropped a marble on the kitchen linoleum, it would immediately seek the east wall. She had long ago gotten used to the old moldy odor that existed full-time within the droopy paneled walls. She watched Travis Tee hold the phone while listening to what would probably be another pissed off employee from AgMotiv Manufacturing. She had long ago become inured to the way the company wrecked horrors upon its workers.

In the beginning, Travis Tee represented an answer to the pain the AgMotiv workers suffered at the hands of its power-hungry managers. Travis Tee was the hero that stood for industrial justice against the tyrannical oppressors. This was what excited Barbara when she first heard him talking at a table next to her at the Broken Saddle Saloon several years ago. He was so passionate about his cause, of which at the time she had no knowledge. She was a hairdresser but had suffered a career-ending allergy to all the sprays and chemicals used to improve her clientele's beauty. This allergy mysteriously turned into a raging case of fibromyalgia that left her unable to hold down a full-time job. Except for occasional visits to the Broken Saddle, her world was never far from her bed, where she could seek respite from a world requiring responsible effort. So this passionate man gave her some vicarious life that she was otherwise denied. And she appealed to his need to save the hapless victims of heartless powers. They quickly married in the cold courthouse, he wearing his yellow union jacket, she wearing her black satin Dale Earnhardt jacket.

But today she was not happy with Travis Tee. He had been acting lost—distant—as if she didn't exist in this world. She understood from the start that he was dedicated to his role of business agent to the United General Laborers International union. This required constant service to the 1,100 employees that belonged to the UGLI union at AgMotiv Manufacturing. Some of this service included random phone calls coming at all hours of the day and night. Today was no different, but there was something else going on to which she wasn't privy. His conversations were unusually abrasive and laced with a high content of profanity. As if on cue, Travis Tee starts.

"You tell them fuckers that you have the right to go into that area and ask whatever fucking questions to whom-fucking-ever you want!" She could see the veins appear in throbbing cords along the sides of his head. His free fist was clenched white on the table.

"Egregious!"

*   *   *

About one year ago, the doctor diagnosed Travis Tee as having a case of low grade Tourette syndrome that caused him to blurt out the word egregious when he felt stress. It was first discovered by an oral surgeon during an operation to extract two wisdom teeth when Travis Tee yelled what came out sounding to the surgeon like "eeee-jesus." It startled the surgeon and dental assistant, who thought they had somehow caused him pain. The surgeon quickly increased his dose of anesthetics and hurried on with their work. Soon they were finished, and moments later Travis's eyes blinked open.

"Egregious," groaned Travis Tee.

"Excuse me?" asked the doctor as he wrote on a white clipboard.

"What?" asked Travis Tee.

"You said 'egregious'?" the doctor clarified.

"What's egregious?" Travis mumbled, trying to clear his head. "Am I done?"

"Yes, we're all done and it went well," the doctor responded. "How are we feeling?"

*   *   *

"Fuck!" He slapped the phone shut and threw it against the far wall.

Travis Tee felt himself under special pressure these days. The management of AgMotiv Manufacturing seemed to be intent on driving him crazy with all the work rules they were trying to enforce. It wasn't that management didn't have the right; it's that many of the rules until recently were loosely enforced. Now day by day, another posting went up on the bulletin board saying they would be enforcing parking rules, break times, how long a union steward can talk to employees and on and on.

He was being pressured to act on this "management harassment" against UGLI's officers, but he had no strategy, no ammunition to fire at AgMotiv. He tried threats to go to the National Labor Relations Board or file endless grievances. He's hollered at them, glared at them, and mustered his stewards to make any and all complaints to the supervisors. Yet they came—rules and more rules. The rank and file were beginning to complain to him and ask why he wasn't doing something about it.

Then the rumors started circulating that the union membership would vote him out and crush his dreams of being a renowned labor hero like Samuel Gompers. Or John L. Lewis. He wondered if Samuel Gompers had to deal with unhappy followers back in the early days in union history. How did big John L. Lewis handle dissention among the ranks? He had heard of how he punched unconscious one such detractor. Maybe he should throw down on a few members.

He overheard people saying things like "he's getting soft" or "he's in management's pocket." They could never understand how tough it was to deal with these bastards. They could not understand that management held all the cards.

*　　*　　*

Mrs. Tee was only mildly concerned about her husband's behavior of late. He seemed a bit edgier than usual. He certainly wasn't sleeping much, and it showed in his puffy eyes and his fits of temper. Although he would hold her hostage while he went on long endless tirades on the evils of corporations and the plight of the working class, he was guarded about the specifics of his union business. She learned long ago that she was not welcome into this part of her husband's life. More importantly, she was finding herself less interested. His battles never ended and varied not a bit. So she returned her attention to the TV and Oprah droning on about her latest book discovery.

"We got nothin' to eat," Travis Tee announced. "Did you go shopping or what?"

"What." Her eyes stayed glued to the set.

Travis glared at her but knew she was immune to his power to demand make-whole resolutions. He did notice, though, that she was starting to act more like those heartless assholes at AgMotiv. Or they were becoming more like her. More and more they seemed to barely respond to his fits and demonstrations of outrage. Yesterday was a stark example of the change he felt in the relations, if you wanted to call it that, between the company and the union.

He had stormed into Joe King's office with as much fire as he could ignite in his eyes. King was at his computer, tapping away at the keyboard.

"You got a big problem out there!" Travis Tee barked while jerking his thumb toward the direction of the factory side of the building. "I got a lot of employees pissed—"

"Just a second. I have to finish this," King interrupted in the distant voice. His thoughts were far away from Travis Tee and his report of severe outrage. This made Travis's blood pressure break the thermometer at the top end.

"Stop what you are doing and listen, goddamn it!"

"Just . . . one . . . more . . . second. There. Got it." King tapped the keys in cadence with his words then swiveled in his chair to face Travis Tee, who was now glowing crimson and moments away from a possible homicide. "What can I do for you today?" A large open smile shone splendidly on King's face. It said he was the ultimate manifestation of customer service. Travis Tee paused so pissed at King's pretentiousness that he wanted so much to knock his teeth into a pile of powder. How dare he treat him, the shop business agent, as if he was some lowly employee asking about his dental coverage? He was the top union guy in this building! He demanded respect and an instant audience with whomever and whenever he so desired.

"Yes. You wanted something? Maybe a cappuccino with fresh biscotti, yes?"

"Cut the crap. You've got a riot situation developing out there."

"Damn. A riot, you say? Well, it's almost lunchtime so I'm sure it will go away," King reassured.

"Don't give me your wisecracks! Your asshole supervisors are taking union stuff down off the walls. We have a right to have our union stuff displayed in the plant. I am going to file a board charge on this company." Travis Tee crossed his meaty arms in defiance and stared down at Joe King. Suddenly, the phone on King's desk rang and he picked up the receiver.

"This is Joe." King paused as he listened, looking up at Travis Tee, who was clearly angry at the interruption. "Oh, nothing much. How's it going with you? Are you going to the game Saturday?"

"Hey!" Travis Tee's face was now purple.

Joe King continued his phone conversation. "Nothing. Someone's talking outside my office. What are you doing for lunch?"

"Fuck!" Travis Tee spun around and walked out of King's office and headed straight for the Director of Human Resources office.

The current HR director is a recent graduate of USC Marshall School of Business and a product of AgMotiv's corporate push to expand its diversity initiatives. Abi Deng, one of the lost boys of Sudan, was rescued from his war-scarred country and resettled in California. His education was paid for by a Catholic foundation in settlement of a lawsuit he brought claiming discrimination based on race and national origin. This would become one of the many lawsuits filed by Deng against the multitude of wrongs inflicted on him by this godless country.

Unfortunately for Travis Tee, Deng considered the union to be a spawn of Satan and a purveyor of despicable ideologies that left God outside in the cold.

Travis walked into Deng's office and sat down in one of the chairs along the inside of the room. Deng glared malevolently at Travis Tee and spoke.

"Why you walk into my office without gaining permission?" Deng spoke in a deep voice with words formed as if by a tongue too big to fit properly in his mouth.

"I have a right to walk into your office." Travis and Deng glared at each other. "You have a problem. Actually, you have two problems. You need to collar that asshole across the hall, one. And two, you need to tell me why supervisors are violating our union's rights."

"You talk to Joe. I am busy now," Deng said.

Travis Tee glared at Deng, who glared back.

"Fuck!" Travis barked as he got up and stormed out of the office.

CHAPTER 5

AgMotiv LLC was Travis Tee's third attempt at a full-time job. His first job had him stocking grocery shelves for a mom-and-pop convenience store in a nearby town. The mom was a chain-smoking hag of a woman who fretted about money all the time. The pop was a quiet mousy man who petered around straightening cans on the shelf and busying himself in the small storage area in the back of the store. Keeping the conversation going in the store was a mouthy Cockatiel named Rosie with a fairly good-sized vocabulary.

Travis was paid minimum wage but had to pay out of his pocket for anything he broke. That too often included items that he didn't break.

One day, he arrived at work to find mom very angry at him. She pointed at the door with broken glass lying about it. "That's going to cost you, buster!"

"Five bucks! Come again," Rosie said followed by a whistle.

Travis looked at the glass, at mom, and back to the glass. His choler was redlining when he finally shouted, "I didn't do that!" His upper lip twitched, and his hands shook as they sought a suitable place to perch.

"You did, and you will pay for it out of your check!" mom sternly stated. She turned and walked away, leaving Travis in a boiling mood.

"Fuck you!" Travis turned and slammed out the door, causing some leftover glass to tinkle onto the floor. Rosie told him to come again.

Later that evening, he spread the contents of mom's jewelry box on top of his bed sheets. There were diamond earrings and necklaces along with jewelry containing a virtual rainbow of variegated trinkets. He would later learn that it was filled with rubies, emeralds, opal, onyx, and a myriad of other valuable gems.

Unloading this trove proved to be a risky venture, for which Travis discovered too late required knowledge and connections he didn't have. Travis was not adept at formulating plans, for he walked right into a local jewelry store and tried to sell the booty outright. The jeweler had been in business at this location for over thirty years and possessed an amazing memory of his sales over that time. He instantly recognized the jewelry as belonging to Agnes Reagan who, along with her husband Beryl, owned Reagan's Kwik Stop convenience store.

After a quick and discreet call to the police, Travis Tee was taken in custody and charged with possession of stolen property. These charges were expanded to breaking and entry and burglary after Agnes filled in the gaps. Travis Tee enjoyed a speedy trial and received five years, which was bargained down to one year in juvenile detention and four years on supervised probation.

$$*\quad*\quad*$$

Travis Tee began his second job on a road construction crew two days after his eighteenth birthday. He considered this a real job because he received medical insurance and paid holidays. The work was physically taxing, but he had grown into a large, well-muscled frame that provided him a reliable and durable tendency toward effortless endurance.

Gradually over a period of time, he discovered that he was working harder than the others in the crew and they were getting the same amount of pay as he. He also started to realize that the other guys in the crew were ignoring him. Sometimes they would swear at him for no reason. One worker the other guys called Snake sat down next to him during a lunch break. Snake told him that he might be making the others look bad by working too hard. He told Travis that he should think about taking it easy because he wouldn't want to make the others pissed at him. He winked, got up, and walked back to where the others were sitting.

Travis Tee discovered that it didn't take much effort to wind down to the prevailing level of productivity resulting in some respect, if not at least tolerance, from his fellow crew members. During a smoke break on a hot summer day, the others in the crew were talking about the possibility of forming a union. He asked about the unions and what that meant for them. He found out that there was a law called the Davis-Bacon Act that made sure people working on federal projects like them were paid the prevailing wage and benefits in the area. He asked that if they were being paid the prevailing wage, why would they need to join a union?

"Because," said Bag (Travis guessed that wasn't his real name but never asked about it), "if we had a union, we wouldn't haf to take any shit offa them. That's one for instance. Another is that we can maybe get paid even if we can't work 'cuz of rain." Bag's eyes widened, and he nodded his head looking at Travis, as if he had just revealed the whereabouts of the Holy Grail. He took a swig of his Mountain Dew, dribbling a good share of it on his dusty T-shirt.

"There are many reasons," added Snake, who glanced at Bag, wondering if he took after his mother or father. "Another is that we can get a pension." The others murmured a weak agreement. Most of them were young, and the thought of retirement was as alien to them as cowboy boots made out of dill pickles.

"And . . . and . . . if we don't like something, we can give 'em a grievance," said Dink (again, not something Travis T was willing to inquire about.) "A friend of mine who's in a union once tol' me that a supervisor was giving him shit and telling him to work harder, and he gave him a grievance."

Everybody stared at Dink, who appeared to be done talking and now found himself locked in mortal combat with a bee that chose him to strafe. Dink frantically slapped at the air around him with both hands. Soon it zigzagged away.

"Then what?" asked Bag.

"Then what what?" inquired Dink, who maintained combat readiness in the event of a second bee sortie.

Bag looked around at the others, who shrugged their shoulders.

"He gave him a grievance and then what happin?"

"I donno. He just gave him a grievance." Dink looked anxious for the conversation to take another route. That help came from Snake.

"The main thing is we can get some respect. The company will have to treat us fair and listen to us," Snake said as he twisted the cap back onto his thermos. "Let's go. Here comes the warden."

The rest of that day, Travis Tee noodled the union idea through his head. He knew a little about them from his dad. His dad never said anything about respect or pensions. He just remembered they helped him so he didn't ever have to work and he still got paid. He also remembered that sometimes the union people stood in front of the business with signs and shouted things. He liked that part for sure.

Travis was fired from the construction job five weeks later when he gave the finger to his foreman after being told to quit talking and get to work. The last thing Travis Tee remembered before walking to his car was Dink shouting to him that if they had a union he could give them a grievance.

*   *   *

He enjoyed his vacation paid for by the state unemployment service. It wasn't much, but it was free money, and he wondered why more people didn't take advantage of it. But he discovered that all wells run dry at some point and his pump was burping air.

He heard from one of his drinking buddies that one of the factories in Fargo was looking for workers; so the next morning he rose from his bed, put on his cleanest work clothes, and drove to AgMotiv Manufacturing. He never imagined that he would get that job with him being fired from the last job but, to his surprise, he did. He was supposed to start the next Monday, so he spent the next few nights celebrating at the Broken Saddle Bar.

CHAPTER 6

Travis Tee was almost late for his first day; and his head was heavy, hurting, and spinning when he arrived at his new job. He spent the first day trying to make it through the videos and explanations during the orientation. Sometimes he would nod off but quickly snap awake with the slightest sound. There were different speakers and videos depending on the subject they wanted to teach.

He stared blankly as the safety man gave his talk. He barely recalled the things he said; but he remembered something about safety equipment, chemicals, locking and tagging something, and lifting shit safely. The one thing he remembered for sure was something called nip points. He laughed out loud during the orientation. The other people just looked at him when he did that. He remembered thinking they were idiots if they didn't think that was funny.

More speakers came and went as he fought his tiredness. He was starting to doze off when he heard one of the speakers start talking about the union. He popped up in his chair, both ears set on record.

He noticed that the speaker was a short, thinly built man sporting a blond mullet hairstyle. He started talking about how the union would watch over them and make sure the company didn't screw them out of anything. He explained that if they joined the union, they would become a part of a large group of people that could push for better pay and benefits. He said that unions were about solidarity. He showed the group his hand, with all the fingers splayed apart. He said that a hand like this couldn't do much good in a fight. Then he wrapped his fingers into a tight fist and looked around the table at each person one at a time in what movie people might call a dramatic pause.

"But together," he intoned, "they become one strong fist." Dramatic pause. "And with this fist, we can fight for our rights! We can fight for respect!" Then he slammed his fist hard on the tabletop. Travis noticed he flinched when he did that and rubbed his hand the rest of the time he was there.

"So," he continued, "today I would like you to make the commitment of your life and sign this card." He passed blue cards around the table, which the new employees picked up with some wariness except for Travis, who quickly filled his out and passed it back to the union representative.

"Do we have to decide today?" asked one person who was wearing a Minnesota Twins cap.

"Why wouldn't you want to join today? Are you thinking you don't need the union?" the representative challenged as he glared at the young man as if he had just called his mother a whore. "Who's going to help you if you don't join?"

"I'll still get paid the same if I don't, won't I?" Minnesota asked and added, "What more help would I need?"

The representative stared at the man with his mouth gaped, as if in petrified horror. Finally, he found his voice again.

"What help?" the representative asked, mimicking Minnesota's voice. "You think you'll be able to learn your job alone? If you don't join the union, it's a safe bet you will be alone."

Travis wondered why Minnesota was hesitant. He could see the others were listening to the argument intently. Mostly, he noticed they weren't filling out the blue card. He couldn't understand why anybody wouldn't want to join a union. It just didn't add up.

The meeting with the union representative ended with two more people filling out the card, but the rest of them, seven in all, holding off. The representative gave the hold-outs a final glare then walked out grumbling under his breath.

Travis applied his lessons learned in his construction job and worked at a minimum pace. He was quickly embraced by the union faithful, which encouraged him to attend union meetings and get involved. Travis Tee didn't need to be asked twice. It didn't take him long to get appointed as a shop steward, which he took as great compliment. Later he was to discover that it was hard to recruit stewards due in large part to the rampant apathy among the union members. It didn't matter to Travis; he knew he would go on to bigger and better things in the union.

CHAPTER 7

Most shop workers at the AgMotiv Company took their lunch breaks at one of the numerous islands of fixed tables throughout the plant. One could choose to stay at their workstation if they wanted solitude, or the cafeteria if they wanted the hubbub of activity. Anita Kloo was one of the UGLI shop stewards who opted for lunch in the busy cafeteria.

She was a very large hipped woman who had to squeeze through the tables to get to her favorite spot, which she shared with two famously lesbian machinists. She prided herself that she represented the fifty or so women who worked in the plant. UGLI steward Anita didn't like men at all. That there had to be men in the union was a heavy cross to bear for her. Her opinions of men were a constant loud commentary that carried throughout the cafeteria. The men quickly trained themselves to ignore her orations like they would ignore a barking dog.

UGLI steward Anita saw any action that went against the wishes of a female worker as discrimination based on sex. If a female lost a bid for a day position, it wasn't because she had less seniority; it had to be because a male-dominated system rewarded its own kind. If a female worker was reprimanded for standing around talking too much, she knew many cases when men were doing the same but not confronted by their male supervisor. If a supervisor watched as a female worker performed her job for even a couple of minutes, it was because he was ogling her. It didn't matter to her if the woman was homely; men are pigs and needed to be dealt with in the sternest way possible.

Any man, woman, beast, fish, or reptile coiled away when making eye contact with UGLI steward Anita Kloo. Her perma-pissed off face was a perfect creation designed to express dedicated abhorrence to everything, everyone, and anything else.

This morning in the company cafeteria, she was pushing her way through the tables toward hers when her expansive hips swept a surprised welder's lunch tray onto the floor in a loud clatter. He bent over to recover the debris when his head bumped into her buttocks. She wheeled around and screamed, "Don't you touch me, you horny pig!" The welder's eyes shot wide open, and he looked around nervously.

"I-I didn't mean . . ."

"I-I-I, you know what you did. You are in big trouble now, pervert!" UGLI steward Anita stood over the shaking welder with her lumpy arms resting on her hips. The two lesbians glared at the welder. Everybody else in the cafeteria watched out of the corner of their eyes with interest, some giggling at the poor schmuck while thanking the Almighty Creator that they weren't actors in this drama.

"I'm sorry. I didn't . . ."

"Don't sorry me, you horn hog. I'm telling HR that you sexually assaulted me." With that she pivoted around and trudged on to her table.

The welder sat frozen to his chair. HR, he thought. He, along with everybody else, feared HR. Nothing good ever came out of that office. Ever since he started working at AgMotiv, he had heard horror stories of the evil Joe King in HR. He had seen him walking through the shop a couple of times. He didn't look like a threatening person, but he never tested that impression. He knew that today he would be called into the office and fired for touching that girl. He was toast.

After break, he shuffled back to his work area and started shoving his personal gear into an olive green duffle bag. Zack Jenson, his supervisor, strolled by and asked him why he wasn't welding. By now, the welder was angry that his employment at AgMotiv was history and told the supervisor that this was bullshit. He shouldered the duffle bag and headed toward the door. Jenson took off after him while wondering what came over this otherwise peaceful employee. He called out to him.

"Dave! What the hell's goin' on with you?" Jenson was one of the few people who actually knew his name. Dave Foster was a dream employee who did his work fast, never had to have his welds reworked, and never caused trouble. Unlike many of the other employees, he didn't take part in the chatty groups that constantly needed to be reminded to get back to work. Although Foster tended to keep to himself, he took his break in the cafeteria because he found it actually provided greater solitude among people.

His coworkers, though, thought him to be aloof and unfriendly. It didn't help that he was an excellent worker that set the bar a bit high for others in his department. Worst of all, most of his cohorts hated the fact that he didn't join the union. AgMotiv was an open shop in a right-to-work state, which meant that he and a number of other employees didn't join the union when they hired on.

For the most part, he was left alone. But occasionally, he would fall victim to some form of harassment due to his nonunion status. Mostly, the pranks were in the form of chalk-written comments such as "scab" or "suck ass" left on the part he was welding. Another time his work gloves were filled with black grease. In time, the other employees didn't get the response they hoped for and lost interest in him.

"Dave! Wait up!" Foster stopped and turned toward the quickly advancing Jenson. Soon Jenson was standing in front of Foster, who was looking down at his own work boots. "What's going on, man? Why are you leaving?"

"I'm going to get fired." Foster looked up, and Jenson noticed his eyes were moist.

"Who's going to fire you? Why?"

"That girl in the cafeteria said I touched her, and she was going to report me to HR."

"You touched a girl? Who?"

"I didn't mean to touch her. I was leaning over to pick something off the floor and my head bumped her."

"So she said she was going to report you for that? Sounds like it was an accident. Who is the girl?" Jenson already had an idea who in his head but waited for his answer.

"I think her name is Anita. She's with the union."

Bingo, thought Jenson. Anita Kloo. Professional victim. Ball buster extraordinaire. Her story was one for the books. She was a homely woman with a homelier attitude.

"Hey, don't take her too serious. She's always accusing someone of something. Forget it. Come back to work."

Foster stood, considering what Jenson was telling him. He seemed undecided. "What about HR? Aren't they going to get me in trouble?"

Jenson laughed. "No. They know about her too." Jenson could tell Foster wasn't convinced. "Tell you what, go back to work and I'll talk to HR. I'm sure it'll be okay."

"Okay. Thanks." Foster walked back to his welding bay.

If Dave Foster was a supervisor's dream worker, Anita Kloo was a supervisor's worst nightmare. She lived every moment of her life in prickly anger, ready to pounce on anybody she thought disparaged her. She found a cozy shelter within the union and was amply protected by the law of the land, which prevented her from discrimination based on her sex.

Jenson watched Foster as he reoriented himself to his area for a minute then walked off to complete his tour of his assigned area of responsibility. Ten minutes later, he headed in the direction of the Human Resources department.

*   *   *

Jenson entered the office area of AgMotiv and felt the instant soothing effect of relative silence. The production floor was a very noisy environment filled with the roar of forklifts, the humming of the air exchange system, the electric sizzling of the welders, and the banging of the shears and punch presses. In the office area, the only noises were the muted conversations from unseen offices and the occasional chirping of a telephone.

The offices of Human Resources were a short walk down the narrow hallways covered with functional beige linoleum that showed black scuff marks that gave evidence of its past use by many production employees since its last cleaning. The walls were painted a no-nonsense gray with a scattering of framed posters of the various models of manure spreaders manufactured in the plant.

He tapped his knuckles on the door frame leading into Joe King's office. King's head popped up from his desk, which was completely covered with paper, the labor agreement spread open and teetering near the edge nearest him.

"Yo, Zack. What up?" Joe King pulled his reading glasses off and rubbed the bridge of his nose.

"It's all cool, homey," Zack said, getting his groove on. King chuckled in appreciation. He liked Zack Jenson's sense of humor and general positive attitude. He got along well with his workers—always a challenge in any workplace composed of tired, hardworking employees. And then you add a union into the mix. But Zack had that laid-back approach to dealing with people that worked well for him.

"What's happening?" Joe King said, putting on his work face.

"Anita Kloo is happening." Zack saw Joe's eyes roll upward.

"She almost caused one of our best workers to walk out," Zack said as he seated himself into the chair across from Joe. "She accused him of accosting her in the lunchroom."

"No shit?" Joe smiled.

"No shit, for sure." Zack smiled back. "Anyway, you can expect a visit from her soon to file her harassment complaint du jour."

"So what happened?" Joe leaned back in his chair and stretched his arm and placed them behind his head. Zack told him what Foster had reported to him. Joe closed his eyes and slowly shook his head in disbelief. "Poor Anita. It must be tough being the Goddess of Beauty. Men just can't keep their hands off her." Both men grinned as they enjoyed their individual mental caricatures of Anita in that role.

They spent the next ten or so minutes catching up on other news before Zack rose to leave.

"Well, I better get back to the floor. Some of us have to work, you know," he said with a wink.

"Yeah. You wore me out and made me miss my afternoon nap. Anyway, have Foster come up and visit me after the afternoon break."

"Roger that."

CHAPTER 8

Jill Hurt was leaning with her arms folded against the doorframe of Joe King's office. Jill had recently attended an environmental hygiene seminar in Atlanta as part of her role as the Safety and Health Officer at AgMotiv. As is usually the case when talking to Joe, the conversation quickly deteriorated to silliness. Just now he had asked Jill with a serious expression on his face if she had heard of the new cure for tapeworms. She responded that she didn't know if there were many cases of that in the U.S. to worry about.

"Oh," he said. He looked at her with a puzzled look. She looked at her watch and decided she had a few minutes to spare.

"Okay, so what's the new cure for tapeworms?" She noticed Joe's eyes lit up ever so subtly.

"Never mind. It's like you said. There aren't that many cases to worry about anymore." He looked away with a look of wonderment. "But I wonder why they would report it in the *Wall Street Journal* if it wasn't important."

Jill was still doubtful but glanced again at her watch and said, "Go ahead. Tell me."

"Well, if you insist." He paused for a short bit.

"Yes?"

"Oh, okay. Well, I guess—and this sort of sounds weird . . ."

"Do tell," she said with a smirk on her face.

"This cure apparently requires six boiled eggs, two cookies, and two bricks."

"According to the Wall Street Journal?" she queried.

"Yes. The Wall Street Journal. They are known for being a credible source of information."

"Yes, I'm sure." She glanced at her watch again.

"Is that a new watch you're wearing?"

"Would you get on with the tapeworm cure? I have a meeting in ten minutes," she blurted. She liked Joe, but sometimes he could wear on your nerves. This was one of those times. She thought it would be best to just cut him off and go to the meeting; but she had to hear the end of the story, as pointless as it probably was.

"Oh, yeah. Well, it's a three-day process, you see. On the first day you take two boiled eggs and carefully place them into the butt of the person suffering from tapeworm."

"Ew, Joe! For god's sake!" Jill's face scrunched up as she covered her mouth with her free hand.

"Yeah, you're right. That's what I thought too. But really, never mind. It sounds ridiculous to me too. You better go to your meeting." Joe was fishing and the fish were biting. He turned back to his computer and started checking his e-mails. He noticed out of the corner of his eye that she was still standing at his door. He looked back at her in mock surprise. "What?"

"You are such a dork. Just finish the story. Please?"

"Are you sure? I mean, I don't want to offend you." Joe's face showed sincere concern. But Joe had an uncanny ability to do this when he wasn't.

"Yes. Just finish. Damn!"

"Whoa, okay okay. So anyway, where was I, oh yeah, so you put those two boiled eggs up the . . . you know." He paused in fake embarrassment then continued. "Then you place one cookie in there too. Then the next day, you do the same, you put two boiled—"

"Yes, yes, the same, go on." Jill was getting flush with frustration and knew she should just walk away.

"Okay then on the third day, you just put the two boiled eggs up in there. At this point you pick up the two bricks and when the tapeworm comes out and asks, 'Where's my cookie?' you crush the bugger between the bricks." Joe crossed his arms and gazed seriously at Jill, who stood stock still with her eyes wide.

Suddenly, her face lit up and she let out a laugh and shook her head. "Joe, you are too much." She was still laughing when she turned to go to her meeting. As labor relations types go, Jill thought Joe was laid-back and was always good for a laugh. It was hard to believe that someone that had to handle the ridiculous complaints from some of the union members could keep a sense of humor. But, amazingly, he did.

Joe had returned to his e-mail with a slight smile on his face when he felt the presence of someone at his door again. He turned back with his smile, which quickly disintegrated when he noticed that Anita Kloo was glaring at him. A visit from Anita was never a good thing. She always suffered problems that defied any swift or satisfactory resolution. Normally, her complaints related to some slight against her that rose to a high degree of legal tort. Joe's day officially became shot to hell.

"Anita! How are you?" He hoped and prayed she only wanted to report that the rack with the vacation forms was empty. Body language being what it is, hers was screaming bloody murder. Although she only stood about five foot nine, her width and horse-long face demanded immediate fear from anyone who dared tread in her vicinity. Her eyes appeared evil due in part to her penciled in eyebrows that angled upward toward her temples. Up close, you could see her real eyebrows that ran horizontal to her eyes so that she appeared to have two tipped-over v's on her forehead. Her mouth displayed sharp rodent-like teeth that were always apparent and ready to gnarl any unwary—and sometimes very wary—prey. Joe hoped he wasn't the prey today. She growled.

"I've been sexually harassed and want to know what you are going to do about it!"

"What happened?" Long day, Joe thought to himself.

"That new punk grabbed my ass in the lunchroom today," she proclaimed.

Joe thought of boiled eggs and felt himself turn pale. He was convinced God was dispensing appropriate punishment for his disgusting joke.

"Who . . . grabbed you?"

"The idiot Foster! You've got a big problem with that pervert." She folded her pillowy arms across her mismatched breasts.

"Please. Have a seat and tell me what happened. When did this incident occur?" Joe pulled a yellow legal pad toward him and clicked open his Parker pen. She sat down in a chair across from his desk and slid it back a bit.

"This incident occurred during lunch in the cafeteria." UGLI steward Kloo emphasized incident as if Joe was unfairly downplaying the crime committed on her person. "He grabbed my ass," she repeated.

"Tell me how it happened."

"He grabbed my ass!" she shouted, causing Joe to jerk back as if he had been slapped. "What more do you need to know? What? Do you think you can get off on the details or something? You're just as sick as he is." She got up to leave. Joe tried to calm her down.

"I just need to know the whole story. What were you doing when he . . . touched you? How did he touch you? Were you both sitting at the same table? Those kinds of things."

"What was I doing? Are you saying it was my fault?" Kloo's eyes pulled into tiny slits under both sets of her eyebrows. She flopped back down into the chair.

"No. Please. I only need to be able to talk to . . . Foster, is that who you said? And to know how to confront him on this information. Now just walk me through what happened." Joe's patience settled in, giving him a sense of control over himself.

Joe's calmness was contagious because Anita also found herself easing down.

"I was walking to my table to eat lunch. When I went by Foster's table, he touched my butt."

"You said he touched you," Joe said as he made notes on his pad. "Earlier you said he grabbed you. I need to better understand exactly how he touched you. Did he grab"—Joe mimed a half-clenched hand—"like this? Or did he touch?" Joe mimed a flat tapping hand.

"I didn't see what he did. He grabbed me when my back was turned," she answered. She seemed to be losing interest and started acting fidgety.

"Okay. You didn't see him, but, again, you say he grabbed you. Do you get what I'm asking?" Joe was tightroping. In reality, he wasn't sure if it was mechanically possible for someone to actually get enough purchase on her wide backside that can be called a handful. Nor did it seem possible that anybody, including someone with diminished mental capacity, would even admit that as a goal of theirs.

"He grabbed me, he touched me. What difference does it make? He assaulted me sexually and I want it to stop!"

"So you were walking by his table and after you got by him, he . . . touched you. Did anybody see this?"

"I'm sure everybody did. It's so embarrassing to get fondled in public." She pulled her arms tightly over her chest in a dramatic gesture of defense.

"Can you give me some names of people who might have seen this happen?" Joe inquired with marked patience. Control.

"Yeah, there was Marsha and Sharon. They definitely saw the whole thing."

"Marsha Sorenson?"

"Yeah."

"And Sharon Barry?"

"Yeah, they both saw."

"Can you tell me the names of anybody else?" He was sure that the two AgMotiv bull dykes would support any efforts to condemn a man, innocent or not. One man gone is good for the cause. Joe hoped to have a more neutral witness to question.

"There were a lot of people in the cafeteria. I don't know any names, but I'm sure they all saw." Anita was winding down and tended toward getting up and leaving.

"Can you remember who was sitting at nearby tables I could talk to?" Joe began to suspect that there were no other witnesses because there was nothing to witness. But something did happen, and he would need to find out what. Anita replied in the negative, saying she was too humiliated to notice. Joe made some more notes.

"Is there anything else you can tell me that would help my investigation?" He sat looking at her, with his pen poised over the legal pad. She closed up saying no. Joe told her he would look into this and get back to her. He also told her to let him know if she remembers anything else later.

UGLI steward Anita grunted and left. Joe stretched back in his chair, thinking about the unholy connection between Anita Kloo and anything sexual. He thought about the time it would take to investigate this incident and the number of people he would have to question. He thought of mafia movies and the code of omerta, which had something to do with not saying anything about anything. He thought of Sergeant Schultz, that rotund Nazi prison camp guard from the old *Hogan's Heroes* television series from the '60s who claimed he heard nothing, he saw nothing.

CHAPTER 9

The loud buzzer signaled break time throughout the plant, and Toivo steered his forklift to the side of the aisle and killed his motor. He propped his boots up and slouched down into the seat. He closed his eyes and let his mind wander aimlessly. He could overhear a group of workers gathered around a break table talking about their weekend plans. One of the workers was talking about traveling to Minnesota and staying in a cabin for a couple of days of boating and fishing.

He remembered his own cabin in Minnesota and Clyde. He missed the conversations they had while working on a project together. They would explore and probe subjects that helped strengthen their father-son bond and hone their conservational and thinking skills. The months spent talking about *Huckleberry Finn* alone created several spin-off conversations, including Huck and Jim's travel down the Mississippi as a metaphor for a search for spiritual as well as physical and legal freedom.

Somehow Toivo and Clyde managed to compare Huck's narrative style to the blues music of Robert Johnson, society's hypocritical acceptance of the status quo, ignorance and love. Toivo listened as Clyde talked about the Jim Crow laws and racism while he varnished a tabletop. As Toivo grew up under Clyde's tutelage, he realized that there was more to Clyde's level of education than he ever let on. It was around the time when Toivo was entering his senior year in high school that he started to wonder about Clyde's past. It was a sweltering summer day inside the woodshop when Toivo decided to find out.

Clyde was in a quiet mood as he was changing a blade on the band saw. John Lee Hooker was filling the shop singing about whiskey and women on the old eight-track player in the corner.

"Where are you from?" Toivo asked, trying to sound nonchalant.

Clyde glanced up, a shiny sheen of perspiration on his face. "Huh?"

"Did you always live here?"

"I'm here now," Clyde said in his low monotone as he returned to his work.

"Did you always live in Minnesota?"

"No. Once I was there," Clyde said, picking a long block of white oak before walking over to the turning lathe. He set it between the spindle and tailstock then paused to light a cigarette.

"Yep. I used to be there."

"Where's 'there'?" Toivo asked as he busied himself with a miter saw.

"There," Clyde said, pointing eastward.

"Wisconsin? Michigan?"

"Just there," Clyde answered in a tone that was a mixture of annoyance and teasing.

"Why are you being all mysterious?" Toivo asked, finally dropping all pretense of casualness. "Are you being the inscrutable Indian mystic today?"

"I could be. God was an Indian, you know?"

"Okay, I'll bite. Why do you think God was an Indian? Because he doesn't know where he's from either?"

"It's right there in the Bible." Clyde took his cigarette out of his mouth and flicked a long ash off. "Job chapter one, verse twenty-one, there."

"I don't know what that says."

"You should read the Bible. Lots of good stuff in there," Clyde said as he extinguished his cigarette in a well-used tuna can. He paused for a long moment then said, "The Lord giveth and the Lord taketh away." Pause. "He was an Indian giver." Clyde chuckled then broke into a hacking cough.

Toivo laughed as well, but his eyes showed some concern over Clyde's coughing fit. Clyde had smoked Marlboro Reds as long as he could remember, but only recently had he witnessed a breakdown in his breathing. He watched as Clyde resumed working the wood on the lathe—his chuckles slowly disappearing like bubbles in a pot of water cooling down after a hard boil.

"So where were we? Oh yes. You were evading my question about your origins," Toivo said.

"Um-hm," Clyde answered distantly while inspecting the newly lathed table leg.

"Look at this work. Nice."

"Yes, it looks good. And you are dodging me."

"Not really. Look at this. It's going to be one of the legs of a dining room table." Clyde brushed over the leg with a couple quick swipes of his large hand. "This used to be part of a tree."

Toivo sat down on a stool and waited for Clyde to continue.

"The tree," Clyde said, "grew from a little acorn."

Toivo waited and watched as Clyde carefully placed the leg near its newly machined mates. It seemed to Toivo that Clyde was done talking on this subject.

"Acorn, eh? So you came from an acorn," Toivo said with a smile.

"Maybe. I, like the table leg, came from something else," Clyde said while brushing sawdust from the lathe. Then added in a distant voice, "I used to be part of something different. I went to school. I read some books. I talk to some people. I rode in some cars. I walked on some roads." Clyde stopped, turned to face Toivo, and added, "I was there. Now I'm here. We . . . are both here."

* * *

Toivo jumped when he heard the buzzer go off and the sounds of the plant returned to his consciousness. He pulled his legs down and turned the key, starting up the engine of his Clark. He pulled away and headed down the aisle toward his next stop.

Clyde Gray Eagle was on Toivo's mind a lot today. This was the tenth anniversary of his death. He missed the time he spent with Clyde, the good times and the bad. Toivo had been a typical teenager with all the self-anointed intelligence and independence that came with it. He had rebelled against Clyde and everything else that wanted to limit his free expression in those days.

"Hey, Toivo!" He pulled over to the side where Steve Elwing was standing. He was a leadman on the assembly line. "Can you pick me up some hose supports next time you come by? I'm running a little low."

"No problem, bro. Be right back." Toivo couldn't wait for the day to end. His body was here, but his mind was in Northern Minnesota.

* * *

The day did end, finally, and Toivo headed home. He stopped at a liquor store on the way home and picked up a twelve-pack of beer. This was going to be a night of drinking and remembering for him. He grabbed the beer and hefted it up onto the counter.

"They say it's going to rain tonight," the elderly clerk said, looking out the window.

"They do, huh?" Toivo asked while wondering who "they" were exactly. He thought they might be a sober-looking group of distinguished white men in black suits wearing black framed eyeglasses sitting high behind an oaken panel. Who else would be qualified to manufacture opinions that prompted the average Joes and Janes of the world to say things like, "They say the war will last forever," or "They say the price of oil is going up again."

Sometimes "they" didn't have all the information. "They don't know how hard it is to run a farm these days," or "They don't realize that living up North is better than anywhere else." Somebody's got to tell "them."

"Yep. I can feel it in my bones," the clerk said. "That'll be $16.25."

Toivo handed over the money. "Well then, stay dry."

"You bet. Thanks."

*　　*　　*

Once home, it didn't take long for Toivo to plop down in his old but comfortable olive-colored easy chair. He left the air conditioner turned off and allowed sweat to collect and run down his forehead. He glanced up and saw the hourglass sitting on top of his book shelf next to a copy of Huckleberry Finn. He studied both objects as his mind wandered off. Soon he found himself young again and living with Clyde in the cabin among the trees.

Chapter 10

A month had passed since Toivo had finished reading about Huckleberry Finn, but the inquisitions about the book continued. Clyde was using what Toivo would later come to know as the Socratic method in the endless questioning about the poor ne'er do well. Clyde was trying to tell him something in his Indian spirit way, but Toivo wasn't getting it. Clyde said it before: Why write a book about this nothing of a person?

Sure, he had a life of freedom and adventure. He thumbed his nose at the proper life and was true to himself. So what? He was trailer trash in Toivo's mind, and the trailer parks were full of those free souls. Quite frankly, he was tired of talking about him.

"Why're you still asking me about that book? I got an A on the report and it's over with. I mean, it's not like it's the Bible or anything," Toivo said in exasperation one day.

Clyde seemed like he wasn't listening, but Toivo knew that he most certainly was. He knew Clyde wasn't given to displays of anger but still felt a feeling of simmering emotion oozing out toward Toivo.

"I mean, there are so many things to talk about. Why are you stuck on that book?" Toivo asked to fill the uncomfortable silence.

After a couple more uncomfortable minutes, Clyde spoke. "Grab your coat. I want to show you something." Clyde threw on his raggedy Carhartt jacket and walked quickly out of the shop. Toivo, taken by complete surprise, pulled his coat off the chair and tugged it on as he dashed through the door. Soon he caught up with Clyde, who was cranking over the old Chevy pickup, and jumped into the passenger side. The old truck smell usually gave him warm comfort, but tonight it just smelled like an old truck—an angry old truck that was about to take him to a place he wouldn't like.

Toivo remained silent, afraid to open up something that should probably remain closed for the time being. The old truck drove down the night road, the headlights revealing its shiny windblown surface ahead. About ten minutes later, the truck slowed and carefully turned into a gravel road then picked up speed again, spitting chunks of ice and frozen gravel up against its side. They drove down that road for what seemed to be about a half hour when the truck slowed again. Clyde continued driving through the tall dark Norwegian pines fencing the roadside from the unknown regions beyond their brittle branches.

They entered a clearing and Toivo immediately saw a smoldering fire pit and next to that a small mound in the center of it all. There were two men, Indians he noticed by their dark braids and cowboy hats with beads around the band, standing next to the mound as if on guard. Clyde stopped and parked and told Toivo in a calm voice to get out. Toivo opened the truck door, which reluctantly opened with a plaintive squeak. He shut the door and stood waiting and wondering by the truck. Clyde exited the other side and walked toward the mound while Toivo remained standing nervously by the truck.

Clyde quietly greeted the two men, and Toivo saw they were talking but couldn't hear what they were saying. At one point, Clyde looked back at Toivo and the other two men followed suit. They went back to talking, and then Clyde walked back to the truck. One of the two men standing guard picked up a shovel off the dark ground and poked at the fire causing a small display of flickering embers. The light created by the sparkling embers allowed Toivo to notice that the mound was actually some kind of small shelter. It looked like a small dome-shaped tent that stood approximately four feet high and four or five feet in diameter.

The other guard opened the flap of the tent for the first one who had used the shovel to dig a glowing stone and placed it into the tent. He placed another stone in, and then another until smoke was drifting out of the top of the tent. Clyde placed his arm around Toivo and guided him over toward the tent.

"Strip down, Toivo," Clyde calmly instructed him. Toivo looked wide-eyed at Clyde, who was already removing his jacket. *So this is it?* thought Toivo. Clyde had cracked and Toivo was going to die. Toivo glanced around at the snow as if to confirm that this wasn't strip-down weather. Clyde was removing his shirt now as the guards watched with no interest.

"Relax, Toivo. This is a sweat lodge," Clyde explained. "Now get undressed."

"It's a what?" Toivo asked while he fumbled at his shirt buttons.

"It's a place to help you remove your impurities. A place to draw close to your spirit world." Clyde paused for a moment then said, "Afterwards, you can tell me how you think this has anything to do with Huck."

Toivo was barely listening. His concern was the tiny tent with the roasted rocks inside and the relationship of all that to his naked body. He stood by the entrance of the tiny "lodge," trying not to watch Clyde crawl in with his butthole out there for the world to see. He glanced around and then crawled in behind Clyde, wondering what the world thought of his anal display. Once inside he immediately felt the suffocating dry heat suck the air out of his lungs. He noticed that the hot stones were piled into a slight recess in the middle of the lodge. Because the area was small, Toivo took great care avoiding the stones before settling into a spot.

One of the guards, or attendants as Toivo would be more apt to describe them now, pulled an inner flap down over the door and heard another layer being placed over that. Now it was dead dark and even hotter, if that was possible. Something light touched his hand.

"Here, hold onto this sage. If you think you can't breathe, hold it up to your mouth. It will help," Clyde reassured. Toivo remained silent as he tried to take it all in. His first thought was survival. But later he would begin to ask why. Outside there was unintelligible talk, then a piercing chant broke through the walls of the lodge. There were no drums like he thought Indians used, but there was an unmistakable cadence to the sound.

"What . . . ?" Toivo started to ask.

"Don't talk now. They are offering a prayer to the four directions," Clyde softly said.

Soon the prayer ended and a silence fell once again inside the lodge. Toivo sat quietly, concentrating on trying to get whatever air molecule he could beg from the Great Spirit of Air. He discovered that if he buried his nose in the bouquet of sage, it did ease his breathing as Clyde had promised. He heard a hiss and realized Clyde had poured water over the stones, causing them to steam and push more heat into the small enclosure. He heard Clyde inhale slightly, then he started talking—it was a prayer. The power and depth of his voice grew with each passing sentence.

"Oh, Great Spirit, whose voice I hear in the winds and whose
breath gives life to everyone, hear me.
I come to you as one of your many children; I am weak . . .
I am small . . . I need your wisdom and your strength.
Let me walk in beauty, and make my eyes ever behold
the red and purple sunsets.
  Make my hands respect the things you have made, and make
my ears sharp so I may hear your voice.
Make me wise, so that I may understand what you have taught
my people and the lessons you have hidden in each leaf
and each rock.
I ask for wisdom and strength, not to be superior to my brothers,
but to be able to fight my greatest enemy, myself.

Make me ever ready to come before you with clean hands and
a straight eye, so as life fades away as a fading sunset,
my spirit may come to you without shame."

Clyde paused, and then in a quieter voice he continued.

"Oh, Great Spirit, oh, my ancestors. I offer thanks from my heart
for Toivo, who you have given to my life. Guide his steps through
the wilderness and fill his heart with wealth overflowing.
Let him be a balm to those left in the dark. Let him be a healer
to the sick of mind and body. Fill his quiver with the arrows
of might to fight ignorance and idleness of spirit. Guide his
inner man nature to learn and serve the lands and the heavens.
Allow him to love. Allow him to hurt. Allow him to see and
hear the Wind Spirit."

Clyde stopped praying, and silence returned to the dark womb of the lodge.
After a minute had passed, Clyde told Toivo to go ahead.

"What?" Toivo said quietly, still trying to master his breathing.

"Say a prayer," Clyde gently answered. He heard more water being poured
over the stones and felt the reinvigorated heat enter his lungs. Toivo tried to
remember a prayer, and all he could think of was the table grace his grandma
had taught him.

"I, ah, don't know any, Clyde," stammered Toivo.

"A powerful spirit is with us now. Talk to him. Tell him what is in your
heart."

"I am . . . thankful for . . . Clyde . . . whom you gave to me . . ." Toivo
squirmed in the dark. He wasn't accustomed to expressing feelings, nor was
he aware until now he had any feelings worth expressing. He paused, realizing
that he was no longer concerned about maintaining his respiratory system. He
heard Clyde urge him to go on.

"I am happy to have my life and . . . to learn about woodworking with
Clyde and . . ." Toivo paused and thought about the cabin he lived in with
Clyde and the warm woodstove that gave off snug warmth and the embracing
smell of birch logs. His mind wandered from there to the snow on the ground
and hanging on the branches of the pines. Although he was inside this small
lodge, he found himself looking up at the stars in the night and realizing for
the first time his insignificance in this universe. He saw his grandma's smiling
face as clearly as if she was sitting right in front of him radiating a silky glow.
Toivo began to cry. "I don't know what to say, Clyde," he finally uttered, his
voice choked with emotion.

"You have said it, Toivo," Clyde said. Toivo and his adopted father sat the next hour in quiet contemplation. For the first time in his life, Toivo was at peace in his mind and body. The heat no longer threatened him as he sat cross-legged and naked in the darkness filled with wondrous visions.

CHAPTER 11

The Swartz brothers sat with Dewey Dumphrey, a union steward at AgMotiv, during work breaks. They shared the same intellectual interests involving snowmobiling, barroom lawyering, and jerking scabs around. They reported for work an hour early every day and met in the far corner of the lunchroom where they would read the newspaper and hatch plans to disrupt the lives of scabs.

The Swartz brothers came into the company about two years apart. Albert "Stinky" Swartz started five years ago, followed by his younger brother Morgan "Hog" Swartz two years later. Both men combined topped seven hundred pounds on the scale, with the weight fairly evenly divided between them. Food. That was their shared love. The source? Lunchboxes, preferably belonging to scabs, but sometimes those brought in by the union brethren.

This business of lunch stealing was one that required much stealth and expediency. Most of the time they would pass through the cafeteria on the way to the bathroom. On the first leg of the trip, they would sneak a peek into the refrigerators to assess the inventory. On the return leg, they would grab a sandwich or container of pudding and stuff it into their shirt.

They honed their skills over the years after many close calls. At first, they would be caught looking into the fridge, but nothing serious could come of it because nobody was sure that they were doing anything untoward. But they would wonder, and that led to the Swartz brothers making sure they always carried a bottle of pop they would say they were putting inside to cool it off for lunch to anybody that questioned them. The prime shopping time was around ten in the morning, when it seemed that everybody would be at the height of their productivity, and so the Swartz brothers would use that time to go shopping.

While slaking their appetites was of paramount importance, lunchroom forays also provided an opportunity to make a statement concerning their union bias to those that they felt needed such information. This would most often be in the form of a roughly scribbled note with editorial comments such as "die scab" or "eat shit scab." Sometimes the Swartz brothers went that extra step, especially Stinky, once making a sandwich at home to place into the lunchbox of the nonunion employee. His recipe was simple: his feces between two slices of bread and inserted into a sandwich bag along with the written invitation to eat shit.

The nonunion victim was impotent in their ability to deter these actions. Complaints were made to union representatives, who would angrily deny that a union member was involved. They would take the complaint as an accusation against union members and threaten legal action against the complaining employee. A complaint to the Human Resources department netted little more than questions about who they thought did it, and unless they knew there was little they could do. And complaining at all seemed to encourage more harassment.

But Dewey was particularly impressed with the extra efforts of the Swartz brothers and bragged to Travis Tee about his ability to motivate union members to action. Travis Tee was at the height of pride with his prodigy at moments like these and knew that Dewey was a true representative of unionism and would go far under his tutelage. He was convinced that actions such as these brokered by Dewey would force scabs to join the union.

Today, Dewey and the Swartz brothers were sitting at their table when Hog suddenly let fly with a belch. "That's not bad manners, that's just gooooood beer," Hog intoned, keeping his eyes on the newspaper. Stinky and Dewey broke out into laughter, even though this same comment was made hundreds of times before. It also didn't seem to matter to them that beer had nothing to do with the burp. If they had the vocabulary to explain this phenomenon, they would have said that it was a comfortable affirmation of their brotherhood. They were union men, and they were the elite of the elite of action men.

Dewey eventually stopped laughing and fell into deep meditation, his eyes glazed as he stared at nothing. Stinky sat to his left, picking his nose and studying the result of his dig. He wiped the booger on his pants and noticed Dewey's absence.

"Whachoo thinkin' 'bout, Dewey?" Stinky asked.

"What?" Dewey said, returning to the present.

"Ya look like you got sumpin on yer mine," Stinky said while turning his efforts toward the discovery of the source of the itch in his armpit.

"Just Anita, I guess," Dewey said.

"Who?"

"Anita Kloo, you know." Hog glanced up from his reading with a look of concern on his face.

"What 'bout her?" Stinky asked. Hog's eyes remained fixed on Dewey.

"I think I like her."

"Fat Anita? Really?" Stinky asked, his puffy face puttied into an expression of shock.

"Are you fuckin' sick in yer mind?" Hog asked.

"Well, I mean. There's something about her that turns me on."

Hog slammed his newspaper onto the table and stormed away. Stinky watched him go then asked, "Yer jokin' right? She's an ugly oinker."

Dewey stared down at the table in thought.

"It's not like you are anything to look at either," Dewey said.

"I'm a dude. I don't haf to look good."

"Well, I don't give a fig what you think. I think she's hot," Dewey said then sat back in his chair with his arms crossed over his chest.

"Yeah, whatever, man."

Both men sat in silence then got up after the starting horn blew.

*   *   *

Dewey passed by Dave Jenson on his way to his work area and noticed he was already bent over a fixture welding on a subassembly. What a suck ass, he thought. The starting buzzer sounded a few minutes ago, and Jensen was already working.

Jenson was under his welding helmet, and the crackle and hum of the welding tuned out all the other sounds around him. That was one of the things that Jenson loved about welding. He was in his own world—an almost Zen state where he and the metal became one. He didn't sense the presence of Dewey nearby.

Dewey looked down and saw that, like most employees in AgMotiv, Dave wore jeans that were tattered with loose threads. Looking both ways, he pulled out his Bic cigarette lighter and lit one of the threads dangling near his groin. The thread caught fire and Dewey quickly left the area. In seconds, he heard Dave scream and curse. He giggled and kept walking.

He didn't look back but could tell from the nearby faces that they were concerned, or at least curious about the ruckus. Dewey walked on down the aisle, thinking about the amount of effort and attention it took to fight for the union. He had heard Travis Tee give speeches at the union hall about how companies are using dirty tactics to keep unions away from their businesses. Travis Tee called out for more blood, sweat, and tears in the union's efforts to raise the level of membership in unions. He called upon the stewards and all members to redouble their efforts to talk up unionism.

Dewey was all too aware of Travis Tee's frustration over the apathy that ran rampant in this local. There were over a thousand members in AgMotiv alone, and yet only twenty to twenty-five members tops came to the monthly union meetings. He had heard Travis Tee say that this was about average for most unions everywhere. Dewey, though, was at every meeting. He knew that he was on the righteous path and knew that Travis Tee appreciated him for that. If he could only find a way to unite the members and get them to come to meetings, he knew that Travis T would be very proud of him.

Dewey blamed the scabs.

The scabs were daily proof that a person could work without unions. Travis Tee called them free riders—people who enjoyed the fruits of labor negotiation without being members. Dewey called them scabs. They were an ugly wart on the beautiful face of unionism. They were a bad influence on the membership. They worked hard to produce at high levels and walked around saying good things about the company. Scabs were spineless pussies. So it was clear to Dewey; they were to be punished as much and as often as possible. They were the enemy. Someday he would do something big to get back at them.

Dewey walked into his work area and realized he should have stopped at the john to take a dump, so he turned around and headed back toward the restrooms. His supervisor, Carl Miller, was walking down the aisle toward him.

"Morning, Dewey. Where you headed?"

"None of your business," Dewey said and walked on by him.

"Dewey!"

Dewey stopped and turned around. "What."

"What did you just say to me?" Miller asked.

"It's none of your business where I'm going," Dewey said, walking right up to the supervisor and standing an inch away from his face.

"What you do on company time is my business," Miller said as he stood his ground, glaring into Dewey's eyes. Miller was a large, well-muscled man who spent a good share of time in the gym. Dewey backed down.

"I'm going to the bathroom. Is there a rule against that?"

"You've only been here five minutes. You couldn't do that before work?" the supervisor asked.

"Now you're telling me when I have to go to the bathroom? What kind of Hitler place is this?" Dewey said, crossing his arms over his chest.

"Go take care of it and get back to work!"

"You can't yell at me! I'm filing a grievance," Dewey said. "I'm a union steward and you have to respect me."

"Yeah, yeah, go ahead and file your grievance," Miller said then under his breath added, "putz."

*   *   *

Hog and Stinky, meanwhile, were still lumbering side by side and side to side toward their work areas. Hog peeled off by the small parts welding area and found his bay that was a shrine to UGLI. Union calendars and bumper stickers covered every available surface around his nest. In the center sat a metal table, where his pieces sat waiting to be welded together. Sitting next to the table was a cruddy-looking stool with a round seat covered in duct tape.

Hog settled heavily onto the stool, which faced outward toward a nearby aisle so that he could keep an eye on the comings and goings around him. Occasionally, he would get a visitor that would share a problem he was having, usually related to a supervisor that was pushing him a little too much. Hog would listen and growl about the "fuckin' assholes" they let be supervisors. This was usually enough for the complainer, who would wander back to his area and return to work satisfied that he had an ally to rely on.

Stinky worked further away from the lunchroom and so was still en route to his job at the takedown area at the end of the paint line. His route took him by the beginning of the paint line, which he noticed was empty of parts. He knew it would soon be full of hanging parts entering the wash area and then on to the primer booth.

Stinky glanced around and noticed the crew was clustered around their supervisor a ways down, probably going over the work plans for the day. Stinky walked over to a nearby worktable and quickly found what he was looking for. He made a recheck of the group, which was still convening.

Walking into the booth, he saw that the walls were dry from the four-hour period of time that the booth was inactive while the line received its daily maintenance. Making one last check to assure his solitude, he raised his white grease marker and started writing.

His hand started moving across the metal walls. He wrote, "Scab Fuckers Suk Cock." Below that he wrote, "Agmotav eat shit." He stepped back and looked at his work and saw that it was good. He heard voices coming closer, so he quickly left the booth and managed to get away undetected.

Out in the aisle, he walked earnestly toward the end of the paint line, where he saw his coworkers taking down dried parts and loading them on carts. He was passing by a break table when he saw a black lunchbox he knew belonged to a scab. Bonus, he thought to himself. He made a quick people check and picked up the lunchbox and dropped it into a nearby garbage barrel. He pulled some dirty paper over it and continued toward his work area.

CHAPTER 12

Toivo Jurva sat with his feet up on the dashboard of his paint-peeled Toyota forklift at break time munching on a bologna sandwich. He looked forward to his breaks and used them to enjoy the relative quiet of an idling factory. The only sounds he heard were the humming of the air exchange system and the lighthearted banter of workers enjoying each other's company.

Most people respected his desire for solitude because they knew him as an okay guy who treated them right. Most of the workers even forgave his nonunion status and secretly admired his independence. His coworkers couldn't even imagine Toivo admitting membership to any organization, much less the United General Laborers International. While he stood for himself, they knew he was ever ready to assist people anytime they needed it.

Two years ago, a fellow forklift driver was killed in an auto accident that left his wife and four children without their main breadwinner. Toivo approached the company, which stated that they would help his widow and children as much as they could. This help amounted to processing his life insurance with the company and forwarding his final pay and vacation to his wife. They explained to Toivo that the company was unable to provide anything beyond that. Toivo then approached the union to ask if they could provide any assistance to the deceased driver's family. He spoke to Ralph Lynch, the president of the local chapter of UGLI, who quickly responded that the driver wasn't a union member and added that scabs could rot in hell for all he cared.

Toivo, always calm and collected, thanked Ralph and walked away. He filed Ralph's comment away for future consideration.

Toivo proceeded to set up a Spaghetti Feed at the driver's church and sold tickets for $5 each. The feed was well attended and netted $1,800, which he immediately turned over to the driver's widow and four children. He noticed a large number of people from AgMotiv who attended the feed, including union members. He didn't notice any of the union officers, though. He filed that away for future consideration as well.

Toivo wasn't through with his fundraising effort. Toivo also set up an event at a local bar that was only too happy to let Toivo use a spacious backroom at no cost. Toivo connected with a well-known local rock band and managed to charm them into performing at a significantly reduced rate. The admission was $10 and included one free glass of draft beer and a chance to win a 50" flat screen TV. This event netted the grieving family $3,000.

At Christmastime, Toivo dressed up in a Santa suit and dropped gifts off at the family's home. This he did out of his own pocket. The mother had tears in her eyes when she hugged Santa, and the children managed to get their eight arms around both of his legs. With a hearty ho-ho-ho, he left them alone to open the gifts. He was fairly certain that none of them noticed the wetness around his own eyes.

He had heard that the widow had found a good job as a receptionist in an insurance office and was working on a sales license. He checked in with the family from time to time but always kept tabs from afar.

This was but one of the reasons he was well liked by his fellow workers. They also liked the fact that he never used his generosity to promote himself. His coworkers took comfort in the idea that he seemed to quietly watch over them—protect them.

Today, as he sat finishing his sandwich, he could make out some conversation about someone being molested. He focused his attention on a nearby conversation in order to know more of this incident. He heard the name Anita and Dave Foster. He heard something about grabbing Anita's butt but figured he mistook that piece of information. He knew Anita and knew that she wasn't, what his grandma would say, a handsome woman. He knew who this Foster guy was but not enough to make an opinion on the probability of his culpability. All he knew of him was that he was quiet and kept to himself. He had never heard any complaints about him.

Something didn't seem right about all this, and it was probably more than curiosity that required him to know more.

The loud buzzer signaled the people back to work and Toivo pulled his legs off the dash and cranked up the Toyota. He drove toward the welding area at his first stop to pick up a pallet of hubs for delivery to the assembly line. He hopped off his forklift in order to adjust the forks in order to pick up the small pallet of parts. He heard voices behind a royal blue plastic welding curtain and the name Foster. Pretending to study information on his clipboard, he listened for more talk. He recognized one of the voices as belonging to Anita Kloo.

"Foster is a scab and he assaulted me," Anita hissed.

"Are you sure? I mean, I know Foster and . . ."

"Now you are siding with a scab? He attacked me because I'm a woman and a steward in the union. Damn!" Her voice was starting to rise, causing others in the area to take notice.

The other voice, who he recalled as belonging to Bill Dirkens, said, "I heard it was an accident. I don't think he meant . . ."

"Cocksucker! Why are you defending that scab?" Anita paused, then in a tone of exasperation barked, "Fuck!"

Toivo watched out of the corner of his eye as Anita stormed away in a frustrated rage. Dirkens walked around to the front of his weld fixture and noticed Toivo working nearby.

"Hey," Dirkens greeted Toivo. Toivo noticed a look of weariness on his face.

"Hey. How goes it?" Toivo greeted back.

"Oh, you know. Same old."

Toivo paused a moment then said, "Sorry, but I heard a little of that. What's this I hear Foster touched her?" Toivo knew Bill was one of the union stewards who relied on a more rational approach to his representational duties. For this reason, he was seldom called upon to lend assistance to the type of people that routinely demanded it.

"Ah, it's just Anita being Anita again." Dirkens paused, recalling that he was talking to a nonunion member. He was one of the many that liked and respected Toivo, but he still exercised caution, lest he be discovered in consultation with a nonmember. Dirkens never referred to nonmembers as scabs. In fact, he always considered them possible future members. This notion got him jeers at more than one meeting at the union hall.

"Yeah, I guess so." Toivo crawled back onto the lift and cranked it on. "Keep on," Toivo said as he backed his forklift.

"Onward," was Bill's response as he turned toward his weld fixture.

Toivo decided to take the long way to the assembly line through the frame welding department. He noticed Supervisor Jenson a short distance away giving him an inquisitive look. Toivo looked at Jenson and waved his clipboard, as if this would explain things. It apparently was enough because Jenson walked off in the other direction.

Toivo drove past two welders who were working under their hoods, sparks shooting around them as the sound of hot wire on steel crackled in the air. He stopped his forklift at the third weld station and dismounted. Foster was busy using pliers to pull welding wire through his nozzle when he noticed Toivo approaching.

"Hi, Dave, how's it going?" Toivo said. Dave looked back at his nozzle and grunted.

"Dave, I heard some weird shit about you and Anita Kloo. What's up with that?" Toivo propped a leg up onto a crossbar of the weld fixture as if he was ready to order up a round at the Fire Eater Bar downtown. He smiled. "You ain't sweet on little ol' 'Nita, now are you?"

Dave grunted again, but a hint of a smile played on his face. Any other person saying this to him would have been grounds for issuing a major league ass kicking but he knew, one, that he couldn't take Toivo to save his own life and, two, although he had hardly ever talked to him previously, he knew Toivo to be a good-hearted person.

"Well, I won't believe for one moment that you would want to touch her with a ten-foot pole. At least not one you would ever want to use again."

Dave Foster glanced up at Toivo then back down to his nozzle.

"It's bullshit," said Dave.

"Cowshit, Dave. Rumor has it she's a female. Females can't be bulls."

"Whatever," Dave said as he set his pliers down and pulled the kink of the welding hose.

"Yeah, whatever." Toivo dropped his feet off the crossbar and turned back to his forklift. He stopped and turned back around. "Hey, nobody believes her, so don't sweat it."

"I won't," Dave said.

"Okay. Let me know if things go hinky with you on this, okay?"

Dave hesitated a moment then said, "Okay," and added, "Thanks, Toivo."

"Hey, no problem, bro." Toivo hopped up onto his forklift and drove off in a propane-powered roar. Heading toward the assembly line he happened across Anita, who was walking in a direction away from her workstation. She glanced up at him when he came near.

"How do cows like you poo?" Toivo asked.

"Excuse me? What did you call me?" Anita stopped walking and stood as if she was General Patton, her fists resting on each hip and her elbows fanned defiantly out by her sides.

"What?" Toivo asked while he slowed his forklift and brought it to a stop.

"I said: What the fuck did you call me?" Her beady eyes glared fire at Toivo.

"I said how do you do?"

"You did not. You said something about cows and poo, you asshole. You called me a cow!"

"Good Lord, Anita, that don't make any sense. Honestly, you need some serious help," said Toivo as he accelerated away. A hint of a smile crept onto his face.

CHAPTER 13

It was a warm Saturday morning as Toivo drove around town taking care of a variety of tasks. He stopped off at one of his girlfriend's home to see if she had time to give him a quick haircut. He wore his wavy brown hair long, parted down the middle and half covering his ears. As part of the payment, he brought her a variety of vegetables he picked up from one of the street-side stands found around town this time of year.

She was home and gladly trimmed his hair, scolding him the whole time for not taking her out on a date. He promised to take her bowling next Saturday, followed by a dinner at her favorite restaurant—The Pita Pit. She asked him what other things they could do on the date, and he assured her that they would figure out something.

After the haircut and promises, he headed down Main Avenue and stopped at the Broken Saddle. He walked through the door and headed straight for the barstool nearest the door and climbed on. He held up one finger toward Roy, the owner and bartender, which served as a greeting and an order for his usual shot and a beer. Toivo glanced around and noticed a table of fellow employees from AgMotiv. They seemed engrossed in a whispered conversation, their heads leaning toward the middle of the table. He noticed that it was a curious collection of employees in that they weren't the usual gaggle of complainers and troublemakers. He pondered that for a moment until his liquor order arrived.

Toivo downed his shot and took a sip from his glass of beer. He noticed one of the regulars sitting at the other end of the bar and gave him a friendly salute. As far as Toivo knew, the elderly gentleman had never missed a day at the Broken Saddle and always sat in the same place. The bartender called him Bernie and often hunched over the bar next to him reading a newspaper and chatting about the day's events.

The jukebox sat silent by the far wall, and Toivo considered bringing it to life but decided the morning crew probably wouldn't appreciate it much. Toivo began to understand why day drinkers went into a daze while drinking. This was the drink and think time—a time to meditate on your life, or what used to be your life.

One of the workers at the AgMotiv table became animated, his voice suddenly rising. Toivo looked at the table, as did Roy and Bernie.

"How you guys doing over there? Can I get you another round?" Roy asked, looking up from the newspaper. The men glanced around at each other while the speaker looked down at the table with a reddened face. Toivo took the opportunity to count the number around the table—there were eight of them.

"I think we're okay right now," said the tallest of the group.

"Hokay," Roy said and returned to his newspaper and Bernie.

Toivo took another drink of his beer and glanced again at the table. He turned his head facing front again, but his ears were tuned to the conversation. He picked out some words but not enough of the substance. Clearly, though, something of deep importance had engaged their attention. As he was trying to focus on the discussion, the door opened, admitting a group of men talking loud and laughing. As they walked by him, he noticed they, too, were from AgMotiv. The loudest talker was Dewey Dumphrey.

"Hey, Toivo! Whacha doing?" Dewey said as he pulled out a chair at a table and sat down. Toivo didn't answer but looked at the others joining him at the table and recognized them as a group of troublemakers and malcontents from the factory. He didn't have anything to do with them at work and even less so outside of work.

"Toivo, are you being anti-unsociable?" Dewey asked, and the others laughed.

"Maybe the cat's got his tongue," said a short, skinny man sitting next to Dewey. The others broke out laughing as if it was the funniest thing they'd ever heard.

"Hey! Look there! A table of scabs!" shouted Dewey when he noticed the discussion group at the other side of the room. They pretended they didn't hear him and went on talking.

"Hey! Scabs! Are you deaf?" Dewey shouted in their direction. Now they looked at Dewey but didn't say anything back to him.

"What can I get you, gentlemen?" Roy asked with a hint of sarcasm on the word gentlemen.

"I'll have what they are having," Dewey said with a serious face. "What are they having, Shirley Temples?" He broke out in laughter along with his cohorts.

"Shirley Temples it is then." And Roy turned to leave.

"Whoa, man. We're just joking. Get us all beers. Jesus, doesn't anybody have a sense of humor in here?" Dewey asked to nobody in particular.

It was silent for a moment, and then Toivo quietly spoke.

"I do."

Dewey looked over at Toivo then around at the others at his table.

"What? Did you say something?" Dewey asked Toivo.

"I said I have a sense of humor."

"Oh, okay, tell us a joke then," Dewey snickered as he glanced around at his tablemates.

"Okay, once there was this moron who came into a bar and didn't know he was an idiot." Toivo stopped and took a drink. Dewey waited, but Toivo didn't say anything more.

"And then what happened?"

"Then he said, 'And then what happened?'" Toivo looked at his beer and waved to Roy for another one. One person started laughing at the first table then all joined in, including Dewey's table. Dewey looked around confused.

"I don't get it." The laughter regained new life as Dewey looked around for an answer. "What?" Dewey asked as his face reddened.

The others at Dewey's table got up to leave, dropping money unto the table. Dewey stayed seated with his mouth hung open.

"Toivo, I don't get it." Toivo looked over at Dewey as if noticing him for the first time. The others in Dewey's party walked out of the bar still laughing.

"Are you looking for a queer to poke?" Toivo asked.

"Wha . . . ? Did you say I'm a queer?" Dewey's face flushed a darker crimson.

"What?" Tovio asked with a mock innocent face.

"You called me a queer."

"I did not," Toivo said defensively. "I said do you want to hear another joke?"

Dewey pulled his yellow UGLI hat off and started rubbing his head. His face was a mixture of confusion and tension. He replaced his cap on his head, rising quickly causing his chair to clutter to the hard floor, and ran out of the bar. He was followed out with a hail of laughter.

"Way to chase my customers out, guys," said Roy, who didn't try to conceal his smile. Even lethargic Bernie emitted a snort of a chuckle.

"Sorry, Roy. I'll make it up to you somehow," Toivo said as he glanced over at the scab table. He arose from his chair and took his beer over to it. "Mind if I join you, gents?"

"Nah, sit down, Toivo. That was quite a show you put on there." Tovio vaguely recalled that the speaker was a finish painter who he rarely saw because his job required him to be fully covered in a hood and paint coveralls and buried in the paint booth. He looked totally different in his street clothes. He looked like a human rather than a paint-speckled yeti. He also noticed Dave Foster sitting in the group.

"Hey, Dave. How goes the battle with sexy Kloo?" The mention of UGLI steward Anita caused one of the workers to spit up his beer. He apologized to the others.

"No, I'm sorry," said Toivo. "I mentioned her name, so I'm responsible. Hey, Roy, can I get another beer here? In fact, why don't you bring us all another round?"

Thanks were offered sporadically around the table. Dave took in a breath to speak.

"That was pretty funny about poking a queer," Dave said.

"Thanks," Toivo said with a grin. "I call that cowpoking." He pronounced it cowpokin. Tentative laughs came from the men.

"Cowpoking?" Dave asked.

"Yeah, cowpoking," Toivo confirmed. All eyes were on him, waiting for a more thorough and satisfying explanation. After a moment, it came.

"It takes a bit of practice, but you say something shitty to a person, like I did, but get out of it by claiming you said something nonshitty." He glanced around the table and was rewarded with bewildered looks.

"So why, you ask," continued Toivo, "would you want to do that? Well, have you ever felt that certain people, like Anita and Dewey, have the upper hand with their phony accusations? Am I right, Dave? You didn't molest that sow, but you're still going through hell trying to prove it, right?"

"Yeah, no shit," Dave answered.

"Doesn't it seem justified, therefore, that they be put in the same spot?" Tovio paused then said, "Cowpoking."

"But couldn't you get in trouble for doing that?" said another man who was wearing a T-shirt with the AgMotiv logo printed across the front.

"I 'spose you could if you're not careful. You need to make sure nobody else is around when you do it. Also, you have to make sure you have both sides of the poke ready."

"Both sides of the poke?" the logo guy asked.

"Yeah, both sides. For example, let's see . . ." Toivo paused and looked up toward the ceiling in thought. "Okay, here's one for you, David, to use on your girlfriend Anita." Toivo smiled and waited a moment for them to stop laughing. A small smile crept onto Dave's face, which was fairly intense for him.

"So, Dave, you walk by her and say, 'You whoring?' The second side of it is 'good morning.' That's what you would claim to say." The group burst out in laughter, causing Roy and Bernie to look over.

"What evil plan are you guys hatching over there?" asked Roy with a smile.

"How to get free drinks on the house," answered Toivo.

"Keep working on that plan." Roy chuckled and went back to his newspaper. The AgMotiv employees sat in happy silence for a moment then Toivo got serious.

"So Dewey Dipshit called you guys scabs. Is it a coincidence that you scabs are all together here today?" The workers knew that Toivo wasn't a union member either, so they didn't take offense to his reference to them as such. Toivo could see that they were a tad nervous as they glanced around the table at each other. Finally, David spoke up.

"We were talking about what to do with all this bullshit the union assholes are putting us through."

"Like what?" Toivo asked.

"Like hiding our tools and spitting Skoal into our pop cans," said a stocky man sitting next to him.

"Writing 'scab' on our tool boxes," said another.

"Drawing a head with a gun next to it in the bathroom stall with 'kill scabs' next to it," said the man with the AgMotiv logo on his shirt.

"They are a creative bunch, no?" Toivo said in a distracted voice—everybody could see his gears were turning inside his head. "Well, let's start with Operation Cowpoke, but be careful. Remember, no witnesses, two sides to the poke, and use only on the main assholes. Leave the followers alone for now. How does that sound?"

The others glanced and shrugged their shoulders in apparent agreement.

"Yeah, cool."

"I'm in."

"Let's rock."

"Groovy," Toivo threw in drawing funny stares directed at him. He smiled back at them. Damn, I'm getting old, he thought to himself.

CHAPTER 14

UGLI steward Anita Kloo hit the cutoff switch on her brake press fifteen minutes before the morning break. She was feeling the urge of a mammoth bowel movement headed down her piping. *God truly is great,* she thought as she lumbered toward the restroom. The other women knew that bathroom would be off-limits for at least two hours after one of her visits. The odor she left was extremely toxic and evil incarnate. But to Anita, her odor was proof positive that she existed, that she counted for something in this world.

She was about fifteen feet from the restroom when Dave Foster walked around the corner and headed down the aisle in her direction. She greeted him with a snarl as he walked by.

"I piss in your shoe," Dave said as he passed. Anita came to a sudden stop, almost falling forward in the process.

"What did you say to me!" she screamed. Others nearby stopped working and looked toward her.

"I said hi Miss Kloo," Dave responded with a wary look.

"You liar! You told me you were going to pee in my shoe, you dick!" Work had totally halted so that nearby people could better hear the exchange. There were some smiles on their faces.

"I did not, Anita. Why are you picking on me? I'm just trying to be friendly is all."

"Kiss my ass, Foster," Anita said in an angry snarl and stormed away, her enormous backside shuffling side to side. She could hear snickering giggles in the nearby work areas, which only stoked her anger.

The normally shy Dave started to feel a rush of excitement and control that he had never experienced before. He wanted to run to Toivo and tell him about the exchange but thought better of it. So this was cowpoking. He liked it.

UGLI steward Anita was soon seated vacuum sealed to the toilet stool, her anger ruining what should have been an enjoyable activity. She thought about the power that had been provided to her by the Equal Employment Opportunity Act that allowed her to take action against any man who dared create an annoyance she felt was directed at her. Often, these men were her supervisors who criticized her productivity and her desire to visit with others outside her work area. These men acted like prison wardens and thought they could get away with their harassment because she was a woman.

Her other targets included the scabs that infested the workplace. She first heard of the term scab when she attended her first union meeting at the union hall about ten years ago. Elmer Arsvold was the president of the local at the time, and he read aloud the definition of scab that was written by Jack London. She was so moved by what he wrote about the evils of being a scab that she swore she would never treat a scab like a human.

She now felt that although she had unburdened her bowels, a real fear of persecution was creeping into her life. She had never felt true helplessness—not like she was now. Even the daily abuse suffered during her childhood at the hands of her perverted uncle didn't match what she was now dreading. Her uncle's dirty damp hands groping her child body was at least a known fear. It didn't make the suffering any less dreadful, and she still awoke drenched in sweat in the middle of the night from frightening dreams haunting her sleep. But this new harassment was an unknown dread, a dark uncertain future slowly revealing its ugly self like the broken pavement in front of the car's headlights on a lonely night road.

UGLI steward Anita was now truly a victim in AgMotiv, not the fabricated one of her hyped accusations over the years. She was coming to realize that she was the boy yelling wolf to the unbelieving villagers. The scabs had stopped running and had turned to face her. They were liars all of them, with their innocent claims of misunderstood greetings. She called upon her union protectors, but they made empty promises to "check it out." She filed an official complaint to Joe King in HR, who asked his questions and looked at her as if assessing her mental fitness to work.

Soon she found herself hiding in her work area all day, only leaving when she absolutely needed to use the restroom. She took her break there, steering clear of the cafeteria and the vending machines scattered around the plant.

CHAPTER 15

Travis Tee had heard rumors on the shop floor that Kloo recently got into it with a coworker. But UGLI steward Anita Kloo was far from Travis Tee's mind today. He had greater troubles demanding his attention than the complaints of that loudmouth sea lion. He had recently come to the realization that AgMotiv was becoming a good place to work, and this was keeping him awake at nights. The rank and file were experiencing job satisfaction and were getting too cozy with the company. He started to see his goal to rise in the union slip away like sand through his fingers.

Travis Tee remembered his first days as a new employee of AgMotiv. The company went under the name of Milton Farm Machining prior to his employment with the company. Since then, it had gone through several changes of ownership and name changes. Currently, AgMotiv LLC was owned by a Belgium conglomerate that despised unions and used every opportunity to show it.

For example, the company would do everything in its power to help employees that didn't go through the union with their problems. But to those employees who brought a steward up with them to discuss a problem, the company would ask too many questions and generally drag the issue out until they were forced to write a grievance. The grievance would be taken and logged in and, basically, thrown into a pile of papers, never to be looked at again until the union asked about it.

Travis Tee had to work through the company labor relations representative Joe King. King didn't need encouragement from the corporate offices to jerk the union around. Resolving grievances with him was like playing tennis in a swimming pool filled with molasses. Travis Tee was convinced that Joe took unions as a personal assault on everything good in America. It seemed like he viewed used toilet paper as a more valuable document than a union grievance.

But he respected Joe King's power to sway the plant leadership in matters of union importance if he believed there was a mutual benefit to them. Joe responded positively to attempts by the union to use a softer, more businesslike approach to problem solving. Any other approach did not work with Joe King. He was impervious to the ranting and verbal tirades by angry stewards. He would put on a hint of the smirk and start his endless questioning: Why? When? Who? Who else? How often? Who witnessed? What do you compare it to? Why is that a problem? How does that violate the labor agreement? It never ended and his stewards would get even madder. Travis Tee would hear all the complaints about King at the next stewards meeting, but there was so little he could offer to help.

To Joe King's credit, though, if there was a clear violation of the collective bargaining agreement, he would do everything in his power to resolve it. But if he didn't think it was a violation, and he didn't with most of them, the grievance went nowhere. The union would be forced to push the issue to arbitration involving a heavy hit to the local's treasury. To make matters worse, Joe King had never lost an arbitration decision.

More depressing to Travis Tee was what happened to the large pile of grievances that didn't get moved to arbitration. They would just sit out there and languish. If Travis Tee tried to bring the issue up for discussion again, the questions would start all over again. Travis would be left to explain to the angry members why their concerns weren't being handled. For a time, he would blame the company for dragging its feet. He would claim that the company lied when it said it would take care of the issues. After a while, the members would no longer accept excuses and demanded to know why Travis Tee wasn't forcing the company to make them whole.

"Take this job and shove it. I ain't workin' here no more. My woman done—"Travis Tee flipped his cell phone open, cutting off the musical ringtone. "Hello." Speak of the devil. He heard King's spirited voice.

"S'up, Tee?" Joe asked. Travis Tee was always amused at King's attempt to sound hip. Joe was in his middle fifties but apparently hadn't received the memo on that fact.

"Okay, I guess. What's going on?" When Joe called, it usually involved someone getting fired or some request he likely couldn't agree with.

"Well, I've been thinking we should have that discussion about the departments we want to eliminate. Unless . . . you . . . ah . . . just want me to handle it." Joe liked to yank his chain. Travis Tee chuckled.

"No, I think you guys definitely need to be watched," Travis half-jested.

"Groovy. Let's plan on two this afternoon." Groovy, thought Travis Tee. At least that's more his era.

"Yeah. Two."

"Ta." Joe hung up.

CHAPTER 16

"Fag," Travis said into the dead phone. Travis Tee turned back to his work when his cell sang out again as he was replacing it in his belt holster. He flipped it open.

"Hello."

"Travis, it's Dewey. How's it going?"

"Good. What's going on?" Travis Tee liked Dewey. He considered him a knock-off of him: brash and eager. Best of all, he annoyed management with his nonstop grievances.

"I just called to see what's up." Dewey Dumphrey giggled with a breathy snuffing sound through his nose.

"Just fighting the injustices of corporate greed."

Dewey loved hearing Travis Tee talk. He used such big words that made him feel like he was an intelligent person just by listening.

"Dewey, you are the bearer of an important legacy. We must always fight big business because they have always tried to trample on the rights of workers. Workers mean nothing more than human machines to be exploited and spit out when they are used up." Dewey could tell that Travis Tee was picking up steam, so he kept quiet and listened on.

"Egregious! The time is now to step up to the plate and run for a touchdown. The ball is in our court to act! We need to take that ball, shove it up their greedy asses! And, and, and . . ."

"And we should be solitary," Dewey offered.

"Yes, we should . . . what? Did you say we should be solitary? Ah, Dewey, my dear sweet naive Dewey. I think you meant we should stand in solidarity." Travis Tee smiled a smile of gentle patience and tolerance. Of course, Dewey couldn't see the smile, but he was happy that Travis Tee would talk to him.

Dewey began employment with AgMotiv about two years ago. For the first few months he was a model employee. Then almost overnight, he gravitated toward the dysfunctional role models who happened also to be a majority of UGLI's officers. He noticed that they could act any way they wanted and management could do little about it. He saw them as free spirits, and so inspired by his epiphany, he went to a local head shop and purchased a nose ring. The next day he signed on as a shop steward.

Dewey was hungrily embraced by the local labor team. For a factory of its size, there was little interest among the members to become UGLI officers and stewards. Most of AgMotiv factory workers became members to avoid trouble with the more threatening members of the union. Others became members because they believed that it was better to have a union than not. They didn't have the numbers readily available to confirm their beliefs, but why take chances? There was some talk that the nonunion AgMotiv plants in other parts of the United States were actually paid more and offered better benefits, but again, no actual numbers were at hand. Sadly, to the union's dismay, all the employees wanted to do was work and go home.

Initially burdened by an upbringing of responsibility and accountability, he was slow to absorb the philosophy of entitlement incumbent upon the officers of the United General Laborers International. Like a drug purchased secretly in the alley behind Central Liquor Store downtown, entitlement slowly absorbs throughout your being until you experience absolute freedom from aspirations of civilization. No more do you need to wear everyday clothing, smile, refrain from profanity, argue logically, show respect to authority, or devise sensible solutions. Your mind slams shut and you allow others of your ilk, but higher in the hierarchy, to decide your opinions. The ego surrenders to the alpha ID.

Plus, you grow an intense love for duct tape. As any representative from other unions that share the Local Lodge building with United General Laborers International will tell you, the UGLI officers take great pride in the use of duct tape in the repair of their clothing. Although employees are paid $150 a year for safety boots, duct tape can lengthen the life of your boots for up to five years. This discovery creates a yearly windfall for the union gurus that can be better invested at the local liquor store.

But boots weren't the only piece of apparel to be adorned in gray tape. Each pair of pants that entered through the lodge doors to cheer for labor strength and prosperity was stiff with layers of tape. Without looking, the wary leaders from the other unions could tell by the creaking walkers what union had entered the building.

The other union leaders tried to not make eye contact with UGLI members. To do so would invite a loud and abrasive diatribe of slobbery union rhetoric long abandoned by the modern unionists. They all knew the leader, Travis Tee, was the role model for this union's leadership. The stories about Travis Tee abounded, from forcing his nephews to run through Wal-Mart screaming "Wal-Mart Sucks!" to threatening a local clinic to forgo his co-pay by picketing them.

Dewey was in love with UGLI. UGLI was the loving mother he never had—to cradle him, to accept him with without condition, to clap her hands when he poops in the toilet. Travis Tee was his fawning father who protected him and taught him how to throw a baseball. Except he didn't wear a cap from a baseball team, instead he wore the bright yellow UGLI cap everywhere he went. He was union through and through.

*   *   *

Yesterday, Dewey handled a disciplinary hearing involving an employee who had asked for a week off but was only allowed two days. Dewey had advised the employee to call in for family emergency for the nonexcused days to round off his week. The company decided to call the employee in to investigate his "family emergency." Dewey told the employee to not say anything, that he would do all the talking. Dewey informed the supervisor that he called in for family emergency because he needed the whole week off and the company would not give it to him. The two company representatives looked at each other.

"Let me get this straight," inquired Supervisor John Johnson, "you advised Cory to call in his absence due to a family emergency when in fact he didn't have a family emergency?" Cory was a new employee hired seven months ago. He sat squirming in his chair and looking at his folded hands resting on the table.

"Yeah. If he would have called in for any other reason, you would have punished him for extending his excused absence." Dewey sat back defiantly in his chair, with his arms folded across his chest. A piece of duct tape grabbed at some hair on his arm, causing him to wince before he pulled it away from the skin and patted it back in place on his jacket.

"Sooo you advised him to lie? Is that what you are telling me?" John's calm eyes looked right into Dewey's vacant ones.

"Yeah."

"Are you aware, Dewey, that providing false information to the company is a serious violation that could result in discharge?"

"That rule is stupid. I'll grieve it."

John Johnson announced a short break, and he and the other supervisor called in to take notes of the meeting, Roberto Gomez, left the room. In a short time, they both reentered the room. John looked at Cory whose hands were visibly shaking now.

"Cory, by calling in your absence and lying about the reason, you have committed a serious violation of a company rule. Therefore, we will be placing you on an indefinite suspension without pay pending further investigation. I will—"

"W-What? You are suspending me? I just did what he told me I should do." Cory pointed at Dewey.

"I told you to let me do the talking," Dewey admonished him, who turned to John, and said, "I'll file a grievance on this."

"But . . ."

"Cory, let me handle it."

"Go ahead and talk, Cory," Johnson advised.

"I . . ."

"I said don't talk!" Dewey glared across the table at Johnson. "And don't interfere with my instructions to my employee!"

Johnson picked up his paper and tapped them against the table to straighten them. "I'm pretty sure that the name on Cory's paycheck says AgMotiv, not United General Laborers International." Johnson rose from his chair. "You can have a few minutes with Cory and then we will escort him out." The two supervisors exited the room, leaving Dewey alone with the fear-struck Cody.

"What am I going to do now?" asked Cory in a trembling voice. "I need this job!" Cory started to get up out of his chair.

"Wait. By contract, we can have thirty minutes to talk."

"What's to talk about? I'm history."

"We still get thirty minutes," declared Dewey defiantly.

After a minute of sitting in silence, Cory rose from his chair and walked out of the room. He was met by Johnson, who walked him to the door. Dewey remained in the room sitting back in the chair with his arms folded. After thirty-one minutes, he left the room and walked to the bathroom, where he spent another twenty minutes. On his way back to his work area, he stopped at the bulletin board where he spent thirteen minutes reading through the postings. He walked a circuitous route toward his workstation that burned off enough time to get his lunch pail and head toward the break room five minutes early.

Dewey smiled to himself. He loved being a shop steward.

CHAPTER 17

Toivo drove his forklift through the large overhead door and headed outside toward the propane storage rack. He released the two clamps holding the tank to the forklift behind the seat. He closed the valve and unscrewed the fitting then pulled the tank off and placed the empty tank into the storage rack. He grabbed a full tank, pulled it from the rack, and clamped it in place on the lift before attaching the hose and opening the fitting. He was ready to roll again.He hopped back up into the seat when he noticed a yellow cap on the ground a few feet behind his forklift. He slid back down off the seat and picked the cap up from the ground. He gave it a shake to remove some dirt and debris clinging to it and recognized it right away as a union cap with UGLI printed in simple block letters above the visor.

He wondered who it belonged to as he turned it over in his hands to see if a name was printed inside. He didn't find a name, but he noticed a label seemed to be peeling away from itself. He tugged the label straight and saw "Made in USA" written on it. Then the tag came loose in his fingers, and he saw it had been glued to another tag that stated the cap was made in China. Toivo wondered how the cap could have been made in two countries. He looked up into the sky and rubbed the area under his chin thinking.

"Ha," he said aloud. Unions would only purchase American-made products and, in particular, union-made products. This cap was made in China but had a tag that was altered to say it was made in America. Toivo chuckled and tucked the cap under his seat and drove back into the plant.

*   *   *

"I need one thousands units shipped today, goddamn it!" Travis Tee shuffled the telephone receiver to his other ear and held it there with his shoulder. He punched the keyboard with aggressive intent and watched as numbers and graphs appeared

on the screen. As he listened, his face grew a grim expression and his lips twisted down in disgust.

"*What kind of outfit are you running there? We have a message to send out and we can't do it unless you get us those caps A-S-A-P, do you hear me?*" He smiled as he heard the nervous vendor squirm at the other end as he promised to ship the caps within two days.

"*And if you don't get them to me by the end of the week, you will have me to deal with.In person! Got it?*" Travis barked before slamming the receiver down.

"What you thinking about, Travis?"

"Egregious!" Travis Tee shouted. His eyes slowly focused on Dewey, who was standing nervously at Travis's car window where he was sitting after work.

"Dewey," Travis said after a brief moment, "how would you like to take on an important project for the union?"

Dewey blushed as a wide smile broke out across his face. Travis Tee was entrusting him with an important assignment for the union. It was an honor to do something, anything, for Travis and the union and he gushed with pride.

"Yessir! I want to help," Dewey spat out.

"What we need to do is get some caps to sell to our union members. You know, with our union name printed on them. We can make some money off this too, Dewey.

"I can do that. What kind of caps?" Dewey asked as he fingered a stray piece of duct tape that was coming loose on the side of his shirt.

"Yellow. With UGLI spelled over the bill," Travis explained. "Will you be able to handle that?"

"Damn right I can. I'll get right on it," Dewey said then turned and trotted off to his own car.

Dewey drove straight to the West Park Mall, a super mall anchored by Sears, Penneys, and Target and located on the busy Parkway Avenue. Dewey made his way to the Cap Country kiosk in the Penney's wing and walked up to the counter. The salesperson was stooped over as she pulled out an armful of merchandise to stock. Dewey pounded loudly on the counter.

"Hey, I need some service here," Dewey said.

The petite salesperson jumped up in surprise and dropped her load of merchandise onto the floor. She spun around to face Dewey who was glaring at her, his face contorted in a frightening scowl.

"Yes, sir. What can I do for you?" the attendant said as she glanced down at the floor and her spilled products.

"I need to order some caps. A shitload of them," he said.

The salesperson looked warily at the hyper man standing before her as he groped at a piece of tape stuck to the crotch of his dirty pants. He looked scary in his scruffy clothes, and he had what appeared to be a grease stain smeared from his upper cheek to his neck.

"Okay. What kind of caps do you want?" she asked in a professional tone of voice.

"I want UGLI caps, about a thousand of them," Dewey said proudly.

"What do you mean ugly caps?" the salesperson said as she glanced around, hoping a security guard was standing nearby.

"I'm an important person with the UGLI union. I want to order caps with UGLI printed on them. And I need them quick too," Dewey said.

"You want ugly written on them? I don't understand. Why would you want ugly written on the caps?" the salesperson asked as she continued her covert search for security personnel.

"Because, dumbass, that's the name of our union. UGLI. U-G-L-I," he said as he looked down at her as if she were a pile of dog feces.

"Can I ask what that means?" the salesperson asked, hoping that he would just walk away and leave her alone. She was buying time.

"What does what mean? Damn, girl, what's wrong with you asking me all these questions? Just get me some caps."

"You want a thousand caps with U-G-L-I printed on them? What color caps do you want?

"Yellow. That's our union color."

"And what color printing do you want on them?" the salesperson asked as she filled out an order form.

"Shit, I donno. Maybe, black?"

"Okay, you want one thousand yellow caps with U-G-L-I written in black letters. Do you want any special font size or design?"

"Goddamn, do I have to tell you everything? Just make the hats. Shit," Dewey grumbled. He was starting to get a headache from all this work. He massaged his temples as the salesperson completed the sales form.

"Okay, this order will come to $4,265.38. How will you be paying for it?"

"I'll pay with a check from the union," Dewey said with visible pride as he pulled out the checkbook and wrote out the check.

"Do you want them sent somewhere or will you pick them up?"

*   *   *

Both Dewey and Travis forgot about the caps until about a month later when four medium size boxes were delivered to the union hall. A member of the electrician's union that shared the facilities signed for the boxes and stacked them by UGLI's office door where they sat for two weeks.

Travis Tee arrived at the union hall to use the fax machine and noticed the boxes stacked up against UGLI's office door. Looking at the shipping label, he saw that they were shipped from in town by Cap Country. He pulled a pocket knife from his pants pocket and slit the top box open and saw neat rows of yellow caps. His hands shook with excitement as he pulled one out to examine it.

He silently congratulated Dewey on a job well done as he turned the cap around in his hands. He pulled the folded cap opened and saw that it was adjustable with a plastic band with small pegs that inserted into holes on the opposite side. He opened the band and set it to the largest setting and tried it on.

Travis Tee walked to the bathroom to look at himself in the mirror. He pivoted in a slow semicircle, checking himself out, then faced the mirror and glared at his reflection with eyes barely visible under the bill. He turned his back to the mirror, looking at himself over his shoulder when a member of the electrician union entered the bathroom.

Travis Tee swung back around to face the mirror in embarrassment that he was caught posing like a model. The electrician gave him a smirk as he walked up to the urinal and unzipped his pants.

"Nice cap," the electrician said.

"Thanks," Travis returned. "Just got them today."

"Is that from the boxes that came in a few weeks ago?" the man asked.

"A few weeks ago? I didn't know that. Why didn't someone call us?" Travis asked, clearly annoyed.

"Is it our job to keep you informed on this shit?" the electrician shot back. "Maybe you should try showing up at the hall more." The electrician turned and faced Travis as he zipped up. "I don't know how you guys get anything done." Travis watched him walk out, stunned that anyone would dare talk to him, an important union officer, like he did.

His annoyance turned back to joy when he caught his image in the mirror wearing the new cap. He pivoted on his feet in front of the mirror then crossed his arms over his chest in a defiant pose. He held up both his arms as if holding a picket sign and walked back and forth as he appraised his appearance.

The bathroom door opened with a loud bang as the electrician walked in. He was holding one of the UGLI caps in his hand, and he looked angry.

"How do you boneheads get off buying caps made in China?" the electrician said, shaking the cap at Travis. Travis stared back in surprise then yanked the cap off his head to look for himself.

Goddamn, Dewey, he thought. One simple project: Buy caps. Did he really have to spell it out to him to buy American? He looked at the waiting electrician, who seemed to be patiently waiting for an answer. What could he say? Finally, the man dropped the cap onto the floor and walked away.

*   *   *

Dewey was hanging around the lingerie department at the Target store when his cell phone sang out. He replaced the black bra on the rack and answered the phone.

"Hello," Dewey said as he watched a lady talking to a store clerk and pointing at him. She probably didn't like him placing the bra against his own chest and rubbing it. Fuck her.

"Dewey! What the hell you doing getting caps made in China?" Travis barked.

"I-I didn't know where they came from. I just ordered them like you told me to," Dewey said. "Can't we buy stuff made in China?"

"Jesus, Dewey. What the fuck's the matter with you? No, you can't order stuff made in China or anywhere else overseas." Travis's voice was a mixture of anger and panic as he tried to talk and process the error at the same time.

Dewey was silent for some time as he listened to Travis Tee's heavy breathing on the phone. Dewey saw the sales clerk talking to another man who was wearing a tie. They both started walking in his direction, so he decided he should probably leave because he knew he wouldn't be able to talk to them and Travis at the same time.

"I didn't even think about that, Travis. We can still sell them can't we?" Dewey asked as he walked toward his parked car. He turned and saw the two men watching him from the entrance door.

"No!" Travis shouted, causing Dewey to wince. Travis was quiet again, and Dewey waited him out not wanting to arouse any more anger from him.

"Pick up the boxes of caps at the hall and bring them over to my place," Travis finally said. "We need to figure this thing out."

Travis Tee disconnected and Dewey slowly put his phone in his pocket. He turned out of Target's parking lot and drove in the direction of the labor hall.

*   *   *

Travis and Dewey carried the boxes of caps into Tee's trailer home and set them on the living room floor. Both men settled into chairs as Travis Tee glared at Dewey, who squirmed and tried to avoid looking at him.

"Well?" Travis said.

"What?" Dewey answered, knowing that whatever he said would result in verbal assault.

"What are you going to do about this?"

"How do you know they were made in China?" Dewey asked.

79

Travis reached into one of the boxes and flipped a cap at him, which bounced off his leg landing on the floor. Dewey reached down and picked it up and held it in his lap. He looked down at the cap and back to Travis Tee with a puzzled look on his face.

"Look inside the cap," Travis ordered.

Dewey turned it over and looked inside. He saw the tag and stared at it for a few moments.

"What does it say?" Travis asked.

"Fits all sizes," Dewey said.

"What else?" Travis said in a patient voice.

Dewey looked at the label again and flipped the label over and saw what he thought Travis wanted him to see. "Oh, Made in China."

"Oh yeah," Travis said. "So? What are we going to do about that?

Travis could see that Dewey was really thinking the problem through. Actually, he had never seen Dewey put that much thought into anything before, and that gave him a feeling of sympathy toward him.

"Can't we just cut the tags out?" Dewey said.

"Cut one thousand tags?" Travis asked. "And besides, won't that look strange that there was no tag in the hat when someone buys it?

Both men sat in silence for about ten minutes before the sound of Travis's wife urinating loudly in the bathroom shook them back into the moment. The toilet flushing came from the rear of the trailer home, and they could hear her settling back into bed.

Suddenly, Dewey shot up in his chair, a smile filling his face.

"I have an idea. My dad used to do printing a long time ago. He used to make business cards and stuff. I think he still has the press in his garage. We could have him print new labels and . . . I don't know, glue them on to the label."

Travis's first instinct was to chastise Dewey for another dumb idea, but he was taken aback by this suggestion and sat staring at him while he mulled it over in his mind. It might work, he thought. They could glue them on the label already in the cap. It would take a long time to do, but hell, they could get a case of beer and make a night of it.

"Good idea, Dewey. Give your dad a call," Travis said as he started feeling the load lift off his chest.

* * *

Toivo drove back into the plant and headed toward the warehouse to pick up some shredder drums to deliver to the assembly line. He noticed for the first time the large number of people that didn't wear the yellow union cap. If they wore caps at all, they showed favor for the Minnesota Vikings or Twins. Some heralded their support for their favorite NASCAR driver or Snowmobile brand. But there were some that did wear the signature yellow UGLI cap.

After dropping off the parts and before heading to the machining area to pick up a pallet of finished parts, he decided to cruise by Curly Wilson, who was leaning against his work bench, apparently asleep as his machine ran through its cycle. Toivo hit the horn, causing Curly to jump.

"Damn it, Toivo. You scared the shit out of me," Curly said as he glanced over at the machine that just finished its cycle. He walked toward the machine and punched a couple of buttons, causing pallets to move systematically into a different location. He turned to Toivo.

"What do you want?" Curly asked.

"I'm just curious. You union guys only buy American, right?" Toivo worked hard to keep the smile off his face.

"Yeah, so? Everybody should," Curly said.

"Uh-huh. What about your UGLI cap? Is that made in America?" Toivo asked.

"No shit. What do you think?" Curly said as he turned to look for a hoist to unload the parts from his machine.

"Are you sure?" Toivo asked. This time he allowed a smile to spread across his face. "Did you ever check to make sure?"

Curly walked over to Toivo's forklift and removed his cap and held it out to him. "It's right on the label: Made in America. Are you happy?"

"Can I look at it closer?" Toivo asked, holding out his hand.

"What are you trying to pull, Toivo? You fucking with me?" Curly said. Curly gave Toivo a suspicious look then handed his cap to Toivo.

Toivo took it and saw the label and noticed that the new label was glued to this one pretty even and tight. But he managed to get a small corner of it and pulled on it.

"Hey, what the fuck are you doing? You're ripping my cap, damn it."

Toivo pulled on the tag a little more before the replacement label came off. Underneath was the Made in China label. He handed the cap back to Curly, pointing out the hidden label.

"Well, at least the Made in America label was made in America," Toivo said as he laughed and drove off on his forklift.

CHAPTER 18

Dewey's eyes came open when he heard the toot of a nearby railroad engine. Day and night he could hear the blasts, honks, and clanking of trains as they fidgeted back and forth behind his apartment house. It was nearly five o'clock in the afternoon when he rolled out of his bed.

He barely noticed the noisy distractions anymore much like a hog farmer pays no never mind to the stink of pig shit. Especially tonight. Tonight had been planned for over a week, and now that the night was here, he felt the juxtaposition of fear and excitement roiling in his stomach.

He had called in absent for the day because he was suffering from a migraine. At least that's what AgMotiv would think. He didn't have a migraine, nor had he ever had one. But a migraine is one of those virtually untraceable medical conditions covered under the Family and Medical Leave Act. He had others to pick from, like depression or a sore back, but he chose migraine because it made it seem that it was caused by too much thinking and responsibility.

Dewey first heard about this law from Travis Tee, who called it FMLA. He told Dewey that it was a gift to the working people who needed a rest from work. Travis Tee claimed that Joe King once told him that if you added all the people who were certified for FMLA among the other eighteen AgMotiv plants around the United States, they wouldn't come near to the number certified for this leave in this plant. This was a source of extreme pride for Travis Tee, evidence that he was using the law to protect his employees from exploitation.

Dewey asked Travis Tee how someone got FMLA and was told that a guy had to visit a local doctor named James Fox, who was very union-friendly. He would certify that you didn't have legs if you wanted him to and watch as you dance out of his office. Travis said that companies were afraid to challenge the law because of the potential legal costs.

Dewey asked what would happen if the company caught you doing something else while you were taking the FMLA day off. Travis Tee snickered and told him that the company wouldn't check on you because they were too busy. Plus, the union would file a grievance and get the person to file a charge with the Department of Labor. Companies hate dealing with those guys.

So Dewey visited Dr. Fox and got him to sign the paperwork, which would allow him to miss work anytime he was "suffering" from migraine without getting dinged on his attendance record. Tonight was the first time he would use FMLA, and the freedom made him feel giddy and powerful.

Dewey rummaged through the pile of boxes and wrappers lying in a messy heap on his kitchen table, which featured one loppy leg and buckled Formica hidden underneath the mess. His hand found an open box of Cheez-Its into which the other hand plunged grabbing a handful of the tiny yellow crackers and stuffing them into his mouth. He stood for a few seconds working his mouth in noisy crunches, crumbs dropping onto the front of his T-shirt. After a moment, he carelessly tossed the still open box onto the top of the hill of debris and wiped his hands on his dirty jeans.

He walked into another room where a mattress covered with a swirl of sheets and a smelly blanket lay flat on the floor neglected and disrespected. From the top shelf of a disastrously organized closet, Dewey pulled down a tote bag, which he dropped onto the mattress. He stooped onto his hunches and opened the bag. He pulled out four rattling spray cans: two flat black and two white. He shook one of them, the marble inside making a rat-a-tat-tat sound. He grinned and replaced the four containers into the tote.

He pulled another plastic bag out of the tote then zipped it closed. Dewey carried the tote and plastic bag out of the bedroom. He dropped the tote near the apartment door then turned to walk back toward the bedroom swinging the plastic bag at his side. He turned into the small bathroom that, among other things, seemed to serve as a museum of malodorous memories.

Dewey extracted a small plastic container of hair remover and a flat cylinder of black shoe polish. Earlier today, he removed his Mohawk, leaving a collection of red cuts. His Mohawk was only one of many looks he was experimenting with in his search for the ultimate bad-ass persona. He had long since discontinued wearing the nose ring due to a severe infection he acquired from it.

Now with only crusty stubble left on his scalp and face, he opened the jar of hair remover and went to work. He slathered the contents of the bottle generously on his face and head. While he waited for the lotion to work, his thoughts drifted to something Anita Kloo had told him yesterday.

She had stopped Dewey outside the break room, clearly upset about things that were happening to her. She spoke in a hissing whisper, something about pigs picking on her. She said that scabs were coming up to her and calling her disgusting names. Her face was a crimson shade of rage, and her eyes were bulging out as she spoke.

He had no idea what the hell she was talking about, but he did catch the part about the scabs and his mind had sidetracked to that trail of thought. He hated scabs because Travis Tee hated scabs. All his union brothers and sisters hated scabs. He heard Travis Tee read a poem about scabs once at a union meeting. He wasn't sure what scabs did to earn that hate, but he despised them anyway the same as his grandpa hated niggers.

He recalled one time when he was young he was riding with his grandpa in his old pickup truck to get some tractor parts in town. They had gone over a hill in the road when his grandpa screamed nigger. It startled young Dewey so much that he almost pissed his pants. Then he saw the black man standing by the side of the road with two old suitcases. One of them was the shape of a guitar.

His grandpa slowed the pickup truck down and moved to the side of the road as he approached the man who noticed this and started to lift his suitcases. When his grandpa got right up to where the Negro was standing, he stepped on the gas pedal, which kicked up a lot of rocks and dust. He heard, or maybe felt, a loud thump against the truck as they sped back onto the blacktop. He looked back and saw the man lying down in the ditch but didn't know if he was alive or dead. One of the man's suitcases was lying partway onto the road, but he couldn't see where the guitar-shaped suitcase was.

He remembered his grandpa slamming his hands hard on the steering wheel and howling with laughter. "Woo haw! Goddamn, I got me a nigger! Hot shit damn if I didn't!" he shouted. He noticed his grandpa looking up and down at the rearview mirror as he giggled all the way into town. Dewey giggled along with him because he wasn't sure what would happen to him if he didn't show the same glee.

Dewey never heard what became of that black man on the side of the road but figured he was probably dead and gone. He grew to accept his grandpa's belief that one less nigger is a gain for the world at large. Even after the death of his grandpa, he didn't dare view black people in any other way.

Even as he lay dying in the nursing home, Grandpa practiced his nigger-hate. Dewey had watched as his grandpa was slowly disappearing because of his throat cancer. He went in and out of consciousness as he lay in his own horrible death stench. His grandpa barely knew that Dewey was standing next to his bed. He noticed that Grandpa hardly acknowledged anybody that came to see him until the last day when a black man in a white uniform came in to check on him.

He vividly remembered how his grandpa's eyes shot open as if startled by the appearance of a malevolent yellow-fanged satanic beast. Grandpa couldn't talk on account of his cancer, but he let out with a loud wet moan, his arthritic hand knotting into a fist and reaching toward the nurse aide. The black man mistook his actions as a call for comfort and approached Grandpa to administer help.

Grandpa growled through his toothless mouth, spitting vile specks outward. The black man attempted to dab at the moisture on Grandpa's chin but couldn't touch down on the thrashing chin.

"Now, now, Mr. Dumphrey, you have to calm down or you gonna get too hepped up. I can't help you all if that gonna happen," the aide said.

Grandpa did calm down but kept his eyes fixed on the aide. His mouth opened, and after a few seconds he moaned something that sounded like nnnaa. He made that sound once again and then died, his eyes still glaring at the aide even in death.

*   *   *

Dewey stood staring into the mirror, his face and head covered with the lotion. He thought about how scabs were like niggers. They were supposed to be hated. It was a natural thing that a person did without second guessing it. Dewey picked up a musty-smelling washcloth and ran some tap water on it.

Wiping the lotion off was a messy process, but the results were what he was hoping for. Though his face and head stung, he noticed they shone cleaned with not a speck of hair to be found. He was Mr. Clean. He also noticed that his face and scalp were a bright red from the procedure but smiled because he knew the next process would take care of that.

After drying his face and head, he opened the container of shoe polish and dabbed some of it onto another crusty but dry washcloth. With a look of intense concentration, he rubbed the polish on his head. Then he rubbed more and more. After twenty minutes of this, his whole head and face was black. His eyes shone white and wide through the black with a set of white teeth slowly making an appearance too. For this night only, he was a nigger, he thought to himself. His plan for tonight required it.

CHAPTER 19

It was 7:15, right on time. He pulled on his black hooded sweatshirt, grabbed his tote bag, and opened the door. He locked the apartment door behind him and headed for the outside door. As he was leaving, he walked by the elderly lady from the next apartment.

"Well, good evening, Dewey. How are you this fine evening?" she warbled. She squinted through her glasses, wondering at Dewey's dark face but wrote it off as a nighttime illusion.

"Very well, Bernice. Thank you." He liked Bernice Schmidt. She always brought a plate of freshly baked cookies for him.

"Well, you have a good night," she said as she entered her apartment. She closed the door.

"Oh, I will, Bernice. I really will," he muttered under his breath as he turned and walked toward his rusty Chevy Citation. Bernice watched him get into his car through her kitchen window as she dialed her rotary phone.

By the time Dewey was driving to his destination, the sun had disappeared from the horizon a half hour ago and the solid darkness of night was displacing the ambivalent color of dusk. The October air became heavier and cooler, so Dewey yanked the cord tight on his hood to contain his body heat. Among other important features, the broken heater in his old Citation relied on ambient temperatures for anything resembling comfort inside.

Soon he found himself approaching the employee parking lot at the rear of the massive AgMotiv building. He killed the headlights and brought the car to a full stop near the fence line that discouraged intruders such as him from entering. To his right, he could see the parking area sprinkled grid-like with incandescent lamps mounted on tall poles.

Dewey allowed for second thoughts to tiptoe through his mind as he looked down at his tote bag. He began scanning the parking area for possible witnesses, focusing closer on the security shack located closest to the building.

Even with the lighting, it was difficult to see moving figures among the conglomeration of parked cars.

After a few more minutes, he was satisfied that he was all clear and slowly opened his car door. The old door let out a plaintive screech, causing Dewey to pause and make another perimeter check. Still not seeing any sign of life, he stepped out of the car with his tote bag in his hand. The interior light was another feature missing from Dewey's Citation, allowing him to leave his door slightly ajar for a quick and quiet reentry.

Dewey trotted off in a crouched posture toward the parking area and headed directly to a black 2008 Ford F-150. This was his first and main target. It belonged to that scabfuck Toivo, who once called Dewey a pee stain on the AgMotiv's underwear. When he told Travis Tee, he laughed so hard he fell off his chair at the union hall. Dewey was humiliated. He complained to that idiot King, who he knew was trying not to laugh himself but promised to talk to Toivo about it.

He knew Toivo would be working the nightshift for a few months so that he could hunt during the fall months. Dewey planned to do a little hunting himself tonight and bag a couple of scabs.

Dewey set the tote bag down next to the truck and took a quick peek to make sure the coast was clear. He reached into the tote bag and fished out one of the spray cans. As carefully and quietly as he could, he shook the can then spelled "SCAB" on the driver side of the F-150. Little trails of paint ran down from the letters. He paused to inspect his work and to enjoy the scent of the paint. If he had any left after tonight, he would take it home and spray some into a paper bag to sniff. It would be an awesome nightcap after his successful mission.

Dewey sidled over to the other side of the vehicle and sprayed "Sukass," and next to that he drew a penis with cum dripping out of it. He fancied himself an excellent artist and had left most of his handiwork in bathrooms throughout the factory and the town.

It took Dewey about thirty-five minutes to hit all the cars that he had targeted. He worked off a list the union kept of the names of the scabs. Unfortunately, he was only going to be able to hit the night scabs. He would figure out another way to attack the daytime targets later.

Satisfied his mission was complete, he glanced around then started back to his car. So immersed in thoughts of his great achievement, he missed the slight noise off to his left. Soon he arrived at the gate and noticed his car wasn't there!

Dewey spun around desperately searching for his car. His stomach pulled into a tight knot and sweat started to break out on his forehead even in the cool October night. This time he clearly heard the sound of feet rushing quickly toward him from behind. He spun around in time to get knocked off his feet and slammed hard onto his back. The tackle took his breath away, which caused him to gasp and cough violently.

He soon realized that there was more than one person involved in his assault. Two of the attackers pinned Dewey to the ground while a third one unbuckled his pants. Soon he felt his pants being pulled down around his ankles and then completely off. His underwear went next along with his hooded sweatshirt and T-shirt.

"What the fuck are you doing? Leave me alone! Who the fuck are you?" Dewey's voice had returned, and he wasted no time communicating his confusion and anger.

The third person took his bundle of clothes and ran off some distance. Soon he heard a car door close and the person could be heard running back toward Dewey and his assaulters.

"Hey! What the fuck! Give those back!" Dewey tried to pull away from his holder, but the person was much too strong for him.

"Let me go, asshole! Who the fuck are you!" Dewey soon realized that his was the only voice you could hear. The attackers never spoke or made any noises. One of the silent kidnappers pulled a strip of duct tape off a roll and wrapped it roughly around his mouth and head. They pulled Dewey's naked body up off the ground and the three of them carried him in the direction of the plant. They stopped outside the employee entrance and set Dewey down by a light pole.

Dewey's arms were yanked back so they were reverse-hugging the pole. He heard more duct tape being pulled and felt it being wrapped around his wrists. More duct tape was wrapped around his ankles and knees making him a semipermanent part of the lamp pole. Finally, a last wrap was made around his chest as he helplessly looked on. Then as if the silent man had remembered something he almost forgot, he pulled out another length of tape and wrapped it around Dewey's pecker. Dewey groaned knowing that would hurt when it was eventually removed.

One of the parking lot marauders trotted off and soon appeared with what looked to Dewey as some kind of poster. He heard the scratching sound of more duct tape being pulled and he could see out of the corner of his eye that they taped the poster on a rack near where he was standing. He watched as one of the men placed his spray cans by his feet.

In the next instant, the three nighttime ninjas took off in a silent run toward the parking lot entrance. He heard the sound of three doors shut and the vehicle drive away. Dewey was now alone listening to the hiss and hum of the industry directly behind him. And he was cold even though most of his naked body was covered in duct tape. His fear and confusion was now being replaced by impending dread and embarrassment. In about four hours the shift would end, and people would be flooding out of the plant to their parked cars. And they would see . . .

Dewey remembered the poster and twisted his head around to get a look at it. He could see that it was a light-colored poster with dark writing on it. It was night, so he had to strain his eyes to make out the words. His eyes slowly adjusted and he could read what it said. In neatly written letters, it said:

I am a steward for UGLI
If you are not a member of UGLI
You are a SCAB
I marked your cars
If you don't believe me
Check my fingerprints on the cans

CHAPTER 20

The night sky began filling with floating snowflakes that seem to suddenly create themselves one hundred feet above the ground. They landed heavily like paratroopers onto the windshield but quickly dissolved into a wet mess.

The police officers had managed to remove Dewey Dumphrey from the light pole with stoic faces. Only Officer Kilmer suffered a bloodied tongue when he bit down hard on it in order to discourage a smile from breaking out on his round face. Now he and his partner, Lew Todd, were transporting Dewey, who was huddled and shivering naked underneath a blanket in the backseat of the patrol car, to the station house downtown. The spray cans were carefully gathered and placed into the trunk of the car along with the sign that was attached next to Dewey on the light pole. For the most part, Dewey lay silently along the length of the seat. Every now and then, a barely audible whimper could be heard leaking out of the folds of the wool bundle. Within minutes, the group had arrived at the station and Lew Todd opened the back door to let Dewey out.

"Let's go, sir. We're here," Todd said.

Dewey moaned but didn't make a move to get out of the squad car.

"Come on, let's go," Todd repeated impatiently.

Again, Dewey moaned but this time added a whine.

"No. Leave me alone," Dewey said.

"Sir, you are going to have to get out of the car. Move it," ordered Todd.

Dewey slowly tilted and rolled toward the door while trying to keep his body parts covered with the blanket. His body, and especially his man parts, still stung from the duct tape removal. Finally, he was out of the car and being guided toward a door leading into the police station. His bare feet slapped along the linoleum floor in the hallway leading to the holding area. A female officer was waiting at the open holding cell and promptly closed it after Dewey was inside.

"My feet are cold. Can't you get me shoes or something?"

"We'll find something for you. Sit tight, Tiger." The female officer's laugh turned into a phlegmy cough as she walked toward the front office area. She was gone for about twenty minutes and returned with a grocery bag and unlocked the door.

"I've called for clothes, but all I could find were these. They should work for now until they come." She dropped the bag on the cell floor and left, closing the door behind her. Dewey heard her croaking chuckle as she walked away. He rose off the bench and picked up the bag. He opened the bag as he returned to the bench and sat down.

"What the fuck! Hey, get back here! What's this shit?!" He banged on the bars and the door pushed open. He looked around, but nobody came in or even appeared to be anywhere nearby. He looked back into the bag and pulled out the contents.

Chapter 21

He looked around before he pushed the cell door wide open and walked out of his cell. Locating an exit door was no great challenge when he quickly found a fire door, and to his good fortune, an alarm wasn't set to go off when he went through it. The Santa Claus boots were very loose on Dewey's feet and were made for size ten feet and Dewey measured out at seven and a half, so running in them was difficult—but run he did. It was about 7:30 in the morning and the sidewalks were crowded as Dewey ducked and dodged through the throng of people heading to their jobs. For the most part, people would move out of his way. Nobody seemed willing to deter anybody whose face was stained dark, wearing a blanket and large black boots.

But cell phone calls were made, and soon the sound of sirens could be heard nearby. Dewey quickly ducked into an alley and hid behind a greasy dumpster as one black-and-white car cruised by.

He heard rustling nearby and looked around. He saw a raunchy-looking man lying under a pile of cardboard and newspapers. The hobo was looking back at him and then at his boots.

"Those are nice boots there, young man," he said in a crusty voice. "Care to part with them for a fee?"

Dewey looked down at his boots and then at the man. "How much a fee?"

"I gotta a buck here," the bum said, holding out a crumpled bill.

"Fuck you," Dewey answered.

"Okay, I'll throw in my shoes," the derelict countered.

Dewey looked down at the man's shoes that looked like they used to be a pair of respectable Nikes in their day. One of the shoes was missing laces. Dewey looked at his own boots and then back at the raggedy man's shoes.

"Okay, I'll take them," Dewey said as he sat down to remove his boots. "And don't forget the dollar."

"That blanket looks warm. How much you want for that?" the man asked.

"It's not for sale. I don't have anything on underneath," Dewey said while tugging it tighter around him.

"How about my pants and shirt?" the old man offered.

"They look pretty dirty," Dewey said.

"I just had them laundered last week. The soiling is fairly recent. I guarantee."

"Well, okay." Dewey removed the blanket then noticed the bum pointing a gun at him.

"Let's renegotiate. I'll keep the boots, the blanket, my shoes, and my clothes and you get your stupid ass out of my alley." The hobo glared at Dewey with a stern face that offered no hope of counterproposal. Dewey slowly dropped the shoes and his blanket to the littered ground. He stood there shivering not sure what to do next.

"I-I'm cold."

The bum looked around where he had been sitting and found a crumpled newspaper. He picked it up and tossed it toward Dewey.

"Here, this should be proof that I'm not totally heartless. Now get out of here, ass-wipe." The bum gestured toward the street with the barrel of his gun. Dewey picked up the newspaper and wrapped it around his middle as best he could. He slowly started walking backward toward the mouth of the alley.

"I'm going to tell the police," Dewey said. The derelict jerked the gun toward Dewey who turned and broke into a dash toward the street. After he was gone, the bum pulled the trigger, causing a stream of water to shoot about three feet away and sprinkle to the ground. He busted out laughing.

Chapter 22

The day was clear and the sun was early morning high, but an autumn chill bathed the air around Dewey whose only possession was the crumpled paper that he held around his hips. Dewey caused quite a stir when he reentered the busy sidewalk.

Cell phones came out again as Dewey hobbled down the sidewalk, eventually finding another alley he hoped would offer him some refuge from any further assaults on his dignity. The new alley was cleaner than the last due to its location behind swanky boutiques and clothing stores. Clothing stores, thought Dewey.

Dewey lurked toward the rear entrance of a store with a simple but professionally printed sign over it identifying it as Andre's Clothier. Standing to the side of the glass door, he peeked into the store and observed an older, neatly dressed man toward the front of the store busily tidying up a stack of shirts. Dewey gently pulled on the door and once again found an unlocked door.

As quietly as possible, Dewey opened the door enough to enter without allowing too much of the outside chill to enter the store and draw attention. Inside, he held close to the wall and paused to assess his safety. He craned his head out from behind a couple of vinyl bags Dewey guessed contained suits. He couldn't see the man from where he was hidden but heard busy noises well away from him.

Dewey scanned the area around his hiding place to see what clothing was available for his use. The only items he could see were the suits next to him and a pair of brown wingtip shoes. He glanced over to a nearby shelf and noticed some neatly stacked sweaters. He started to venture out toward the warm-looking sweaters but stopped when he heard the sound of steps on carpeting moving toward his position.

Panicking, he swung his head from side to side looking for a better place to hide. He noticed the edge of a door behind a group of trousers hanging by the rear door. He sidled toward the partially hidden door and found the handle. He opened the door, the light from the store briefly lighting the interior. He ducked inside into a small restroom and closed the door, again shutting away all light, worried the old man was standing right outside.

After listening for a few minutes, he heard the steps returning to the store front. He leaned the back of his head against the door and felt soft fabric. Turning toward the door, he felt the clothing identifying them as pants and a shirt. His heart leapt for joy. He pulled the pants off the hanger and immediately put them on. Next he grabbed the shirt causing the hanger to bump noisily against the door. His heart jumped and he froze. He leaned his ear against the door but didn't hear anything.

He resumed dressing, putting on the shirt then feeling around the floor in hopes of finding shoes. He got on all fours and slowly and methodically traced the floor but found nothing. Then he remembered the wingtips outside the door. Carefully, he opened the door and saw the shoes on the opposite wall.

Crawling slowly out of the bathroom, he reached out toward the shoes. He heard before he felt the handcuff clap around his wrist. He jerked away in surprise. "Well, there you are." Dewey looked up and saw the familiar face of the policeman that took him to the police station. He looked at the gold name tag on his chest with the name Lew Todd engraved on it. The old man he saw earlier fidgeted behind him.

"Shopping are we?"

CHAPTER 23

"We better get your picture before you leave us again," the female chortled through her curtain of phlegm. Dewey stood against the height chart, relieved that he was fully clothed at last even though the suit they gave him to wear was a bright orange. At least the slippers they provided him were an improvement over the Santa boots.

The policewoman finished adjusting the camera and turned her attention to Dewey, who was fidgeting against the wall. "Okay, say cheese. Hold that board up a little higher, tiger," she said, indicating the identification board with Dewey's name and assigned prisoner number.

After the photo was taken, Dewey was taken to another part of the station where they inked his fingers and rolled them onto a card. Afterward, he was escorted in handcuffs to a somber-looking room furnished with a square table with metal legs and four chairs that should have been replaced years ago. Dewey was directed to one of the chairs and his cuffs removed.

"Now you sit here and behave yourself," the policewoman advised. She turned to leave.

"What going to happen now? I didn't do anything," Dewey said.

"A nice man will come in and ask you some questions," she answered. She gave Dewey a sincere smile and exited the room leaving him alone. He recognized the two-way mirror and knew that people might be watching him like on TV. He waved at the mirror.

Soon he was joined by a man who introduced himself as Detective Adams. The detective sat down and placed a folder onto the table in front of him. He wrote some notes on a yellow tablet then looked up at Dewey.

"Well," the detective said. "You've had quite a day of adventure, haven't you?"

"Why am I here?" Dewey asked. "I didn't do anything. You should go after those guys that taped me to the pole. I'm the victim here."

"I'm afraid it's a little more complicated than that. We checked your fingerprints against the ones on the spray paint cans. They're yours." Detective Adams paused and looked into Dewey's eyes for a few uncomfortable moments then asked, "Why did you spray paint those vehicles?"

"What's the big deal? Just make me pay a fine and let me go. It's not like I killed anybody," Dewey said and looked away.

"Some people wouldn't agree with you and then there are the other charges," the detective said as he opened the folder.

"What other charges?" Dewey asked with a surprised look on his face. He knew he was busted on the graffiti but was unaware of any other law he might have broken.

"Well, let's see," Adams said while looking at the open folder. "We have escaping from custody, unlawful entry, attempted theft, and indecent exposure."

Dewey looked at the detective, his mouth gaped.

"I want a union steward," Dewey said.

"Excuse me. You want what?" Adams asked.

"I'm a member of the UGLI union and I demand a steward." Dewey sat back in his chair and crossed his arms defiantly across his chest.

"Ugly . . . ? Do you mean a lawyer?" Adams asked.

"I said what I want. This is union animus."

"This is union . . . what?"

"You are picking on me because I'm a union member."

"Mr. Dumphrey, you have been charged with crimes. I don't think this is a matter for your, ah, union."

"It is so. I painted those cars because they belong to scabs. That is official union business."

"Are you saying your union put you up to this?" Now Detective Adams sat back and crossed his arms. As a member of his own union, the Police Officers Union, he knew something about unions. He knew what scabs were. And although his union was rather low-keyed, he had heard of unions that were militant and used scare tactics against management and especially on nonunion workers. But for a union to openly commit crimes as a course of business was something he thought only happened in movies.

"Okay, Mr. Dumphrey, who should we call?"

Dewey smiled triumphantly. "It's in the phonebook. Look it up."

"Who's in the phonebook?"

"The union is, Einstein. UGLI. United General Laborers International.

"All right, I'll be right back." He got up then leaned over the table toward Dewey so that he was an inch away from his nose. "And it's Detective Einstein to you. Got it?"

Dewey reared back with genuine concern on his face. "Y-yes, I got it."

Adams smiled and winked at Dewey then left the room.

CHAPTER 24

Officers Todd and Kilmer rolled to stop at the AgMotiv Plant around 9:00 on a chilly Thursday morning. Kilmer called in their presence at the plant, and both men got out of the patrol car. They approached the small security shack and informed the nervous guard that they needed to see one Travis Tee and Ralph Lynch. The security guard made a phone call to someone in the plant, and within minutes a supervisor approached the officers and introduced himself. The officers followed the supervisor into the plant while the security guard pulled his own badge away from his uniform and looked at it. Someday he hoped he would be able to trade it in for a police badge.

The supervisor guided the policemen into a lunchroom filled with two rows of tables covered with small dirty lunchboxes and newspapers and magazines. The floors looked as if they hadn't been mopped in years, and the walls were in need of a new coat of paint, perhaps something other than the crusty blue that currently surrounded the room. The officers decided to remain standing rather than risk ruining their uniforms on the dusty grease-covered chairs scattered loosely around the tables.

In a few minutes the supervisor returned with a stocky man wearing a dirty yellow T-shirt and jeans with pieces of duct tape randomly placed on it. "This is Ralph Lynch. Travis is absent from work today," the supervisor said. Lew Todd thanked the supervisor who left the room and turned to Ralph who stood with his legs apart and arms folded.

"What's this about?" Ralph asked with an edge of contempt in his voice.

"Mr. Lynch, my name is Sergeant Todd, and this is Sergeant Kilmer from the police department. We'd like to ask you a couple questions concerning one Dewey Dumphrey."

"Dewey. This must be about his escapades last night. I don't know anything about it," Ralph said then turned to leave.

"Mr. Lynch, we still need to ask a few more questions. Why don't you have a seat?"

"I told you I don't know anything about that," Ralph said.

"We never said what this was about. Please, sir, have a seat. It shouldn't take long." Todd sat down himself against his better wishes. Kilmer selected what he hoped was a relatively clean chair and eased himself down into it. Finally, Ralph grabbed the chair nearest to him and plopped down into it. Kilmer noticed that it was one of the filthier ones.

Both officers flipped open notebooks and clicked their pens in unison. Todd spoke first.

"I understand from talking to Mr. Dumphrey that you are the president of the local union here."

"Yep." Ralph slouched in his chair with his arms folded across his chest.

"Mr. Tee is the business agent for this plant?" Todd continued wondering for the first time if he was named after the black actor that got his start in a Rocky movie.

"Yep."

"Mr. Dumphrey said . . ." Todd flipped the notepaper and stopped at a page. "He claimed that his spray painting of the vehicles in the parking lot was union business."

"Oh shit." Ralph looked at the floor to his side and rolled his head back.

"What did he mean by that? Did the union tell him to spray those cars?"

Ralph snorted. "That's stupid. Why would the union tell him to do that?

"That's what we want to know."

Ralph paused then said, "No. If Dewey spray painted those vehicles, he did it on his own. The union doesn't condone that behavior. We protect workers. Not fuck them over. Shit."

"Dewey said he did it because the owners of those vehicles were scabs. Do you take adverse actions against these nonunion employees?"

Ralph smiled. "You guys are in a union, aren't you? What do you think of scabs?

Todd glanced at Kilmer.

"This isn't about us, Mr. Lynch. I asked you a question. Does your union condone taking adverse actions against nonunion employees?

"Nah. We don't take adverse actions against scabs," Ralph said with a smirk.

"Why do you think Mr. Dumphrey implied that the union sanctioned his actions?"

"He's a confused young kid. He means well."

"You think vandalism is a good thing?" Todd glared into Ralph's eyes.

"This is bullshit. Am I being arrested or something? I'm going to leave now," Ralph said as he arose from his chair.

"Sit down! We aren't done yet."

"This is bullshit," Ralph said as he plopped back into his chair.

"Did the union in any way encourage or suggest that Mr. Dumphrey spray paint anti-scab comments on the vehicles last evening?"

Ralph leaned forward in his chair and looked Officer Todd into his eyes. "No."

"Are you aware if Mr. Tee encouraged or suggested Mr. Dumphrey spray paint on the vehicles?"

"No." Ralph continued glaring at Todd.

"You're not aware but he might have?"

"No. You're twisting my words. We don't do that shit. Okay?"

Todd paused as he made notes then flipped his book shut.

"Okay. Thanks for your cooperation," Todd said. All three men stood up, and Ralph quickly exited the room. Todd looked at Kilmer and smiled.

"So. There it is."

Outside, the officers approached the security guard and asked him to notify the supervisor that they were done. The guard said, "Yes, sir" and picked up the phone. He watched with a smile on his face as the officers returned to the patrol car.

"Someday," he said to himself.

CHAPTER 25

Judge Winston Fredericks wasn't in the best of mood this morning. He received a call from his son the previous evening stating that he had been arrested in Baltimore, Maryland, for possession of a controlled substance and resisting arrest. He had curtly demanded, not asked, for bail money while claiming he was set up by the "fuckin' pigs."

Fredericks had always considered the police a hierarchy of armed bureaucrats who closed ranks when one of theirs was in trouble. This included lying in open court when they thought it necessary to cover up a procedural slipup. But for all their faults, he respected the work they did and appreciated the danger that faced them every day they showed up for work. He never considered them pigs, fuckin' or otherwise.

His son, on the other hand, had started down the path toward a life of aimless hedonism and recklessness. This downward spiral began during his junior year in high school when he started hanging out with a crowd of losers who would show up at his door and parade right past him without permission or greeting up the stairs to his son's room. Soon after obnoxious laughter and loud music, if you could call what comes through his door music, spilled outward and made normal thinking and conversation difficult.

His mother would caution the judge to be patient and let his son spread his wings and let him explore his life. He would outgrow his exploration in time, she would say. That was six years ago. Since then he began his journey of exploration hitchhiking around the country until he finally landed in Maryland. He rarely telephoned home, and when he did it was to ask for a "loan" that he would pay back as soon as his deal went through. When asked about the deal, he would laugh and say it was a business investment and change the subject. And now he needed bail money. The pieces were coming together.

He wasn't sure he made the right decision when he told him he was an adult and he needed to solve his own problems. That thought hung over his head as he pulled into his parking space at the rear of the courthouse. Today he would be hearing cases similar to his son's, and that made him feel hypocritical—him passing judgment on people no worse than a member of his own family. Was there hope for his son? Would his son learn responsibility? Was there hope for the people in court today?

His first case was nothing like his son's. It involved a bushel basket of charges, including escaping custody, attempted theft, vandalism, and indecent exposure. This made him feel a little better about his son's trouble. At least he hasn't fallen this far. He couldn't wait to hear more about this case.

The uniformed bailiff rose from his chair and called court into session, introducing the judge in a loud voice. The clerk of court seated to the side of the bench then read from a document.

"The first case is the State of North Dakota versus Dewey Dumphrey on charges of vandalism, destruction of property, escaping custody, criminal trespass, attempted theft, and indecent exposure."

"You had a busy day, didn't you?" the judge said without humor, glancing toward the defendant's table.

"I . . . ," Dewey said before his court-appointed lawyer placed his hand on his arm and got up from his chair.

"I will be representing Mr. Dumphrey in this matter," said defense attorney Miles Martin, who was one year out of law school and earning his stripes as a court-appointed advocate.

"Hello, Miles. So. How do we plead today?" Fredericks said nonchalantly with his head down while making notes.

"This is complicated case, your honor."

"I'll bet," the judge said with a smile. The scattering of people in the courtroom giggled, resulting in a quick tap of the gavel. Quiet returned.

"Although Mr. Dumphrey didn't leave the clothing store with any products and so couldn't rightfully be found guilty of theft—attempted or otherwise. And although Mr. Dumphrey was indecently exposed through no fault of his own. We wish to plead guilty to the charges based on our discussions with the States Attorney Office," Martin said.

"Hmm. And the states recommendation?" Judge Fredericks asked, looking at the assistant district attorney.

"The state accepts the guilty plea of the defendant in return for a deferred imposition for 360 days. The state understands that the defendant has no priors and was caught up in a series of events that got out of hand."

"Interesting. I believe we have a felony or two included in the charges. This offer seems to be a bit lenient, don't you think, counsel?" Fredericks asked the ADA with a look of bemusement.

"Your honor, if I may, this was a prank that went awry," Martin interjected. "He panicked and fled from custody. During this time he was robbed of his clothing and—"

"Robbed of his clothing, you say?" the judge asked with a puzzled look on his face. "How does something like that happen?

"Well, your honor, he, ah, was wearing only a blanket and, ah, Santa boots when he—"

"You're serious, aren't you?" The judge looked over at the bailiff with a confused look and then had to gavel laughers in the gallery.

"Yes, your honor, he—Mr. Dumphrey—was taken into custody wearing no clothing." The young lawyer paused to refer to his notes. "He was stripped of his clothing by unknown assailants during a prank spray painting several vehicles at AgMotiv Manufacturing."

Judge Fredericks stared down at both the lawyer and Dewey in rapt attention. This was quite a way to start the day. He had forgotten his son's problems under the twists and turns of this case.

"Go on."

"Anyway, your honor, he was duct taped to a light pole in his nakedness until the police arrived. A nearby, ah, handwritten poster claimed that he had spray painted the vehicles, so he was taken in to the station for questioning. During that time, he managed to escape, ah, leave through an unlocked door."

The judge caught the bailiff glancing at his watch and took that as a clue that a full day of cases lay in wait on the dockets.

"Your honor, the defendant has no prior—"

"Yes, yes, I understand," the judge said and paused, looking down at his notes. The courtroom was still for what seemed a little long before the judge looked up and turned his gaze toward Dewey, who slouched nervously in his chair.

"Mr. Dumphrey, things got out of hand for you, didn't they?

"Y-yes, sir. I won't do anything like that again, for sure," Dewey said then looked down at his folded hands.

Judge Frederick's son's face appeared in his mind as he sat pondering the case. He made some notes then looked down at Dewey.

"I'll accept the state's recommendation with the addition of two years' probation. Any further mischief from you and these charges will be restored. Do you understand?"

Both the young lawyer and Dewey looked at the judge with surprise.

"Yes, sir, your honor. Thanks, sir!" Dewey said.

"Just keep your nose clean, son." Judge Frederick tapped his gavel.

"Next case."

CHAPTER 26

"This is Barry Arnold, plant manager. Leave a message."

"Barry, I mean, Mr. Arnold, th-this is Dewey . . . Dumphrey. I just wanted to tell you that I would like to keep working at AgMotiv. I've always liked working there. I-I was let go from jail and I'm on probation. I know I did a bad thing there and I want to make it up. I will pay for all the cars I p-painted on. Please let me come back. I promise I will be your best worker and I won't cause any problems. Will you call me at 701-555-1432? Please call. Thank you very much, sir."

* * *

"What? You're joking, right?" Joe King said in a voice mixed with confusion and anger.

"No. I don't joke," Abi Deng said.

"But, but that's crazy. He's a lousy employee and a troublemaker. Why would we bring him back to work?"

"We return him because Mr. Arnold says so."

Joe King was frozen in disbelief, his mouth hung open and his arms were extended out from the elbows with the palms of his hands up. "I don't get it. Why? It doesn't make sense. This was a golden chance to rid ourselves of the poor performer. A troublemaker."

Abi Deng rose from his chair and walked out of King's office without another word. King watched as Deng strode back to his own office, his mind racing. He rose from his chair and walked into Deng's office and sat in a chair.

"Yes," Deng said in a flat voice.

"Abi . . ."

"Mr. Deng," Deng corrected.

"Mr . . . . Deng, this causes several problems for us if we bring him back. This will become past practice for other people we terminate. What is the basis for returning him to work? The next person we fire can—"

"Call him and tell him to come back to work," Abi Deng said.

"But . . ." Joe King stared into Deng's eyes and saw he wouldn't budge from his position. What did Arnold tell him? Deng held all the cards in this job with his race card lying face up ready to play every day. Why didn't he push back on Arnold? Why would Arnold want him back?

King's biggest headache came not from the union members, but too often from the unpredictable and rash machinations of the plant manager. He was known for dropping in unexpected, coffee cup in hand, planting himself in a chair and barraging the overloaded department manager with accusations masked as questions. Halfway through the answer, he would grab up his coffee cup and walk out of the office with a knowing smirk.

Joe King, not a fan of the union, knew that managers like Barry Arnold justified its existence. His lies, manipulations, favoritism, and reckless abuse of the labor agreement caused many uncomfortable meetings with the union leadership.

King wondered what drove his decisions. Arnold seemed to see himself as a mafia don who punished and rewarded at his whim. There seemed to be little logic involved in his thinking—only emotion. He could become angry for any unintended slight or as in a case of an employee coming to him hat in hand, the magnanimous father figure. Mostly he was merciless and always lobbying to have somebody fired sometimes simply because they didn't return his greeting. But Dewey, for god's sakes! What the hell was he thinking? The dimwit wouldn't last a week before he's stirring up shit again. King was so aggravated he wanted to grab Arnold's toupee off his head and slap the bejesus out of him.

"Call him," Deng repeated.

King returned to his office and picked up the phone. Finding Dumphrey's phone number, he dialed.

"Hello."

"Dewey, this is Joe King."

"Yeah."

"I'm calling to inform you that you are to return to work starting tomorrow,"

King said with his head resting on his other hand.

"Took you long enough." King could feel his blood pressure racing upward. "But I won't be able to start until Monday."

King hung up without offering a good-bye.

CHAPTER 27

Travis Tee walked briskly toward the spinning doors of the hotel with an escort of four bodyguards. He acknowledged the appreciative clapping and chirping whistles of the hotel staff with a quick wave.

Outside he was greeted by the city smell of trapped car exhaust heralded by their hollow honking sounds echoing off the tall buildings within the canyon of commerce. This was the odor of money and avarice—the belching, gurgling gluttony of corporate greed.

He was quickly coaxed into the back of the limousine and found himself wedged between two massive stone-faced men that dwarfed the husky Travis Tee. He felt something hard poking his hip and assumed it was a weapon hidden within the folds of the guard's overcoat on his left. The limo rushed confidently through the traffic as the men sat silently concentrating on moving chaos that was Chicago traffic. The cacophony of the metropolis was absent within the plush interior of the limousine. The only sound was the sporadic murmuring of the guards into the microphones hidden in their collar.

Within twenty minutes of leaving the hotel, they found themselves pulling up to another large hotel with a large mob of sign holders milling around the large awning-covered entrance. Soon eager fingers started pointing in recognition toward the limousine as people realized the great Travis Tee had arrived.

Travis Tee slowly pulled himself out of the back door of the limo and found himself immediately barricaded within the four bodyguards. Hands seeking to touch him were brushed away as he was pushed and pulled into the hotel. Inside he was met with a wall of cameras held up over the heads of the reporters, the flashing lights causing him to flinch.

He was directed down a long corridor, which ended with a door that they quickly passed through. He heard the growing roar of a large audience as they approached a double door. The guards shoved the doors open and the crowd noise fell out into *the hallway. The noise suddenly increased into a frantic crescendo when it became known that Travis Tee was present among them.*

Again, he was manhandled by his bodyguards when they rushed him to the side of the stage and gently pushed him up toward the rostrum. He saw that the Rev. Jesse Jackson was already in the middle of a speech.

The massive audience pushed forward toward the large stage in order to get a better view of the Rev. Jesse Jackson, who was in town to support the candidacy of Travis Tee to the presidency of the AFL-CIO. By now, the United General Laborers International had been readmitted to the federation as a result of Travis Tee's adroit political acumen.

He gained recognition by the other union labor leaders upon the publication of his book, Bad Business: Corporate's War on Workers. *The book shot to number one on the New York Times Bestseller list and was favorably reviewed in all the major magazines.* Newsweek *called Travis Tee the new voice for American labor. Even the conservative President Bush remarked that the "wonderful ideas presented in this work of art has caused him to rethink his opinion of unions."*

It was no surprise that the powerful and righteous Jesse Jackson was moved to humility when he turned and bowed to the seated Travis Tee behind him on stage. Travis Tee barely acknowledged Jackson as he sat erect in his chair with a resolute expression of erudition and power on his face. He watched out of the corner of his eye as Jackson turned back to the crowd. Jesse Jackson began addressing the crowd again, which went wild with a thunderous pandemonium of chants and cheers.

"My fellow working Americans," he began, "we are united here on this glorious day of redemption. Brothers and sisters of all colors join together today to salute a hero and to damn the oppressors."

"Salute a hero! Damn the oppressors!" chanted the throng of people. Travis Tee's neck stiffened as he lifted his chin and slowly swept the crowd with his piercing eyes.

"The world is ready for a hero!"

"Yeah!" responded the crowd.

"The world is ready for a savior!" Jesse Jackson pronounced it say-vee-your.

"Oh yeah!" a supporter shouted from the audience.

"They neeeeeeds a true savior!"

"Amen, brutha!" The crowd was swaying back and forth, each with one arm outstretched overhead.

"Brothers and sis-stas! We are on fire with desire!"

"Woobie woobie wah!" a black woman screamed from the front row.

"We's gonna rock and we's gonna roll. We's gonna shimmie rights down to our soul."

"Oh you all that Jesse!" the same woman shouted, bringing a wink from Jackson.

"You can sing all you please 'cuz we gonna bring da man down to his knees!"

"Yeah, yeah, to his knees!" the crowd responded.

"And now . . . and now," Jesse Jackson panted and wiped his forehead with a black kerchief. "We all knows the pain and sufferin' of the working person. We all knows the load we carry on our broken backs. We all knows the sorrow of our weepin' chillen who only ax for a lil crumb of bread. The boss man, he doan know the trouble he gives us. He doan know how he breakses our hearts. He only cares about the all-mightly dolla. He wants the dolla bill!"

"Dolla bill dolla bill dolla bill!"

"My peoples, the end is near. The light is at the end of the tunnel and it ain't a train a'comin' this time. The rain that falls from above is the rain of redempshun! The army of the peoples is a marching forward to rectify our miserable condition! We are being invited into the leemozeen of dignatee!"

The roar from the crowd was deafening and surely could be heard from many miles around. Travis Tee knew it as the sound of justice. It was the sweet sound of power given back to the people. Travis Tee listened as Jesse Jackson started to speak again.

"And who be the driver of dis here leemozeen, my peoples?" Jesse Jackson dramatically shrugged his shoulders and looked side to side in mock confusion. He paused again to wipe the sweat off his brows. "Why, the driver be none other than masta Travis Tee! He be the driver! He be the savior!"

The crowd went wild chanting, "Travis Tee, Travis Tee!"

"Travis!"

"Egregious!" Travis Tee was startled awake from his reverie. UGLI steward Anita Kloo was standing in front of him by his idling lathe, with her massive legs straddled and her heavy hands resting on her hips. Her odd-sized breasts were covered by a greasy Hillary in '08 T-shirt, with the larger breast causing Hillary to look like half her face was swollen.

"I want to file a grievance."

Travis took his work gloves off and rubbed his shaved head with a hand. "What's wrong?"

"What's wrong?" she repeated. "What's wrong is the scabs are after me. What are you going to do about it?"

"What scabs? What are you talking about?" Travis hated how she always started at the end of a conversation and made the listener struggle for background information.

"Jesus testicles, I'm talking about that dumb Finn Toivo and his band of creeps."

"Okay. And what are they doing?"

"What they are doing is saying shitty things to me." Travis Tee noticed her larger boob slightly swaying in her shirt. He felt his stomach start to fetch up bile.

"What are they saying to you, Anita?" Travis asked as calmly as he could in order to balance his voice with his reflux system.

"They are calling me a cow, slut, whore, and all kinds of things like that." A tear started to show in one of her eyes.

"Have you told Joe King?" Normally, Travis T wouldn't recommend union members use Joe to help solve problems; but in this case, he felt the need to share the wealth.

"Yeah, I told that loser and he won't do anything," she said while flailing her arms around. Her bigger boob shook, his bile oozed.

"I'll talk to Joe and see what we can do." Travis swallowed hard and grimaced.

"Oh, you'll talk to Joe, huh? Shitburger, you two won't do crap! I should go to the board and file a failure to represent charge on your sorry ass!" She turned and waddled off.

"Crap," Travis T muttered under his breath. She knew the buttons to push. The failure to represent complaint to the National Labor Relations Board posed a serious threat to unions. He knew most members had never heard about that course of action but, of course, Anita had. Now he was forced to take a more aggressive position on Anita's complaint. He put his gloves down on the work bench and headed toward the HR office. Jesus testicles, he thought.

CHAPTER 28

Joe King was sitting at his desk typing on his keyboard when Travis Tee strode into his office and fell into a chair. Joe glanced over at Travis Tee and greeted him with a quick nod. In a moment, Joe finished typing and pivoted around to face Travis.

"Aloha," Joe said with a big smile.

"Got a big problem," Travis Tee said in a somber tone.

"Is there any other kind, my man?" Joe grabbed a legal pad and pen.

"This is about Anita Kloo," Travis Tee said with a hint of frustration in his voice. Joe picked up on that right away.

"Oh my, what's up with her?"

"Yes, oh my. She says some guys in the shop are calling her names." Travis Tee looked down at the desk while he talked.

"I see." Joe King made a steeple with his fingers. "Tell me more."

"She says they are calling her a slut and whore."

"Ouch, that's not good." Joe winced. "Who's calling her that?"

"She said it's the sca . . . nonunion people in the plant."

"All of them?" Joe said then began silently counting on his fingers. "Jeez, there must be about fifty or sixty of those out there. Was she more specific?"

"All she said for sure was Toivo."

"Ah, Toivo Jurva. So he's calling her these names? What's that all about do you suppose?" Joe King didn't think Toivo would call people names, but he might be up to something. He knew Toivo could be creative from earlier discussions he'd had with him.

"I don't know, but he should stop. She can make life difficult for both of us," Travis Tee said with renewed authority in his voice.

"It sounds like we have accepted as fact that he's said the things she accuses him of," Joe King innocently proclaimed.

"All I know is that she will make it a big deal and we will both suffer."

"Hmmm . . . so should I fire Toivo?" Joe was fishing with live bait.

"I don't think you need to go that far. How about you just suspend him?" Travis Tee looked at Joe with a look of hope.

"I think we should fire him. I mean, if Anita says he did it, well, by golly, that's good enough for me." Joe picked up his pen and wrote on his pad: Terminate Toivo. Out of the corner of his eye, he could see Travis Tee's face go pale. "Done and done."

"No, now stop it. He doesn't need to get fired. Forget it. Let me go talk to him and see what he says about this," Travis offered.

"Talk to him, hmm . . . yes, yes, I think that might just work. You go talk to him and let me know what he says," Joe said with a look of absolute seriousness.

*   *   *

Travis Tee located Toivo stooped over a pallet of parts loaded on the prongs of his forklift. He appeared to be adjusting the parts on the pallet.

"Hello, Toivo."

"Hyva Paiva, T-man." Toivo gave the standard Finnish greeting with gusto.

"Call me Travis."

"Okay . . . Travis, what can I do for you this fine day?"

"I got a complaint from someone that you are calling her names," Travis said in a quiet voice.

"What? I can't hear you. It's loud out here. Could you speak up?" It was indeed loud in the plant when all the machines were running, which required people to wear earplugs. As a matter of fact, Toivo did hear Travis.

"I said, we got a complaint from someone that you are calling an employee dirty names!" Travis loudly repeated.

"Thirty names? I don't understand," Toivo asked with a puzzled look on his face.

"Dirty names!" yelled Travis, leaning forward toward Toivo.

"Who?"

"You!"

"Somebody called me dirty names? Why?"

"No, you called someone dirty names!" Travis Tee was beginning to show the effects of weary frustration.

"I called someone dirty names? I don't get it. Why would I call someone dirty names?" Toivo asked, with the palms of his hands outstretched by his sides.

"I don't know why you would call someone names." Travis felt himself getting absolutely nowhere, but then he recalled Anita's threat to go the board.

"But you gotta stop it! Right now!" With that, Travis walked quickly away and back to the relative comfort of his job.

Toivo went back to his work when Rod Olson walked up to him from behind. "Hey, Toivo. Joe King needs to see you up in HR," Olson told him.

"I'm a popular guy today. All right, I'm on my way." Olson walked away as Toivo hopped into the forklift and cranked it up.

*   *   *

Toivo knocked on the open door to Joe's office. "Joe, you need to see me?"

"Yeah, Toivo, come in. Have a seat," Joe said, gesturing toward the chair across from his desk.

"What did I do now?" Toivo asked in half-jest.

"Well, it appears that you have been mentioned in a name-calling incident," Joe replied.

"Yes, so I heard."

"Oh, you know about it already?"

"Yeah, Travis already confronted me with it," Toivo said.

"I see. And what was the outcome of that discussion?" Joe asked.

"I'm not sure. He told me to stop it and walked away."

"Well, have you been calling her names?"

"Oh, Joe, you know I have more class than that." Toivo hoped Joe didn't recognize the nonanswer.

"Why do you suppose she is saying what she is saying?" Joe felt a little uncomfortable that he didn't really answer his question.

"I have no idea except that I'm not in the union and that bugs her."

"Yeah, I see. That could be it," Joe said pensively then added, "so you haven't called her names then?"

"Come on, Joe. Would I do that?" Again, the nonanswer.

"All right, well, let me know if you hear of anything with this situation." Joe watched as Toivo got up to leave.

"You know, Joe," Toivo said before walking out of the office, "I think Anita might have some serious issues. I've seen her having run-ins with other employees a lot these days. She's creating quite a hostile work environment out there."

"Oh, yeah? I haven't heard about that. Who else has she mixed it up with?" Joe picked up his pen. As Toivo talked, Joe wrote several names down on his legal pad. He knew he would have to follow up with them in the near future.

CHAPTER 29

UGLI steward Anita Kloo was no stranger to the grievance procedure at AgMotiv. She had, in fact, written one hundred twelve of them in her twelve years with the company. Twenty-one of those grievances were written by her on behalf of other union members in her role as shop steward. The other ninety-one were written on her own behalf for injustices heaped upon her over all these years. Of those grievances, seventy-five were written for sexual harassment and/or sexual discrimination. None of those grievances ever reached the level of an arbitration hearing but remained open in a latent status. Joe King referred to those grievances held open indefinitely as the bone pile.

Unions are a highly political entity that must give the appearance, at least, of providing service to its members. This bone pile is a safe way to deal with grievances that the union local knows have no merit but which the grieving member sincerely believes does. The grievance-handling members of the unit are often afraid to tell the grievant that their complaint isn't valid, so they will place the grievance in a "union hold" and hope that everybody will forget about them. After a few years have passed and nothing was said about the grievance, it will quietly be dropped from the list and buried.

When UGLI steward Anita Kloo stomped into Joe King's office with a paper in her hand, he could smell another grievance being filed. For sure he smelled something unpleasant. She flipped the sheet of paper toward King, who was sitting behind his desk. The paper hitched upward in the air then boomeranged back and made the long orbit around Kloo's massive thighs landing about three feet behind her. Her anger increased as she wheeled around and bent over to retrieve it from the floor. Joe King wasn't able to look away in time and received a light-eclipsing view of Kloo's buttocks.

This time she slammed the now crinkled document on top of King's desk with a loud thump. She stood glaring down at the passive King while panting from her recent exertions.

"Can I help you?" King asked.

"I doubt it," Kloo countered.

"Okay then."

"Okay what?"

"You doubt that I can help you."

"I doubt you can."

"Okay then."

"Are you fucking with me?"

King's stomach twisted and hitched. "No."

"Well, there's my grievance," Kloo grunted.

"I see. Do you want to give me some details on it?"

"It's on the grievance. Can't you read?"

"Yes, I can," King calmly answered as he looked at her.

"Well, read it then."

"Okay, let's see," Joe said as he picked up the document. He held it up and started reading it aloud.

"Nature of grievance: Harassment of sexual nature. Articles violated: Actical two—"

"Actical? It says article. What? You can't read?"

"I can read. It says actical."

"No, it doesn't," Kloo said.

"Yes, it does I'm afraid. It says actical."

"Bullshit!" Kloo grabbed the grievance form out of King's hand, causing it to rip into two uneven pieces. "Shit. Now you ripped it."

UGLI steward Anita Kloo's eyes moved over her half of the form. Then she reached over to snatch the other half that was still held by King. That half also ripped in half again.

"Shit! You ripped it again." Anita's face was the color of dried blood. Her lower jaw trembled.

"Here, take this piece too before it gets ripped," Joe offered in a soft voice.

Kloo snatched the scrap, which held together this time. She started puzzling it back together on the desk. She restored it to its right form and looked at King.

"Well?"

"Yes?" Joe said, his innocent eyes wide as he looked at her.

"God damn it! Do you have any Scotch tape?"

"I do." King reached across his desk and picked up the dispenser that was sitting by Kloo's elbow. She winced.

"Watch yourself, Bub," she warned. She pulled some tape out and tried to break it off on the cutter, but it folded onto itself. She grunted and wadded it up and attempted to drop the wad, but it stuck stubbornly to her fingers. She uttered a curse and tried again with no success. After a few wild attempts at removal by shaking it, she grabbed the wad with the fingers of her other hand, this time the wad agreeing to make the transfer. But liking its new home, the wad firmly held thwarting her attempts to flick it off. It finally agreed to attach itself to the desktop, allowing her to make another attempt. By then, Kloo was through trying and stormed out of the office.

Joe King reached across the desk and retrieved the pieces of the documents and proceeded to restore it with tape utilizing a skill honed by years of office work. In less than a minute, he had it back together and soon after had logged it into the grievance list with the number 09-198. The 09 represented the year 2009, and the 198 represented the 198th grievance of that year.

At first, King thought it related to the Foster butt-bumping incident. Instead, her beef concerned employees making profane comments to her. Through several tearful meetings, she alleged that several employees told her she smelled like farts or something about cows pooping. She claimed other similar comments being made to her during the workday, but to King they made no sense.

Nonetheless, it is the company's policy to investigate all such cases, which meant King had to make a list of her alleged verbal assaulters and call them in one at a time for questioning. He expected and received denials and confused looks. Next, King called in employees that worked in Kloo's general work area along with those that worked in the alleged perpetrator's areas. More denials and more confused looks.

In the end, nobody confirmed (or denied for that matter) hearing that anything unusual was said to her. He could only discern from the sighing and eye rolling that Anita was a tiresome fixture of the company. Most of the people he talked to, in fact, said that they tried to keep a safe distance from her. He had to verbally reprimand one employee when he referred to her as One-Point-Two Kloo, which he explained was the number of breasts she had. King told him that he didn't want to hear that term again or there would be serious consequences.

*   *   *

A few days after his last meeting with Kloo, King contacted her supervisor to request that she report to his office at two in the afternoon to give her the results of his investigation on her grievance. Although not required to, he told her she could have a steward present with her. King made certain he had someone from the management side in the room to witness the proceedings. He chose the only female supervisor, Melissa Swan, to sit in and take notes. Kloo showed up in King's office fifteen minutes early and proceeded to interrogate him on the results of his investigation. He instructed her to have a seat outside his office and they would start at two. She objected, claiming she had a lot of work to do and didn't have time to dillydally.

King said, "I think this is important enough for us to take the time. Please have a seat and we'll start soon."

"You're going to tell me I'm wrong, aren't you?" she asked, the question coming out more like a statement of fact.

"Please have a seat and relax," King repeated patiently. Kloo sat down in the chair in front of King's desk. "I meant in a chair outside my office."

"You don't believe me, do you?" Kloo asked.

"Anita," King said, pointing at the chair outside his office, "sit there."

"Did you just call me a shit bear?"

"What?" King bellowed.

"You called me a shit bear."

"Oh for Christ sakes! You know what, Anita? I'm starting to get the picture here. You want to know what I think. You are making all this stuff up about people calling you names. You just proved that to me." King glared at Anita.

"You can't talk to—"

"Your complaint is without merit. Your complaint is unwarranted. Go back to work," King ordered in a slightly raised voice.

"But—"

"Now!"

UGLI steward Anita Kloo huffed and quickly walked out of his office.

CHAPTER 30

Dewey Dumphrey walked hurriedly down the plant aisle and crossed an intersection, which caused a forklift to screech to a sudden stop. The driver barked out for Dewey to watch his stupid ass, but Dewey kept walking, oblivious to the near miss. He came upon a pallet piled about a foot high with cap parts and proceeded to hop over it. His foot caught one of the caps, and he fell hard to the ground striking his left knee. Dewey jumped up and kept moving, this time with a limp. Dewey was HR bound with a grievance form in hand. The noted reason for the grievance was age discrimination.

The investigation report stated that the alleged incident leading to the claim of age discrimination occurred last evening about 7:00 p.m. when Production Supervisor George Burnside noticed Jimmy Bosch, an employee assigned to the paint line, sitting on a stool eating a banana on work time. Burnside approached Bosch and instructed him to get back to work. Bosch looked up while continuing to eat his banana and acted like he didn't hear. Burnside then said, "Hey, kid, get back to work now." The employee immediately asked for shop steward Dewey Dumphrey in order to file a complaint. Bosch informed Dewey of the incident and told him that he didn't like to be called kid. Dewey then filed the aforementioned grievance citing discrimination language in the collective bargaining agreement as well as the Age Discrimination Act he had heard Travis Tee talk about at a union meeting.

Dewey finally limped into the Human Resources department and approached Joe King, who was just leaving his office for the day. He noticed his limp and asked him about it. Dewey told him about how he hopped over a pallet of parts on the way to HR.

"You hopped over a pallet of parts?" Joe said incredulously. Only two weeks since Dewey was returned to work from his discharge, and he was back at it without missing a beat.

"Yeah, I was in a hurry," Dewey said matter-of-factly. Just then, Mark Fosse, a maintenance employee, walked into HR and over to where Joe and Dewey were standing.

"There you both are," Fosse said, looking back and forth at the two. "I want to complain about Dewey here. He walked right in front of my forklift, and I fucking near ran his ass over." Fosse's anger was apparent in his body language: leaning forward, eyebrows severely knitted over flame-thrower eyes.

"Well, maybe you need to watch where you are going," Dewey replied.

"I was, you twerp. It was you that wasn't watchin'," Fosse said.

"Okay, guys, come into my office and let's discuss this," said Joe, who was disappointed that he couldn't leave for home. They all moved into the office, and Joe shut the door. "All right, Mark, start over. What happened?"

"I was heading over to deliver some parts and do some repairs on the Mazak and this goofball—"

"Hey! That's harassment!" Dewey said in a raised voice.

"Let's watch the name-calling. Go on, Mark," Joe said, looking at his watch.

"So this . . . guy," Fosse said, pointing at Dewey, "walked right into the intersection and didn't even slow down or look for traffic. I almost ran right over his ass."

"Maybe if you slow down you wouldn't be a danger to everybody," Dewey said in a righteous tone.

"I was driving normal speed," Fosse shot back.

"Okay, guys, let's do this. Dewey, you make sure you look before you enter an intersection."

"I always do!" Dewey responded.

"The hell you do, pinhead," Fosse argued.

"Name-calling, Mark. Let's not resort to name-calling," Joe cautioned. "Okay, again, Dewey, watch out for vehicles. Okay?"

"Yeah. And Mark needs to watch his driving," Dewey said. Fosse glared a moment at Dewey and quickly walked out of the office and back to the shop. After Fosse was gone, Joe turned back to Dewey.

"Dewey, two things. First, I have a problem with you hopping over the pallet. That is an unsafe act."

"Big deal," Dewey grumbled.

"And two, this issue of stepping out into traffic."

"So you're just going to believe that asshole?" Dewey sniffed.

"Consider this a warning concerning unsafe behavior," Joe stated. "I'll have to notify your supervisor. You need to know that if there is any more of this, we will have to step up the discipline."

"That's bullshit."

"Nonetheless, you need to take care and make sure this type of thing doesn't happen again," Joe said. He paused then continued. "What did you want to talk about when you first came in?"

"Age discrimination," Dewey said with defiance.

"Age discrimination," Joe repeated, raising his eyebrows to signal attention.

"Yeah, one of your supervisors is discriminating against a worker. He is in big trouble, buster," Dewey said, sitting down and crossing his arms across his chest.

"Go on," Joe said.

"Burnside discriminated against Jimmy Bosch," Dewey said with an eerie smile. "Big trouble here," he added.

"Jimmy Bosch? I don't get it, Dewey. He's in his twenties, isn't he?" Joe was flabbergasted.

"Yeah, so? He called Jimmy a kid."

"Dewey, that isn't discrimination," Joe stated. "First off, age discrimination pertains to people forty years of age and older."

"It does?" Dewey asked with a confused look.

"It does." Joe King stood up to leave. "Do you still want to file a grievance?"

"Damn right I do. Burnside can't go around calling people kids."

Joe sighed. It had been a long day and he wanted to go home.

"Okay, fill it out and drop it in my box," Joe said. "Now if you excuse me, I need to get to another appointment."

CHAPTER 31

Dewey left the Human Resources office and entered the factory while reading the grievance he intended to submit. He didn't know about the age discrimination rules but knew in his heart that there was a grievance somewhere in this case. He didn't look forward to telling Jimmy Bosch that his grievance wasn't valid. Jimmy was big and mean and had a way of glaring at you for a long time without blinking. Jimmy disturbed Dewey.

But if Dewey could think of something else that could be used for a grievance, maybe Jimmy wouldn't be too mad at him. Maybe just general harassment would work or union animus. Dewey liked grievances for union animus. The way he understood it, management could be accused of disciplining someone because they were in the union.

Dewey remembered that Travis Tee always claimed union animus anytime the company made any kind of statement to him that he didn't like. He recalled Travis Tee telling him about a time when he walked outside to make a phone call to his wife. After about twenty minutes on the phone, his supervisor looked out the door and told him to get off the phone and get back to work. Travis Tee said he went back to his work area and filled out a grievance for union animus and turned it in to Joe King. King asked Travis Tee the reason for him being on the phone instead of working. Travis Tee said that he told him it was none of his damn business, that he was the business agent for the shop and didn't need to check in with management every time he needed to conduct union business.

Dewey was lost in thought about how much he admired and worshipped Travis Tee when suddenly he heard screeching tires and a crashing of falling metal. His heart was pounding as he looked to his right at the mess that was lying a couple of feet where he was walking. Hot rage replaced panic as he hopscotched through the fallen parts toward the driver.

When he got to the side of the forklift, he noticed the driver had a bloody nose and was rubbing his head. Rage turned to fear when he saw Mark Fosse trying to clear his head, rapidly shaking it back and forth. He turned to leave too late. He heard Fosse's voice.

"Where you goin', asshole!" Fosse roared, causing Dewey to freeze in his spot. "Look what you did! Now you can pick it up, shit-for-brains!"

"I'm not going to—" But before he could finish his sentence, he felt strong hands grab him and violently shove him sideways causing him to hit the floor and slide about ten feet. He looked behind the quickly approaching Fosse and noticed people watching in the aisles and from behind their machines. He felt his face flush hot and was sure he was red with embarrassment. Soon Fosse was standing over him again, his eyes were burning coals and blood from his nose was smeared around his mouth creating the image of a psycho killer.

"You-you can't touch me. I'm a union stew—"

Dewey found himself being hoisted up and suspended by his shirt in front of Fosse, his boots barely touching the floor. His shirt was cutting into the back of his neck as both his hands struggled to loosen Fosse's tight grip on him. He wasn't sure if it was pain or fear that was bringing the tears to his eyes.

"I'm reporting you to HR. You are assaulting me. You're goin' to get fired," Dewey croaked, his throat partially blocked by the knuckles of Fosse's grip.

Fosse jerked Dewey's body forward so that their faces were nose to nose. Fosse smiled with his teeth showing. "You would rat on a brother?" Fosse let go of his grip, and Dewey tumbled to the floor.

"Nah, I don't think you will." Fosse turned away from Dewey, who was trying to reset his shirt, then turned back. Fosse raised a fist. "Solidarity, brother. Asshole."

Dewey took a moment before finally getting up off the floor. He looked around and found the grievance lying a short distance away, which he retrieved. The audience of workers continued to watch him as he pulled himself together. He focused on the grievance, as if immersed in important business.

The grievance. The last thing he needed right now was to deal with Jimmy Bosch after this current episode.

CHAPTER 32

Travis Tee walked with purposeful strides pulling a wheeled briefcase behind as he headed toward the large meeting room where the negotiations were to take place. Behind him, trying to keep pace with Travis Tee, were his obsequious assistants, who talked hurriedly into cell phones or jotted last-minute notes.

The group barged through the double doors and spread out along the long oak table opposite the timorous management team. Travis took a seat across from the head negotiator for management and opened his briefcase, extracting reams of documents and spreading them out in front of him. Satisfied that he had everything and was fully prepared, he looked up and glared at the head negotiator for the management team. His glare told them that he was leaving with a deal acceptable to the union or the heads of management strung out in an oversized necklace.

Travis Tee had just recently concluded a successful contract negotiation for a new local in Sisseton, South Dakota. Neither the representatives for the employees or the management team had any experience in labor negotiations, which put Travis Tee at a great advantage. He was able to hammer out a contract settlement that allowed for much higher wages and benefits than the employees currently had. The management negotiators had heard horror stories about the power of Travis Tee and wanted to get the negotiations done and him out of town as soon as possible. He was feeling good about himself.

"William Drexel," *Travis said in the hissing voice through closed teeth.*

Drexel looked furtively at the union leader.

"Good morning, Mr. Tee, sir," *he whimpered.*

"Travis Tee," Joe King said with a smile as he sat down in the chair opposite him.

"Egregious," Travis Tee said as his eyes came into focus at the people around the table. Everybody looked back at him with small smiles on their faces.

Joe had a premonition that this meeting with the union grievance committee would include some drama and excitement because it was taking place about two weeks after his short meeting with UGLI steward Anita Kloo. In some deep part of him, he looked forward to the entertainment it offered.

The meeting participants included the union grievance committee and Abi Deng, the Human Resources Manager, and himself. Kloo was in attendance as one of the members of the union grievance committee, and her harassment complaint was one of the grievances scheduled for discussion. The three other members of the union committee were Travis Tee, Curly Wilson, and Wade Green. Curly started to speak but suddenly sneezed instead, leaving a delta-shaped pattern of chewing tobacco splattered across the table and onto Joe King's shirt. Joe King was startled but quickly regained his composure.

"Okay. With that introduction, let's begin." Joe King looked across the table at Curly, waiting for an apology that didn't come. Instead, Curly chuckled as he placed another clump of tobacco into his mouth.

"You deserved that," Kloo grunted.

"I deserved to have saliva-drenched tobacco spewed all over my shirt?" King asked.

"Yes." Anita's shoulder shook as she enjoyed a rare laugh, causing her larger boob to jiggle underneath her greasy T-shirt. Everyone from both sides of the table looked away for a moment as they individually attempted to hold down their most recent meal.

After another minute had passed, Joe King coughed into a Kleenex, thus helping him to gain control of himself, and started the meeting. The group discussed the first grievance over the color of the aisle lines in the plant. Currently, the lines were white, but the union believed they should be yellow. After about ten minutes of intense debate, both parties agreed to put the grievance into joint hold for further study. So off to the bone pile it went.

The next six grievances were dealt with in a similar manner until they finally came to UGLI steward Anita Kloo's issue. The group decided to take a short break and reconvene in about ten minutes. Even though the group managed to stretch the ten minutes into twenty minutes, the time passed quickly and they soon found themselves back at the table.

"The next grievance, number 09-198, concerns Ms. Kloo's complaint of verbal harassment." King paused then went on. "Based on my investigation, Ms. Kloo was not a victim of verbal harassment."

Silence, then a whimper began slowly building and growing into a heart-wrenching wail emanating from within the very soul of UGLI steward Anita Kloo. It sounded like a culmination of all the suffering endured by women throughout the history of the world concentrated into the martyred countenance of Kloo. It was pain incarnate. It was horror upon horror and then some more. Suddenly, silence again. The union and the company representatives united this one moment in mutual shock.

UGLI steward Anita Kloo's chin was downturned as she appeared to be in silent prayer. Her breathing was even and her eyes were closed. Then she spoke.

"I have been disrespected."

Another moment of silence.

"I have been dishonored."

More silence.

"I want, no, I demand satisfaction."

Both sides of the table looked beseechingly across at each other. Then they looked at their team members, not sure what to do next. Abi leaned close to Joe King, his large lips almost touching his ear.

"Iss she ahkay?" Abi Deng whispered.

Across the table Wade Green leaned into Travis Tee and whispered, "What the fuck?"

Both sides resumed their silent vigil. After a few minutes, Kloo silently stood up and walked out of the room, leaving the others sitting like a small replica of the Easter Island statues. Finally, Joe King broke the silence and asked the union representatives how they intended to proceed with the grievance. The union members snapped awake, and Travis Tee told them that they had no choice but to move it on to an arbitration hearing.

CHAPTER 33

Robert Kowalsky felt proud of his duo status as a cell leader and shop steward at AgMotiv. He didn't have the power to hire and fire or even issue discipline, which was as it should be. He saw his role as one of the union shop stewards as a foil to management's efforts to issue discipline to employees—the union members anyway. He didn't give toad shit about the scabs. Management could do whatever they wanted to those rats and he wouldn't stand in its way. But he was fortunate that there were no scabs in his department. What troubled him and his fellow union officials was that his department had the highest level of productivity. This made the other departments look bad, and that's not a good thing among his cohorts.

Secretly, Kowalsky felt a twinge of pride in his association with the stellar department. They were good workers and consistently received recognition in the form of a monthly steak dinner in the fancy product display area. But that wasn't all. His department also led the others in safety numbers and low absenteeism. More steak dinners, caps, and jackets.

Kowalsky kept a low profile at the union hall during the monthly steward meetings, but the subject of his overachieving workers always came up. He would try to downplay the matter, but mostly he tried to keep his mouth shut and wait out the coming storm. Travis Tee normally used most of the meeting to wax eloquent on the glorious privilege of being a steward to the UGLI members. Kowalsky would use this time to think about his weekend projects: hunting, fishing, or organizing his sock drawer. Travis Tee was a union drone that had mastered all the time-tested speeches on the benefits of unionism and the evils of corporate America. He noticed that sometimes his eyes would glaze over and he seemed to go into a trance. Then he would suddenly snap out of it and bark out the word egregious. It was the damnedest thing he ever saw.

Today he glanced over and watched Dewey Dumphrey, who seemed mesmerized by Travis Tee's oration. He wore an ear-to-ear smile as he sat there, and Robert noticed that his elbows were moving back and forth. Furrows grew on Robert's forehead as he discretely leaned forward for a better view. His eyes quickly widened when he saw Dewey rubbing his groin with purposeful determination. Robert sat back and looked around at the other stewards who seemed to be on mental shopping trips to Home Depot. He watched out of the corner of his eye as Dewey continued on with his project for another minute then suddenly stopped. Dewey's head tilted back and his eyes were shut. He was smiling the satisfied smile of a job well done. Kowalsky's stomach coiled.

Kowalsky pushed his chair back as he got up to leave. The chair made a screeching sound as it rubbed its metal legs against the dirty linoleum floor. He saw Dewey tip his head to the side to look in his direction, that sappy smile still on his face under his sleepy eyes. Travis stopped talking with his signature "egregious" sign off.

"Where you going, Bobby?" Travis said in a voice full of challenge. Kowalsky stopped and turned toward Travis Tee and saw everybody looking at him.

"I gotta be somewhere," Kowalsky said, turning to leave.

"Going back to work, maybe?" Travis asked with open sarcasm. Dewey giggled.

Kowalsky turned facing Travis Tee and stood with his legs apart and hands resting on his hips.

"What the fuck's your problem, Travis?" he asked, giving a hard glare. Kowalsky happened to notice that the duct tape covering his broken fly was hanging out away from his pants like a flat grey penis. He ripped it off with a jerk. Dewey giggled again.

"You're the problem, maybe," Travis Tee spoke, his eyes dark slits. "Maybe you are becoming a company man. Maybe you're planning to move upstairs."

"The fuck you talking about!" Kowalsky spit back.

"Seems to us like you are trying to break records in your department. We have a problem with that."

"Well, maybe the other departments need to step it up," Kowalsky said, but his face quickly reddened. Everybody gasped.

"Step it up? Step it up?" Travis Tee shouted over the loud murmurings of the stewards.

"Hey, man, look, I didn't mean that. It's just that, well, it's just that the people in my department don't know how to slow down. They just go all day long, man."

There was a long pause; then Travis asked, "What are you going to do about it?"

"What do you mean what am I going to do about it?"

"What are you going to do about it? We can't have your guys making us look like shit," Travis reasoned, the other stewards grumbling their agreement. "You need to slow it down, dude. And your guys gotta start missing some work too."

"How the hell can I control that shit?" Kowalsky asked, relieved that he didn't get jumped by the whole group.

"That's your problem, Bobby. Just get your group in line or . . . I don't know what," Travis threatened.

"Yeah, okay," said Kowalsky, glancing at Dewey, who reminded him why he was leaving. He turned and walked out of the lodge, letting the lopsided door bang shut behind him.

Kowalsky climbed up into his new Chevy Silverado and sat behind the steering wheel, his hand holding the keys. He was filled with confused thoughts. He thought of himself as a loyal union member but also took pride in his work group. He knew it was he, and not the ever absent supervisor, that made work move in his department. He knew he was at a crossroads and needed to make a decision one way or the other.

Kowalsky had grown up in a union family. His father drove a truck for thirty-five years and was a Teamster all of that time. His grandfather had been a member of the boilermakers union in the Bremerton Shipyards in Washington. His wife's father was a member of the machinists union but did prison time for violence he committed on a picket line and never returned to the union after he was released. Her grandfather was a business agent for the commercial food workers union in a meat-packing plant in Iowa. There were uncles and aunts too numerous to list who were union. So the thought of not being a union member was something he couldn't even imagine. There were no scabs in the Kowalsky family tree, plain and simple.

A loud knock on his window startled him. He saw Travis Tee's large head glaring in at him, so he lowered the window to see what he wanted.

"I thought you had to be somewhere," Travis Tee said while lighting a cigarette. He picked something off his tongue and wiped it on his dirty pants.

"I do. I was just thinking," Kowalsky said.

"'Bout what?"

"The meaning of it all."

"The meaning of what all?"

"Fighting with scabs, arguing with management, sitting in a stewards meeting, watching Dewey jerk off."

"What the hell is the matter with you, Bobbie? Unions are important. Unions give workers a voi . . . Did you just say Dewey was jerking off?" Travis Tee said with a gasp.

"Ah, never mind," he said then started up the truck and backed away, leaving Travis Tee staring in wonder at him.

*　　*　　*

The next day, Kowalsky reported to work at his usual time but didn't sit and have a prework coffee with his team. Instead, he found a stool near a box of parts and sat waiting for the buzzer to signal the start of work. He could see the people from his work cell talking at the break table, occasionally breaking out in laughter over some story.

The buzzers resounded throughout the plant, and sounds of industry slowly whirred to life around him. He walked over to the table as his team began getting up to start work.

"Hold up, guys," Kowalsky said. "Let's meet for a moment."

The workers stopped moving and gave Kowalsky confused looks.

"Sit."

"We need to start work, Bobby," said one of the workers.

"We will. Let's sit and talk about what we have to do today."

"We already know. We have the daily work orders," said another.

"Well, I heard the supervisor say that we aren't, ah, doing our jobs right."

"What? What did he say?" said the first worker.

"He said we, ah, mislabeled a bunch of parts yesterday and he's pissed."

"We did? Which ones?" said the only female in the work cell. She was short and thin but demonstrated an unusual physical strength in her work. Mostly, Kowalsky enjoyed looking at her large chest hidden under her coveralls. She had had to remind Kowalsky more than once the location of her eyes.

"He didn't say for sure."

"He didn't say?" said the second worker.

None of the cell members noticed Carlos Perez, their supervisor, walk up to them from around one of the storage racks.

"Hey! Que pasa, people? Let's get shakin' here," Perez said in a not too unfriendly voice as he walked by.

The work team hopped up to leave, but Kowalsky told them to sit down. They stared at him like he had lost all hold on his sanity but ignored his command and began walking to their stations. Meanwhile, Perez stopped suddenly as if he had just stepped into a bear track. His upper body was a little slow getting the message to halt, causing him to teeter forward before he righted itself. He spun around and returned quickly to where Kowalsky sat with his arms folded over his chest. The others had begun working, but their attention was fixed on the drama unfolding before them.

"Excuse me?" Perez said.

"We were having a meeting. We have a right to assemble," Kowalsky said.

"You . . . what? Get your ass to work, amigo," Perez said.

"You are interfering with my rights as a union member," Kowalsky calmly said.

"What the fuck are you talking about?" Perez didn't need this shit so early in the morning.

"You are swearing at me. That's harassment and union animus."

"Okay, let's do it this way. Get to work or you're fired," said Perez.

"You are going to fire me for being a union member?" Kowalsky asked.

"No, I'm going to fire you for refusing my order to work."

"Then fire me. I will report your ass to the National Labor Relations Board."

"One last time: Go to work or you will be discharged."

Robert Kowalsky sat with his arms folded, looking calmly at Perez.

"No."

Perez grabbed his cell phone off his belt and dialed HR. He told King that he would be escorting Kowalsky to the door. He listened for a moment, answering unheard questions with yeses and nos. At last he holstered his phone.

"Kowalsky, you are being discharged for insubordination. Do you want to talk to a steward before we walk you out?"

"No," Kowalsky said in a quiet but determined tone.

"I'll need your ID badge," Perez said. Kowalsky silently unclipped his badge and handed it over.

"Grab your personal stuff."

At last Kowalsky rose from his chair and walked over to his work bench. Calmly, he picked up his Igloo Playmate, took down a photo of his daughter from the back panel of the bench then looked at Perez.

"Okay. I'm ready."

"Let's go," Perez said as he started off toward the plant exit, with Kowalsky trailing close behind.

Both men looked straight ahead as they silently walked down the main aisle. People stopped working momentarily as they passed by, knowing full well that Bobby got fired. They observed the body language of both men as being cold and determined. An employee walking next to a supervisor and carrying his lunch container this early in the day is not a good sign.

Kowalsky lost his escort after he went through the exit but felt Perez's eyes watching him as he walked toward his truck. Perez couldn't see the smile on his face. He knew that he would need to find another job; but for now, after fifteen years with AgMotiv, he was free of UGLI, Travis Tee, and Dewey, his masturbating monkey.

CHAPTER 34

She felt all alone after walking out of the grievance committee meeting. The company, those bastards, of course, didn't believe her; but neither it seemed did her own union. They just looked at her as if she was crazy, and none of them would comfort her or join in with her complaint.

UGLI steward Anita Kloo lumbered toward her work area, lost in her miserable thoughts, wondering how she could gain back control. She had lost it somewhere along the way. Where did her power over others disappear to? People avoided her before, and that was okay because she took that as a sign that people respected and feared her. Now, though, they barely noticed her when she beelined through their work areas.

She cut through the robot weld area without noticing one of the operators stooped down adjusting a catch. He stood up and stepped backward, colliding into Kloo as she passed closely by. The operator was a large man, and the force of his weight pushed her such that she almost fell into a nearby garbage container.

"Goddammit, you clumsy fuck!" she screamed.

"I didn't see you coming," he said with anger in his voice.

"Did you just call me a dummy!" she said, pulling in close to his face. Her rank halitosis caused him to blink as he turned his head to the side. The vapors filled his eyes, causing them to tear up.

The operator sputtered, "What?" Suddenly, he felt a stinging pain rush from his groin into his stomach after Kloo violently buried her knee between his legs. Before he could recover, he felt her hand push him hard on his chest causing him to trip over an empty pallet. He fell hard, smashing his head into the large metal frame tube that was loaded onto the robot. He was out cold.

Two workers standing nearby heard the shouting and saw the operator fall backward. They heard the sickening sound of his head hitting the steel and rushed over in time to see Kloo kicking at the motionless body lying on the ground. They pulled the screaming and struggling union steward off the unconscious man and were rewarded with some of her fists and elbows.

In a moment, others had joined the fray, including the supervisor who phoned for a security guard to the area. He also called for an emergency medical technician and the business unit manager, both of whom appeared moments later. The nervous security officer arrived in time to see the two employees holding the writhing Kloo against a partition. One of the men looked at the hesitant guard who was frozen where he was standing, his eyes wide in shock.

"Don't just stand there, goddammit!" the worker yelled. Kloo managed to wiggle out of his hold long enough to deliver a jab to his face.

"Call the police," the manager said to the guard as he held a cloth on the back of the operator's head while the EMT was at work removing gauze from packages. Another first responder arrived and located objects to place under his feet in order to elevate them. The medical work continued while Kloo screamed in the background.

The dazed operator came to just as Kloo was being escorted out of the plant in handcuffs. Work came to a stop throughout the plant as its workers stood watching in amazement as the police rushed the protesting Kloo down the aisles and out the door.

The EMT and first responders managed to walk the operator to the medical office and help him lie down on the examination table. The decision was made to call an ambulance when the operator wasn't able to give his name or the day of the week.

CHAPTER 35

Travis Tee heard the high-pitch wailing first. He looked up from his metal lathe and scanned the area for the source. He immediately saw people scurrying around in an array of confused panic. He shut the machine down and walked hesitantly toward the heightening chaos. As he walked down the main aisle, he saw two women clutching each other, their shoulders shaking. He could see tears streaming down their eyes highlighted by misguided eye makeup creating a look of creepy clowns. His observation was interrupted by a man crouched down on all fours, with his forehead resting on the cement floor. He pounded the floor in front of his head, crying like no man Travis had ever heard cry in his life.

He continued his tentative walk, looking this way and that at the devastation of unknown source. Three workers ran in his direction, the first passing him before Travis's arm could catch him. He did manage to gather up the second runner, bringing him to a sudden stop. The third runner crashed into the second, causing him to spin and fall sideways, cracking his head against a metal parts rack. He fell solidly to the ground where he lay motionless. A wet pool of blood grew under his head.

Travis Tee snapped his head back toward the second runner, who was now sobbing uncontrollably in his grip. Off in a distance he heard a gunshot and responding screams.

"What's going on?" he shouted at the worker who was now growing limp. Travis Tee shook him violently. "What the fuck is going on?"

"They, they . . . oh my god!" The worker fainted away, and Travis Tee guided his limp body to the floor. He saw a group of workers holding hands in a circle. They appeared to be praying. He rushed over to them.

"Hey! What's happening here, goddammit!" He could hear they were chanting Kumbaya. One of the chanters looked up at him and warned him to not curse.

"What is going on?" Travis Tee was beside himself with frustration. Finally, one of the chanters spoke up in a voice of strained courage.

"They posted it on the board."

"They posted what on the board?" Travis feared the answer so much his fist clenched and his gut tightened. His eyes fixed on the chanters, and he repeated in a whispered voice, "They posted what?"

"We have to work on Saturday!" The chanter broke down sobbing. "We have to work on Saturday!"

Travis Tee was frozen where he stood. Rage filled his face, turning it red. His teeth clenched together in any ugly grimace, causing his jaw muscles to tighten into hard knots as witness to the effects of injustice against the working man. His rage grew, causing his feet to move him urgently toward the office area. He slammed through the door with the stern look of righteous indignation. The door bounced off the adjacent wall rebounding toward Travis Tee, who instantly slapped it away again. He stormed down the narrow hallway toward the Human Resources office and burst through its door. He spotted Joe King sitting at his computer plucking away at the keyboard.

"King!" Travis Tee's roaring voice fairly shook the walls, causing the HR receptionist to scamper away.

"Travis? Wh–what's wrong?" Joe King had the frightened look of a mouse cornered by a hissing cat crouched and hungry.

"Where the fuck does the company get off thinking it can force employees to work on Saturday? This is pure unadulterated bullshit!"

Joe King shivered in his chair, his hands shaking.

"It couldn't be helped," Joe King sobbed. "It couldn't be helped. I–I tried to talk them out of it, but they just said no." He sobbed and buried his face in his hands. "Oh god, I just couldn't stop them," he cried in words muffled by his hands.

"Travis?"

"Egregious!" Joe King was standing in front of Travis Tee, who was sitting in a chair outside King's office.

"It's all egregious, Travis. The world is a cold and hostile rock, hurling through space with no concern for us little creatures trapped like ant corpses in a dirt clod." Travis smiled. "So? What's going on?"

Travis shook his head to clear it, which Joe King took as a reproach for his philosophical comment.

"Okay, maybe not ants."

"Jesus, King, don't you ever get tired of your bullshit? What's with the overtime on Saturday?"

"Yeah, so?"

"Isn't it short notice?"

"Don't you ever look at the bulletin boards, Tee? It's been posted for three days per contract." Joe King paused then said, "And it's only for four hours. What's the big deal? Are people complaining?"

"It's about to blow up on the plant floor." Travis Tee's eyes grew wide with concern. "You're going to have a riot on your hands."

"Oh my god. I better call the National Guard. I wonder if I can get air support from the Air Force," Joe said with pointed sarcasm. "Christ, Travis, it's been posted for three days. I've been out there at least five times since then, and I haven't heard a peep. In fact, everybody seems to be pretty mellow out there these days." Joe tilted his head a bit to the side with a look of genuine concern. "Are you okay? You seem stressed. Do you want to talk to someone? I can give you the number for employee assistance."

CHAPTER 36

Toivo knew that something about this day was off, but not enough to ponder it any further than if he was hearing the faraway buzz of a chainsaw. He was working in the shop with Clyde, who was unusually quiet—even the eight-track wasn't producing old blues music.

Toivo glanced back from his work on a dark oak dresser top and saw Clyde slowly sorting through a plastic drawer filled with wood screws. He noticed his eyes were directed slightly above the screws, as if he were trying to recall a missing thought. Toivo stopped what he was doing and turned to watch Clyde, who had now stopped fumbling with the screws and stood frozen.

"Clyde?" Toivo said then moved toward where Clyde stood statue-like in front of the work bench. "Clyde, are you all right?" The old Indian staggered in place upon hearing Toivo's voice and turned, his knees trembling.

Toivo watched with helpless shock as Clyde crumbled toward the floor in slow motion. Toivo found himself reaching out toward his father to guide him the rest of the way down. "Dad! What's wrong?" he shouted.

Clyde's face was turning blue-gray, and Toivo watched with a mixture of fear and wonder as a painful smile broke his face.

"Y-you've . . . never . . . called me . . . that . . . before." Clyde forced the words out, white spittle formed in the corners of his mouth.

"What?" Toivo's eyes were wide with fright.

"Dad." Clyde panted. "You . . . you never . . . called . . . that." Now Toivo could see moisture fill his eyes. Clyde's eyes closed as he took in a shuttering breath. "There is . . . a key . . . in your . . . b-book." Clyde took in another gasp, his dirty hand reaching up to hold his chest, as if something was trying to jump out.

"What key? What are you talking about?" Toivo was hugging his stepfather now, his own tears now mixing with Clyde's.

"Toivo . . . I love . . . you." Clyde created a final smile then closed his eyes.

136

Toivo managed to lift the large Indian off the sawdust-covered floor and carry him down the snow-covered path toward the cabin. Clyde's gray and black hair was a moving shadow in the dark night as it swung side to side with Toivo's step. Toivo reached to the doorknob and was able to click it open and flip on the light switch by the door using his elbow.

Toivo carefully laid Clyde's body onto the sofa then positioned his arms and legs so that it looked like he was taking a nap. Toivo dialed 911 on the old rotary telephone and told the dispatcher what happened. While he waited for someone to come, he pulled up a nearby chair and sat near his father's head. A tear ran down his cheek as he pushed Clyde's stray hair off his face. Slowly he came to realize that he was gone and wasn't coming back. The crushing finality of it all hit him hard in the stomach, and he laid his head on Clyde's chest and started sobbing. It hit him with a rush that all that was his world was gone: the long conversations in the woodshop, the hours spent in front of the fireplace reading in communal silence, and all the other moments that make up a life shared.

Then regret trickled and collected inside Toivo as he recalled the struggle and anguish he caused Clyde during his high school years. It didn't take long for Toivo to feel the folly of his youthful rebellion against his guardian and mentor, who would tell him, if he was alive, that it wasn't anything he didn't expect. As he listened to sirens increase in urgent rush toward the cabin, he realized that his role had changed. He no longer had the option of being under the watchful guidance of his stepfather who nurtured and cajoled him toward adulthood. He knew that he was under his own care and had to walk alone down the path of life.

Toivo looked into the peaceful face of his Indian father with a heavy heart and knew he would soon be taken away in the ambulance. He heard the ambulance pull up and the doors slam shut outside. He rose and walked unsteadily toward the door and opened it for the EMT personnel, who rushed in with their cases. He waited for them to confirm what he already knew: Clyde Gray Eagle died at age sixty-eight of a massive heart attack.

"Do you know this man?" one of the technicians asked.

"Yeah, he was my father," Tovio said, looking at the lifeless body lying on the sofa.

The technician gave him a curious look.

"We'll take him to the hospital. Do you want to meet us there?"

"Yeah." Toivo's voice barely registered. He saw the other attendant pulling out a large blue body bag, which caused him to emit an audible gasp. The first technician saw this.

"Let's get him on the stretcher and get him to the hospital," he said to the other man, who looked at Toivo's face and understood immediately. Both men carefully lifted Clyde onto the gurney and secured him with straps. In another moment, they were moving him with clockwork efficiency out the door. Toivo followed them toward the ambulance and stood there watching as they pushed the bundle into the back of the vehicle, the collapsible legs giving way underneath the gurney.

The rear door shut and the two men turned toward Toivo, who stood stock still looking at the ambulance.

"We'll be at the hospital in a few minutes. Will you be okay getting there on your own?" The EMT spoke in a gentle voice learned over time from many such encounters with grieving survivors. It was all too easy to forget that there is a human cost to these ambulance runs that EMTs become hardened to after some time on the job. When they treat injured or diseased victims, it is done with a sense of professional calm that too often came off as indifference.

"Sir? Will you be okay? You can actually ride with us if you want to."

"Yeah, no. I mean, I can go myself." Toivo turned and walked toward Clyde's pickup truck, which brought renewed sorrow. The truck belonged to Clyde even though Toivo was allowed to drive it whenever he needed to. Now the truck sat there as if the there wasn't anything new happening in their little family. He climbed inside and turned the key that was never removed from the ignition. Toivo had once asked Clyde why he left the key in the truck, and wasn't he worried that it would be stolen?

"I would like to meet the person that was willing to steal this truck," he chuckled, taking a drag off his cigarette. "I would give him gas and food money too."

Toivo remembered becoming aware of Clyde's complacent attitude toward the potential theft of his pickup truck as an epiphany of his philosophy toward his material existence. He scoffed at ownership saying that "nobody owns anything," adding that a person doesn't even own the clothes he's buried in. "The worms get the clothes along with everything else in the casket." The ambulance moved slowly down the gravel driveway and turned into the paved road that led into town, driving at a casual rate of speed. Toivo followed even as the ambulance soon was magically transfigured into a charcoal gray hearse on its way to the graveyard south of town.

CHAPTER 37

Toivo was surprised at the number of people that showed up for Clyde's funeral, enough to fill the small country church. Clyde was probably rolling in his grave that he was in a church, much less that he didn't have a say in the matter. But Toivo would never know that this event at this location was a compromise between two opinions in his family as to how he should be sent to the spirit world. Those that remembered Clyde knew that he would have liked to have been bagged and dropped into a hole in the ground among trees with a pack of cigarettes. The other side believed that his Indian heritage demanded a true tribal ceremony with the obligatory chants and prayers.

The service was short, and Toivo found himself standing outside the church with a group of people from Clyde's past, some family members and other characters who knew him once upon a time. He observed that the assemblage of people were very comfortable standing in complete silence. At first Toivo thought that his presence among the mourners created an uncomfortable feeling often brought on by an intrusion of an unwelcome person. He came to realize that these Native Americans socialized in an unspoken way—a sort of quiet communion of family and brotherhood. So he stood among the grieving family members and felt a tacit acceptance of his presence.

After some time had passed, he wandered away from the group toward the edge of a stand of nearby trees. He found himself focusing on the tree and being reminded of Clyde's love for the trees and the beautiful furniture he would produce from their wood. He could almost see Clyde wandering through the trees looking for fallen wood that could become a decorative walking stick or a rugged wall clock varnished to a splendid sheen. Feelings of loss returned in a rush, and he felt tears filling his eyes.

"Clyde loved you," a woman's voice said, causing him to jump. He jerked around to find an older Indian woman dressed in a navy blue dress. Her gray hair was pulled back and held by a black-and-blue beaded braid. The only jewelry she wore was a small brooch depicting a silver hawk in flight pinned above her heart. She had a somber but serene face, as if she had seen and experienced all the pain and joy of the world and allowed it to settle peacefully inside her soul. "I miss him," Toivo answered. He looked down at the ground to hide his red eyes.

The woman moved closer and gently touched his arm. "There's no shame in sorrow. We all loved him in our own ways. But he expressed his desire to be left alone, so we all honored that wish. We knew it wasn't about us—his family—but something changed when he came back." She looked off in the distance as she spoke all the while tapping his arm as if emphasizing certain things.

"Came back from where?" Toivo asked with a confused expression. The woman's face turned toward him, and her eyes searched into Toivo's.

The woman looked around and spotted a fallen tree nearby. "Let's sit," she said. "My legs are tired." They walked over and sat down on the log.

"What did you mean when he came back?" Toivo asked again.

"He didn't tell you," she said this as statement rather than a question. "He was in the Vietnam war. He never talked about it, but he needed help when he returned. Before he went there he was a rowdy young man, full of piss and vinegar as some vulgar people put it."

Toivo was transfixed by this image of Clyde. He realized his mouth was hanging open and he shut it. He found that he couldn't think of what to say next, but the woman started talking again.

"Anyway, he returned and spent time at the VA Medical Center in Minneapolis. We were told that he was suffering severe psychological trauma from the war." She paused for a long moment, studying a chirping finch that was hopping from branch to branch. "They wouldn't tell us much, but another man said he served with Clyde and that he was in a battle with him during a Vietnamese Holiday. It was called Tet, I think." She never took her eyes off the finch while she talked, but after it flew off, she turned to Toivo.

"The young man told us that he served honorably and saved a lot of soldiers. But he lost many too, and he blamed himself for their deaths."

Toivo looked at the woman but didn't say anything. What could he say? This was a whole other side he didn't know about Clyde.

"And that included the deaths of the people he was fighting," she continued. "The vet told us that he just shut down one day and said he wasn't going to kill anybody anymore. So they sent him home and put him in the hospital. He was there for two years before they let him out. But he stayed away from people after that, and I think it was because he didn't want to get close to anybody again for fear of losing them."

Toivo remained speechless but listening with all his attention focused on this woman's story.

"Then we heard about you. We were happy that he found someone that he would let into his life." She looked deep into Toivo's eyes. "He loved you more than anybody that I know of."

"How . . . how did you know him?" Toivo asked.

"I'm his sister," she answered. She remained composed throughout her discourse, but now Toivo noticed her eyes pooling up. She wiped at her eyes with a tissue then turned toward Toivo and embraced him. He held her in his arms as she quietly sobbed. "Thank you for being in his life, Toivo."

*   *   *

The family didn't know what to do with Clyde's estate since they couldn't find a will. Certainly, Toivo didn't know about anything to do with property rights and planned on moving out of the cabin. Again, the family was divided on this issue of his property, half-wanting to sell everything and split the proceeds with the relatives and the other giving it to Toivo, who had brought happiness to his life. Again, they reached a compromise and allowed for Toivo to rent the property after his graduation.

Toivo accepted the arrangement for lack of any other immediate options. Certainly, he was competent enough as a woodcrafter that he could continue Clyde's business, at least until the pending work was completed. But every day was a painful reminder of Clyde's absence from his life. The things that surrounded him only had meaning when they could both enjoy them, and now they were a reminder of what once was. Toivo remained at the cabin long enough to wrap up the business obligations then decided to move on—to where he didn't know. Nor cared.

CHAPTER 38

The attractive stenographer sat posture perfect studying her polished fingernails waiting for the arbitration hearing to begin as both sides flipped through their exhibits. She had sat through many of these hearings between AgMotiv and the United General Laborers International before. Although she wore a practiced face of indifference, inside she was always entertained by the dramatic arguments between these two adversaries. She was particularly amused by the antics of the union side and the crude behavior of some of their witnesses. She was raised in a blue-collar family; but her father would cringe if he was forced to sit and watch, even now, as a large moppy-haired union witness sat staring blankly ahead while he probed deep into his nose with a finger buried to the first knuckle. Her eyes moved over at the young man sitting next to the nostril spelunker, who she noticed was staring straight at her with a goofy smile on his face. She quickly looked away and acted as if she didn't notice his friendly overture.

To busy herself for the moment, she checked the paper in her stenotype as well as the flash drive jutting out the side of her laptop. She adjusted her seat down, then back up to its original position. Thankfully, she heard the arbitrator clear her throat causing the representatives from both sides to snap to attention in their chairs.

"We'll go on record, now," she said, looking at the stenographer, who had started gliding her fingers over the abbreviated keyboard. "Do the parties have any joint exhibits?"

The company and union representatives spent the next few minutes agreeing to add various documents as joint exhibits in a jovial manner that belied the upcoming combat fraught with accusations and biased logic. As they puttered around with the joint exhibits, the witnesses on both sides of the tables, which were arranged in a u-shaped set up, stole furtive glances at their counterparts. They fidgeted in their seats, waiting for their turn to be called to sit in the hot seat in front of the arbitrator to give their testimony. Everybody had been prepared to say their part and hoped they wouldn't blow it for their side.

Only ex-UGLI steward Anita Kloo seemed relaxed as she sat stony still with a wicked smirk on her face. She had waited for this very kind of event most of her life, and now she could bring down her enemies in ignominious defeat. She was confident that she could prove she was treated in a discriminatory manner for being a woman and abused due to her involvement with the union. She knew that this would only be the beginning of her vengeance on a society that mistreated successful women such as her. Win or lose, she would go all the way to the Supreme Court with this case. Her name would become as famous as Jane Roe of Roe v Wade. It never occurred to her that Jane Roe was a pseudonym for Norma McCorvey. As she sat waiting, she imagined Kloo v AgMotiv becoming the benchmark for all injustices perpetrated against women who fought for justice in the workplace. Talk show pundits would debate the layered meanings hidden in the principles enshrined within the case for years to come. She even saw her picture on the cover of *TIME Magazine*.

"Are there any stipulations I need to consider before we move forward?" the arbitrator asked. Kloo's thoughts were interrupted by the relative insignificance of this event to her future prominence in labor history. She glared at the arbitrator, who she saw as a member of the establishment that oppressed common workers such as her. In her eyes, the arbitrator was a woman in an important role but doubted she got there on her skills but rather on the number of men's asses she had to kiss. The fact that this arbitrator was a tenured professor of law at the University of Minnesota and authored several books and articles on women's rights and challenges in the work force eluded the novice gender-warrior.

"As the moving party, the company maintains this hearing to be limited to her actions leading to the decision to terminate grievant's employment." The company representative, Lynn Baker-Samuelson, was a tiny, neatly dressed attorney who spoke in a soft voice and directed her questions to opposing witnesses in a nonconfrontational manner. She would raise her eyebrows after each question, as if she was filled with wonder and curiosity. Her strategy was to pull out as many sound bites from the witnesses that she could include in her written brief. That was where arbitrations were won and lost, she believed, not in the hearing itself.

The union spokesman, Austin Santini, shook his head. "The union believes that her termination was based on trumped-up allegations and was based on her earlier complaints of harassment. The union asks for wide latitude in its testimony in order to discover the real reasons for her termination." The nose picker burped as he nodded his head in agreement. The arbitrator glanced up from her note-taking and glared at the union side of the table. She turned her gaze toward the union spokesman.

"I'm going to require that you instruct your witnesses to observe some basic manners while in this hearing."

"I apologize. Consider them instructed," the spokesman said as he glared at the offender with a scowl.

"I will allow some elbow room for both sides to make their case. But I will cut it off if I don't see a viable path developing." The arbitrator paused then said, "Are the parties ready to begin?" Both spokespersons nodded. "Let's start. Does the company have an opening statement?"

"Yes, we do," Samuelson said while pausing a moment to arrange some notepaper in front of her. "The company will show that the grievant attacked and struck another employee which is in violation of Company rules. We will show that the grievant was not provoked to any degree that would justify her assault. The company will show through witnesses and signed affidavits that the grievant was the clear aggressor in this case and has intimidated other employees in the past. The company asks that this grievance be denied in whole."

"Thank you." The arbitrator turned toward the union side. Arrayed down the table were the typical union lineup of somber-to-grouchy-looking people wearing jackets and shirts adorned with union insignias and sayings. She noticed printed on one of the shirts a depiction of a cartoon rat standing upright while a hand was choking it around its neck. "Do you have an opening statement?"

Santini took a deep breath and sighed. "We are here to counter the company assertion that a harmless person"—he gestured toward Kloo, who sat with doughy arms crossed over her chest—"would risk her own safety to attack a strong man without extreme provocation. Clearly, the company is headhunting here and I, too, will be having witnesses testify to prove that the grievance should be sustained in its entirety and the grievant returned to full duty with back pay."

The arbitrator looked over at ex-UGLI steward Anita Kloo, who sat glaring defiantly at her. She felt an unsettling feeling of antipathy directed toward her, which she was unable to account for. As a neutral arbitrator, the parties usually treated her with a respect that was borne out of their need for her to reach a decision favorable to them. She tried to ignore such obsequiousness and would rely only on the testimony heard in the hearing to arrive at a decision. Secretly, she enjoyed the deference given to her by the parties in these hearings. But today, she was receiving focused energy from the grievant that was as hot and burning as sunlight condensed through a magnifying glass. She returned her attention to Samuelson.

"The company will proceed then," the arbitrator instructed.

"The company calls Joe King," Samuelson said. Joe arose from his place along the table and walked toward the seat near the arbitrator and the stenographer. The arbitrator swore him in; and Lynn began her questions starting with his name, job title, and years of service with AgMotiv. She passed exhibits to him that included the employee handbook, Kloo's disciplinary letters from her file, tables showing the past history of disciplines issued for fighting, and so on. Her main purpose, as alluded to before, was to enter them into the record so they could be referred to in the posthearing brief. After about fifteen minutes of such testimony, he was turned over to Santini for cross examination.

Without looking up, he asked, "Do you make all the decisions on whether to discharge an employee?"

"I have input into the decision," Joe answered. He and all the company witnesses were instructed to make all the answers short and only answer the question—don't volunteer information.

"Is that a yes?" Santini pressed.

"Decisions are made by a group of people."

"Who is part of this, ah, group?"

"The employee's supervisor, the business unit manager of the area, the manager of human resources, and, of course, me."

"So the only one that has any information concerning the grievance, I'm guessing, is the employee's supervisor. Is that right?"

"He did the initial investigation," Joe answered.

"Initial investigation. So there were others?"

"I don't understand your question," Joe said, knowing he was probably referring to other investigations, but he had long ago learned not to assume the meaning behind cryptic questions.

"Other investigations. Were there other investigations?" Santini asked with a slight hint of patronizing tone in his voice.

"Yes."

"And?"

"And . . . What?" Joe answered with a poker face.

"How many other investigations took place?" Santini was becoming irritated. He had questioned Joe in other hearings and didn't enjoy the weary back-and-forth sparring that usually took place between them.

"It depends how you define an investigation."

"Investigation! You getting information concerning Anita Kloo's alleged fighting!" Two large red splotches grew on each of Santini's cheeks.

"One," Joe said.

"One investigation? Only one investigation for such an important matter? How much time did it take for this one investigation?" Santini hoped he could come out of the gate showing the company failed to conduct a fair investigation. He was sure that the arbitrator would see one little investigation could hardly be considered fair.

"Approximately one week," Joe answered with a calm voice.

"You-you investigated for a week." Santini broke the axiom to never ask a question without knowing the answer beforehand. He took a risk and got sucker punched in the first round. All he could do now was to pick at the quality of the investigation.

"Did you talk to any witnesses beside the supervisor who, by the way, I understand, did not actually see this so-called attack?" He glanced at the arbitrator to see if she saw the hole in the company's case.

"Yes," Joe said.

"And?" Santini's voice rose, signaling an increase in his frustration with this witness.

"I don't understand the question."

"Who are the witnesses?" Santini belted out.

"The victim and two other employees in the area."

"Two other employees?" Santini looked sideways at the union members with a confused look. Travis Tee looked sheepishly back at him with wide eyes and shrugged his shoulders.

"Yes," Joe said.

"Why are we finding this out now?" Santini glared at Joe, who continued sitting with a look of peacefulness, his hands resting on top of the other on the table.

"I don't know."

"You don't know," Santini said, repeating each word separately. He paused for effect then asked, "And why don't you know?"

"I can't account for the investigative abilities of the union."

Santini's face turned purple.

"I have no further questions for this . . . witness." He spat out the last word.

The arbitrator turned her attention to Samuelson. "Do you have any further questions?"

"Yes. Just one." She finished writing a note on her pad then looked at Joe.

"Joe, you were asked about the investigation. You said you did one investigation. So that we all understand"—she looked over at Santini"—give us a brief overview of how you went about investigating this issue."

"Certainly," Joe answered. "Upon first hearing of the incident, I talked to the victim to get his side of the incident. Afterwards, I talked to the grievant to get her side. I asked her if she was aware of any witnesses that would confirm her account of what took place. She said there weren't any witnesses. I visited the area in the shop where the incident occurred and talked to employees in the nearby workstations. I found two employees who said they saw the whole incident. I brought them to my office to have a more in-depth interview. I had a second discussion with the grievant to get explanations for some of the disparate accounts."

Now he's a bubbling brook of information, Austin Santini thought to himself as he listened to Joe King talk. Santini was raised in a union family and sympathized with the plight of the workers. He was proud to be part of the struggle between the haves and the have-nots. But it frustrated him when he had to defend a case when he didn't have all the facts as was becoming apparent in this case.

"Thank you, Joe." Samuelson looked over at the arbitrator. "I have no further questions."

"Does the union wish to recross the witness?" the arbitrator asked.

"Yes. Why didn't you tell the union about the other witnesses? Don't you think that would have helped both sides understand this case better?"

"The union didn't seem interested in the case until two days ago when—"

"Okay," Santini interrupted, "I have no further questions."

What Joe had started to explain before getting cut off was that the union only requested a copy of the grievance form itself two days prior to the arbitration. The union had not requested any other information, which had always puzzled him. For one, he never understood why the union would not request a history of terminations to discover inconsistencies in the application of discipline. For another, the union witnesses always took the whole week off prior to arbitration to prepare. What were they doing in that week to prepare for the arbitration if they never researched past practices that could be supplied by the company records? Drinking beer? Playing cards? And in this particular case, why didn't the union locate potential witnesses as he had done?

The arbitrator looked over at Samuelson, who said, "No further questions."

"The witness is excused."

CHAPTER 39

Joe King was in a good mood. He had just received a notice that he would be receiving a 5 percent increase in pay. This was on top of an NLRB decision he received in the mail this morning that ruled in the company's favor.

The complaint by the union involved a notice Joe King had posted on the plant bulletin boards explaining the "right to work" statutes of the state. Joe had heard from employees that they thought they were required to join the union. The notice went on to explain that employees who felt their rights were violated by the union could contact the district Labor Relations office and it gave the phone number.

The posting caused a flurry of resignations from the union ranks as well as calls to the NLRB requesting help from neglected union members. Panicking, Travis Tee filed a complaint with the board charging union animus and union busting. The board reviewed the case and issued a letter finding no cause or wrongdoing by AgMotiv.

Later in the day, after returning from lunch, King found a letter from Constance Roth-Nagel, Arbitrator in his mail slot. He had been waiting for this letter for over two months and it had finally arrived. Receiving arbitration decisions, even if you felt you presented a good case, always put a knot in King's stomach. You could win outright or, God forbid, you could lose. Sometimes the decision was split. A few months back, the company had received such a split decision. That arbitration involved a grievance written based on an employee the company had suspended a week for deliberately missing work after having his leave of absence request denied to attend a bowling tournament out of town. The arbitrator upheld the company's right to discipline for this infraction but ruled that the weeklong suspension was too severe and reduced the suspension to three days. The company was required to repay the employee for two lost days.

As he held the envelope in his hands, he wondered the worst: Would Anita Kloo be allowed to return to her job? If that happened, she would feel validated, and King shuddered to think what horrible behavior that would unleash upon AgMotiv. Maybe she wouldn't return. Maybe she would take her back pay—if that was what she was awarded—and quit. King knew that there was no way she would get a total award. No way. At the most she would be returned to work without back pay. A split decision. But there was no way the company would feel satisfied with that decision. King chuckled to himself thinking that the company would rather pay her the back pay and not have her return.

The answer lay in the envelope he held in his hands. He wanted to know but dreaded opening the envelope.

"What do you have there, King?" He snapped out of his thoughts. Travis Tee.

"A letter," King answered. "What's up?" King pocketed the letter but not before Travis saw the return address.

"Is that the decision on Kloo? What is it?" Travis Tee was excited.

"I haven't opened it yet."

"Fuck, why not? Let's open it." Travis Tee was half-reaching for the letter, his hands opening and closing as if he was milking a cow.

King sighed, pulled the letter from his pocket, ripped the envelope open, and pulled the documents out. Travis swung around behind King to read over his shoulder. King pulled the last page away from the rest of the bundle and read the decision to himself. "The Company had just cause to discharge the Grievant. The grievance is denied."

"Yes!" King said.

"Yes!" Travis said. His face immediately flushed when King shot a curious look at him. "I mean, goddamn. Now I gotta tell her." Travis did an about face and walked off. King watched as he left the office and then looked at the decision again. His smile returned to his face.

"Yes," he muttered again. He went back to his desk and pounded the keys of his computer e-mailing the message of Kloo's news to the management staff. He almost ran across the hall to tell Abi Deng then remembered he didn't care about what went on in the office. The workday business of the HR department only annoyed him, and it was better for all to keep it and all things away from him.

What a day, and it keeps getting better, King thought. No more Kloo and her drama, and he allowed this feeling to permeate though his mind. He ignored his subconscious that told him that someone else would take her place. There always was and there always would be. But he brushed that thought aside. Kloo was gone. That was all that matter at this moment in time.

CHAPTER 40

"Oh my god!" she howled over the phone. "Oh my god!"

"I'm so sorry, Anita," Travis Tee said. He didn't expect this reaction. He had told her that the arbitration had ruled against her and expected to feel the nuclear heat of her anger. He didn't expect this response at all and was now speechless; sympathy giving was not something found in his social toolbox.

"What-what am I going to do now?" she sobbed. Travis Tee felt the tears pouring through the telephone.

"I don't know what to say," he whimpered. "I thought for sure we would win. It just isn't right."

"My god, oh shit, my god!"

There was a long silence, both sides wandering frantically through their own thoughts: Anita in shock and Travis Tee trying to calculate how he could end the conversation.

"What am I going to do?" she asked, calmness coming into her voice. Travis Tee calmed along with her and wondered if he was getting to a closing point in the conversation.

"I don't know, Anita. I-I think it's maybe a good time to look for something else. This place sucks, you know," Travis said.

"Well, they aren't getting away with it. I'll sue them. This is bullshit!"

Anita's anger was returning, and the heat Travis dreaded was starting to pour out. "Somebody's going to pay for sure."

Travis wondered who else but the company would have to pay. He recalled the arbitration as a fiasco that left Santini leaving town in an angry mood. The arbitrator was outraged as well, and Travis had never seen an arbitrator express any emotion in all the times he'd been involved in arbitrations. He knew then that their case was toast, and secretly he was happy that Anita would be gone. She was a colossal burden to bear for him and everybody else, friend or enemy. But now he had a nagging fear that somehow her leaving wouldn't be easy.

Maybe she would hold the union at fault with a failure to represent charge leveled at them. They didn't need that now with everything else going on.

"Maybe you should keep fighting, Anita. Maybe you should file a discrimination charge with the Department of Labor," Travis Tee said. He would rather she just go away, and even deflecting her to the DOL would somehow drag him and the union in. But it bought time and it gave her some hope, enough anyway to let him get off the phone.

"You goddamn right I am," Anita barked. "Right now too." She hung up and Travis breathed a huge sigh of relief.

*   *   *

"You can't resolve issues as a union so you pass the buck to the DOL?" Joe King's voice was elevated as he shook the DOL document in front of Travis Tee's face. Travis sat back in the chair in front of King's desk, trying to appear calm and self-assured. But it was starting—the union was being sucked back into Anita's case.

"Hey, she has the right to file whatever complaint she wants with the DOL," Travis Tee said.

"Yeah, did you read the complaint? She states that you suggested she file it," King said, his face a mask of anger. "Discrimination based on sex and gender? This is horseshit!"

"Fuck, what could I do? She wouldn't stop complaining."

"So you took the pussy way out? Man, you guys are gutless." King was skating on thin ice here and he knew it. You want union animus? Here it is, you loser, he thought. "Well, just so you know, I plan on pointing them in your direction too. Do you remember the union's behavior at the arbitration? Hardly good representation I would say. Maybe Kloo needs that pointed out to her."

"Shit, don't blame us. You were the ones that whacked her."

"Right, well, maybe we should bring her back. How would you like that? We could tell her that we don't think she was represented very well and felt she needed a break. Would that work for you?" Joe said, still holding the document in his hand. He knew that Travis knew the company would do no such thing, but it felt good to say it.

After chasing Travis Tee out of his office, Joe walked across the hall and tapped on Abi Deng's open office door. Joe could see that he was doing some church work again, more specifically he could see, compiling a roster of names of church members and their assigned date to greet people at the postworship coffee and cookie social.

"Yes," Deng said with annoyance. His attention never left the computer screen as he continued typing.

"I just wanted to let you know I would be contacting Lynn to handle a DOL charge."

"Yes." Deng continued typing, and Joe was sure he could have told him that a six-foot platypus wearing a scuba diving outfit just fondled Jill Hurt's breasts and he wouldn't notice.

"Yeah, okay. I'll give her a call then," Joe said and returned to his office and made a note of the date and time of his conversation with Deng. Joe wanted documentation in the likely event that Deng would question the reason for the bill for legal advice and forget that he preapproved it.

AgMotiv was a major client of Lynn Baker-Samuelson, and one of the many privileges enjoyed by Joe King was his ability to use the direct line to her office rather than having to work his way through the receptionist. He picked up the receiver and punched buttons.

"This is Lynn."

Just hearing her voice soothed Joe's anxiety. He had lost many night's sleep on a previous case involving a "victimized" female employee who, like Anita, decided to make a federal case out of her termination. In that instance, the employee was fired for insubordination. The case dragged on for four years and involved a marathon deposition that lasted all day. Lynn had told him he did well in it, but he still felt as if he was a criminal on trial for his life. They ended up settling the case for $5,000 and a nondisclosure statement just to make her and the case go away.

"Hi, Lynn. Joe."

"Well hello, Joe. How are you?"

He read Kloo's DOL charge to her as she interrupted with sporadic questions on pertinent details. Thankfully, she had represented the company in the arbitration on this matter and so was familiar with the case. For this reason, she had a stake in the outcome of this complaint even though she had successfully argued the case and received the favorable arbitration decision.

"This shouldn't go anywhere. Fax the complaint over and I make some calls," she said in a confident tone.

"Thanks, Lynn. I don't want to sit through any more depositions, if you get my drift."

"Got it. Don't lose any sleep over this. We'll make it go away."

*   *   *

Within a month, the North Dakota Department of Labor ruled Kloo had no case and issued a "right to sue" letter. So Kloo sued. Another two years of investigations and depositions resulted in a dismissal of the lawsuit from a summary judgment, leaving Kloo only one more target: the union.

The union, fearing a failure to represent charge from Kloo, offered her a no-show job that would pay her without her having to perform any actual work. She would show up at the union hall anyway, and so they allowed her to open mail and answer the rare phone calls. Unfortunately for her, she lasted only a month before being discharged for her constant negative diatribes against her former union and unionism in general to anyone who came near her.

At this point ex-UGLI steward Anita Kloo gave up as depression set in. She filed for unemployment benefits, which weren't challenged by the union. Her attempts to find work were met with a frustrating lack of success. Her job interviews, when she could get them, were catastrophic at best. She came off to her interviewers as a bitter person who hated her previous employer and did everything she could to take them down through the legal system. It never occurred to Kloo that future employers would be frightened to put such a person on their payroll.

Her job search was put on hold one wintery day in December when she injured herself after slipping on a patch of ice in the Kmart parking lot. She broke both her legs when they collapsed under her large frame; the double snap could be heard all the way across the parking lot. Her ample shanks, unfortunately, didn't cushion the severe trauma to her spine that folded like a sailor's squeezebox.

The hospital put her back together the best they could and fed her painkillers that had the double benefit of mitigating her pain and quieting her constant howls of pain. She was released from the hospital after two weeks and restricted to at-home rest. Her pain continued but was relieved through her daily doses of OxyContin.

Ex-UGLI steward Anita Kloo gradually felt the walls of her apartment closing in around her as boredom and restlessness set in. She watched television but couldn't get into the daytime lineups. She tried reading, but that only served to make her tired and caused her to frequently nod off. She didn't have many friends—her only outside contact was with her former union brothers and sisters, and even they brushed her calls off. She mostly ate cookies, salted snacks, ice cream—anything she could lay her hands on went into her mouth. She hardly noticed she was gaining more weight and began wheezing when she limped across the room.

Mostly, she spent her days transporting herself from one window to the next in her second floor apartment, hoping something noteworthy would occur to help alleviate her ennui. After spending another restless day padding around her apartment, she settled into her couch in the late afternoon with her remote control and started scanning the stations. There was an eternal sameness to the programs: talking heads, home repairs, jewelry, cartoons, old TV shows, more talking heads, medical shows, Oprah, politics, wild animals, tame animals. She clicked off the television and made her way to the bathroom and grabbed the amber-colored container from the medicine cabinet. She popped an OxyContin and returned to her sofa.

She flipped a well-thumbed copy of an old UGLI newsletter; she had stopped receiving new ones in the mail long ago. She tossed the newsletter on an old end table and limped over to her apartment window and stared out at the passing cars.

Her apartment had become a prison cell. She had nowhere to go and nobody to visit. A single tear ran down her cheek.

CHAPTER 41

Yesterday, Phil Lundeen got the good news that he would receive an extra $50 on his paycheck due to the resolution of a grievance that had been pending for about five years. The grievance involved his suspension for his long drinking binge that required his weeklong absence from work. The union filed a grievance for unjust discipline and demanded back pay for his two-week suspension. The company finally decided to pay the $50 to resolve the issue once and for all. For the company, $50 was small potatoes compared to two weeks' pay. For the union, it was a big win—a rare win—and justification to its members that the union was there for them.

The jubilant Phil proposed to his friend Ray that they invest the money wisely—Ray being the union treasurer and all and an avowed expert on the subject of money. Phil offered the idea that they quickly liquidate the money, and Ray concurred. Haywood Park was nominated and selected as the site in which to consummate the matter. Both men called in their absence on Friday of the following week, which was both protected under the Family and Medical Leave Act. Phil's certified condition related to a herniated navel, and Ray's allowed for intermittent home rest for his onset of carpal tunnel pain in his right wrist.

Phil purchased two cases of Budweiser at the Broken Saddle for a premeeting summit at his apartment after work. Ray the treasurer arrived with a Kwiky Mart bag filled with a cornucopia of salty delectables and a couple of videos from his personal stock of art films. Without as much as a hi-how-are-you, he stuck in Jurass I Pork into Phil's VHS player and plopped down onto an overstuffed chair. The chair was a product of many successful repair efforts involving the liberal use of duct tape. To Ray, it was a throne fit for a king.

Phil was accustomed to Ray's inattention to the work involved in nurturing a friendship with something as simple as a greeting. So Phil offered a hello and passed him a can of beer as he sat in a less comfortable chair nearby. Phil had long ago gotten over the discourtesy of Ray taking his favorite chair whenever he came over. Both Ray and Phil started work at AgMotiv on the same day and were now in the retirement red zone. Like an old married couple, they had integrated the other person's annoyances into the normalcy of their lives. And like long married couples, their conversations were reduced to functional one-word sentences and sounds. So the evening passed quickly and quietly into history with the two men eventually conked out in their chairs.

A new day greeted both men around eleven the following morning. Both were seasoned in the art of overindulgence, and a quick trip to McDonald's was all it took to get them into shape for a serious session of drinking. They stopped at the Broken Saddle again, this time purchasing a fifth of Captain Morgan, a 750 ml bottle of Jägermeister, and another two cases of Budweiser. With that supply, they drove off giddy in anticipation of an afternoon and evening of chemically assisted meditation.

They soon arrived at Haywood Park, which was situated on the east side of town. Being that it was a workday, the park was empty, except for a lone college kid driving around on a mower with headphones wrapped around his head. They maneuvered the old Chrysler down a maintenance road that broke away from the main parkway. The car chugged down a decline and then belched smoke as it labored up the backside of the dip, finally making it to the top where Phil angled the car and shifted it in park so that it was facing an overlook that was secluded from view of the park.

The two old friends groaned in unison as they disembarked from the car and opened the back doors. A large Igloo cooler came out one side and the Kwiky Mart bag out the other. Next, the two found themselves behind the car opening the trunk and extracting two rickety lawn chairs. Phil used his right elbow to nudge the trunk lid down as Ray broke rank and started down the steep slope, his body at a slight angle while his feet skittered quickly and carefully underneath. Ray was already seated and cracking open a beer when Phil reached the bottom. They wasted no time getting to the business at hand and within the first hour had finished the Morgan and a good share of the Jägermeister. The beer was judiciously used as chasers but started taking a more prominent level of importance on the agenda in the next hour.

Their favorite spot was secluded at the bottom of a decline that sloped toward a narrow part of the Red River. The stream there was agitated by a small dam nearby causing the green water to eddy and bubble. The noise it caused was urgent but relaxing against a backdrop of silence where they were surrounded by trees. The trees were an eclectic collection of unkempt Dutch elms, box elders, and a variety of conifers populated by a scattering of dull sparrows making lazy conversation with each other.

Today a rogue swan drifted by a wrinkled Burger King bag that was caught on a partially sunk branch. Phil found a good-sized rock and heaved it, but it fell well short of the swan. The swan continued its slow float downstream, unaware or unfazed by the threat posed by the two visitors. The swan took its time letting the stream transport him safely around the bend and behind a grove of trees.

"I never seen a swan here before. What do ya suppose he doing up here in North Dakota?" Phil mused.

"I think they live in all fifty-two states," Ray said as he crumpled his beer can and chucked it into the stream.

After a minute passed by, Phil said: "They ain't but fifty."

"Fifty what?"

"They's only fifty states."

Another minute passed before Ray said, "What about Alasky and Huhwhy?"

"Oh yeah. I forgot 'bout dem," Phil said then added, "I wish I woulda finished high school like you."

"You shouldn't. It's a big burden to be smart. Evybody's always buggin' you 'bout things."

"Yeah, and you gotta do that treasure works too."

"It's a burden."

Ray burped as he popped open another beer can with a hiss. Both men lay back against the curve of the hill and closed their eyes.

"So whadda think of Dewey?" Phil asked.

"Dumphrey?"

"Yeah, him."

"He's a turd."

"Did you hear that Toivo called him a pimple on AgMotiv's ass?" Both men laughed hard; Phil sprayed beer through his nose.

"That fucking Toivo is funnier'n shit," Phil chuckled.

"Fucker's a scab, though. Nothing worse than a scab." Ray pulled on his can and swallowed. "Ya can't have anything to do with a scab."

Moments passed.

"Too bad he's a scab. He's pretty cool," Phil said.

Of the two longtime employees of AgMotiv, Phil was the only one who sensed the presence of their car lumbering down the decline toward them. Ray was snoring next to him, so he was oblivious to the squeak and groan of the car's springs.

* * *

The police were unable to determine with certainty how the old Chrysler's parking gear malfunctioned causing it to start its accelerating descent down the hill. It appeared that the two victims were totally unaware of the approaching vehicle that plowed over them at about forty mph according to the traffic accident and reconstruction analysis report. The autopsy showed nothing more than that the men died of radical spinal injuries and severe head trauma. The presence of a high level of alcohol was also noted on the report. Foul play wasn't ruled out, but the case didn't receive any significant attention after a few weeks.

CHAPTER 42

AgMotiv allowed for excused leave for any employee who wished to attend the two funerals. Twenty-three employees requested the leave, with six of them actually attending each funeral. The six employees that attended the services outnumbered the balance of those that came to pay their respects. Only Ray had a living relative, an aunt in Oregon who was in her nineties and suffered from Alzheimer's. She was unable to attend.

Although both men were longtime union members, no union representative was in attendance. Instead, several seized on the excused day off to meet to discuss a replacement treasurer. Travis Tee successfully lobbied to have Dewey Dumphrey placed into the position until the regular election scheduled to occur in a little over a year. The other members in attendance had doubts about whether Dewey was capable of counting the number of fingers on one hand, much less account for the influx and disbursement of union funds. Nevertheless, they went along with Travis Tee because it was the path of least resistance and that is always the best path.

Travis Tee went to work and had Dewey sign the necessary authorization forms at the bank. This entire process was completed before the final amen at the last funeral.

The first check Dewey wrote was to Travis Tee in the amount of $200 to cover transportation to the bank and loss of earnings to handle the transfer of authorization. The second check in the amount of $300 he wrote in his own name for the loss of earnings to assume check writing authority. In the next two months, Dewey would write a total of thirty-two checks amounting to nearly $10,000. It was toward the middle of his fourth month as a union treasurer that he received his first overdraft notice. Dewey quickly crumpled it into a ball and tossed into the waste basket. He did that with the second and third one as well.

Dewey didn't bother opening the fourth letter with a return address of Union Fidelity State Bank. If he had, he would have known that the account had been frozen and authorities had been notified of the irregularities occurring with the union account. He did, however, answer his cell phone a couple of days later.

"Hello," Dewey grumbled with his mouth full of potato chips.

"Good afternoon, Mr. Dumphrey, this is Roger Williamson from Union Fidelity State Bank," the voice said. "I would like to talk . . ." Dewey interrupted with a loud wet belch. This was followed by a short pause; then Williamson tentatively continued.

"Mr. Dumphrey, I understand you are the authorized signatory for your union's checking account." It was more of a statement of fact rather than a question, but he waited for a confirmation, which came back as a crunchy "um-hm."

"Ah, Mr. Dumphrey, I am concerned about the number of overdrafts occurring on this account." Williamson heard a click. "Hello . . . hello."

Dewey was home on union leave when he answered the call from the bank, coincidentally and presumably, to perform treasurer duties. He was happy that he received the call because that would justify his leave in his own mind. Dewey started to realize there were things about being a treasurer he didn't understand such as overdrafts. Also, being a treasurer meant getting lots of mail from the bank, the union, and one that he had to sign for from the U.S. Labor Department's Office of Labor-Management Standards. He opened that one but didn't see a check inside, so he tossed it in his overflowing garbage container that emitted an odor of stewed debris. Curiosity rather than fear about all the letters caused him to call Travis Tee, who he knew was also home on union leave. Travis Tee picked up on the fourth ring.

"Yeah." Travis Tee's voice crackled. The call had pulled him out of the abyss of sleep and dropped him into an ugly hangover.

"Hey, Travis!" Dewey fairly yelled into the phone.

"Jesus fuck, Dewey! Lower your fuckin' voice. I was sleeping, goddammit!" barked Travis Tee as he rubbed his face.

"Oh, sorry, Tee. Should I call back later?" The last thing Dewey wanted on earth was to annoy Travis. Dewey knew that someday if he was lucky, he could be an important union leader like Travis.

"Fuck. What time is it?" Travis sighed as he swung his feet off the bed and sat slouched on the edge.

"It's, ah . . . wait a minute. It's two and fifteen, sixteen, seventeen . . . twenty. It's two and twenty minutes."

"What the fu . . . you have to count to tell the fuckin' time! Jesus Hannaford Christ!" Dewey flinched as Travis yelled through his earpiece. Travis sighed again, exhaled, and then asked, "What do you want?"

"Well, it's about the bank," Dewey said with reluctance.

"Yeah?"

"They said we had something like an overdraft." Dewey was talking business with the great Travis Tee. He was in heaven.

"Egregious! We have a what?" Travis screamed.

"An overdraft," Dewey whispered. "They said we have an overdraft. I don't know what that means."

"You . . . Dewey, fuck! What the crap-queen do you mean you don't know?"

"I never heard that word before," Dewey answered.

"It means . . . Dewey, shit. It means we spent more money than is in the account." Travis was standing up now, gesturing with his free hand.

"But don't the bank keep money in the . . . account?"

"Fuck, Dewey." Travis paused a moment, the silence settling on Dewey's chest like a half ton bar of steel. "What else did they say?"

"Who?" Dewey asked.

"The bank, shitbird! What the fuck did the bank say next?" Dewey started to feel tears well up in his eyes. Travis had never called him a name before. He felt his world starting to crumble down around him.

"They didn't say anything 'cuz I hung up on them." Dewey realized that there was a distinct possibility that he was in some big trouble. Travis Tee didn't say anything for what seemed to be an eternity. After a couple more eternities, Dewey said, "Travis?"

"What?" Dewey took heart that Travis Tee sounded more collected now.

"I don't want to be treasurer anymore," Dewey said with sorrow in his voice.

Travis flipped his cell phone shut cutting Dewey off and walked out to the living room. He fell into the sofa causing a couple pieces of synthetic foam to blow through a tear into the air. His wife was out somewhere visiting one of her friends in the same trailer park. Right now, he didn't care if she was banging one of her neighbor's husbands, which she probably was. His power in the union had provided more than enough sexual release than sex ever would these days. But he felt the weight of responsibility closing in like a hard angry grip of some unseen monster. Dewey had told him he didn't want to be treasurer anymore. Right now, Travis Tee didn't want to be the business agent anymore. He wanted to curl up in a fetal position inside the coat closet and stay there forever.

Travis Tee remained frozen to the sofa where time sat quietly with him. No thoughts entered or exited his consciousness. His mind was stuck in a screensaver mode—objects oozed and morphed into meaningless shapes in front of his eyes. Soon the shapes shifted into more recognizable objects causing his stomach to seize up. He began seeing policemen, handcuffs, the angry glare from UGLI members, and some important-looking men from the national committee. Fear turned to anger as the shape of Dewey's face appeared, goofy grin and all.

"Egregious! Fucking Dewey," Travis Tee hissed to himself.

Over time Travis Tee had become leery of Dewey's contribution to the union but tolerated him because of his eagerness to serve. But he had come to realize that Dewey represented more of a liability to the cause than an asset. Other members had complained that it was he who brought anger from management, resulting in stricter enforcement of rules. It was he who gave members counsel resulting in their suspension or discharge. Now Travis Tee knew that Dewey would be his undoing unless he did something soon. He realized that now was the time to get Dewey out of the way.

Travis Tee's first thought was to call the police on Dewey and have him arrested for the overdrafts. Travis instantly recalled that his was the required second signature on all checks putting him in the role of an accomplice. Why did he presign all those checks? The next thought brought a sobering reminder that the bank had probably started the wheels turning with the call to Dewey. Travis felt panic set in as time seemed to move into hyperspeed.

Travis Tee sat hunched over on his sofa, with his head buried to both his hands. His shoulders started to shake as tears filled his eyes. This was not what he had dreamed of when he became the business representative for UGLI. He told himself that his aim was noble, that he wanted to help the helpless. He wanted to be the strength for the weak, the guardian for oppressed. That was what he wanted—not to be a criminal. It was just like Joe King had said; nowadays unions are out for themselves. He said corruption had always been part of the history of unions and it's no different today.

Travis Tee remembered the "off-the-record" debates he had with Joe King about the value of unions. King would make offensive statements about unions only taking care of the liars, loafers, and losers. The three L's he called them. He cited cases of union abuses from the monthly *Union Corruption Update* newsletter on the Internet.

His counter to Joe King was that Corporate America was continually financing a smear campaign against working Americans. King would sarcastically correct him by asking if he was including all workers or just the dues-paying members of unions.

Now, he dreaded King's reaction to this situation if it got out. He dreaded seeing the smug look as Joe King would dramatically shrug his shoulders with his arms stretched out as if saying, "See? There you are." But King's reaction was only one of the shitty things that would come out of this quagmire. He knew he needed to think of something, and he knew he was all alone in this.

For the next hour Travis Tee sat and thought. He didn't recall ever thinking this hard in his life. He massaged his shaved head with both hands as he gazed in deep concentration at the worn carpet on the floor. The path to a solution was long and filled with barbed bushes and loose rocks. The path to a solution finally led to a face of a high cliff, sheer and impossible to scale. He was screwed.

CHAPTER 43

"Well, mother fucking ay!" Travis howled. Travis Tee had been lounging on the sofa flipping through the newspaper as his wife, Barbara, busied herself in the small trailer home kitchen. Now his mammoth body amazingly defied gravity when he flew off the sofa and danced around holding the newspaper over his head. His wife poked her head around the corner, her face revealing a mixture of surprise and annoyance.

"What the hell, Travis," she said.

"The workers at Rich Creamery are going out—they're going to strike the motherfuckers!" Travis Tee shook the newspaper at his wife.

"So?" Barbara shrugged her shoulders and stared vacantly at Travis Tee.

"So?" Travis shrieked. "So? They are going to do what our pussy members couldn't. They are going to stick it to management."

Barbara remembered the deep disappointment Travis Tee felt when nearly three years ago the union and management reached an agreement over the terms of a new contract. In fact, the members voted almost unanimously to ratify the proposed contract. Many felt that, although the union members didn't get everything they wanted, they managed to see a respectable improvement in wages and, more importantly, they were able to maintain health coverage that wouldn't hurt their pocketbooks.

Barbara joined with the feelings of the majority and was glad that there wasn't a strike. She had been listening to Travis's complaints of corporate greed for years but couldn't for the life of her understand what that had to do with them. They were living comfortably and had plenty of food. She would never say so out loud, but she felt Travis was paid well, considering he had no particular skills.

But she knew that for the handful of members like Travis Tee, the belief was that the members had bent over and let management give it to them up the ass. Management needed to be shown that the workers were in control and a force to be reckoned with.

"Okay," Barbara said, "but what does that have to do with you?"

"It's a sign! The tide is turning! The workers of the world are uniting!" Travis Tee prophesized, spittle flying out of his mouth. Travis Tee stood before Barbara, his chest heaving and beads of sweat were appearing on his shaved head.

"Yeah, okay . . ." Barbara was relieved when she saw that Travis Tee had turned away from her and was punching numbers on his cell phone. She returned to the kitchen shaking her head.

"Dewey! Drop your cock and put on your socks! We're going to walk the picket line!" Travis barked into the phone.

"I didn't know—it's just a saying. Goddamn, don't tell me that, Jesus!" Travis thought he heard his wife giggling in the kitchen.

"Never mind, get ready, I'll pick you up in fifteen minutes." Travis flipped his phone shut and grabbed his yellow UGLI jacket and started for the door.

"Hey, get me some beer and smokes while you are out," Barbara said as Travis Tee walked out the door.

*   *   *

Travis Tee saw Dewey standing in front of his apartment looking in the opposite direction as he drove up. He tapped the horn and Dewey's head snapped around. He jogged over toward the car as Travis Tee pulled to the curb. Dewey opened the car door and got in.

"Where's your jacket?" Travis asked as the car idled in park.

"I am wearing a jacket," Dewey answered as he looked down at himself.

"Your colors, dude. Your union jacket," Travis said.

"I . . . lost it."

"You lost it? What do you mean you lost it?" Travis glared at Dewey.

Dewey sat speechless while looking ahead through the windshield.

"Where—shit, never mind. Let's go."

Dewey was relieved when Travis Tee started driving away. He didn't know how he would be able to explain what happened to his UGLI jacket. Several weeks ago after he went to his locker to get his jacket and go home from work, he noticed his jacket was gone. He did a quick search of the area around his locker, including a couple of lockers that, like his, weren't locked. It was gone and he was pissed. He remembered thinking the goddamned scabs stole it.

He recalled grabbing his lunchbox and noticing it was heavy. He thought that he had food left over, which brought a smile to his face. He was feeling a little hungry, and the thought of a quick snack before he got home would be good. He opened his lunchbox and was shocked to find shreds of yellow cloth packed inside.

As he pulled the strips of cloth out, he quickly realized they were what was left of his union jacket. He looked around with a growing sense of fear. He had an uneasy feeling that he was being watched, but the only people nearby were walking out the exits with no apparent awareness of his crisis.

He shoved the shreds of cloth back into his lunchbox and hurried out of the plant. For the next several days, he would search the faces of his coworkers for clues leading to the perpetrator of the mutilation of his jacket. But he was certain he wouldn't tell Travis Tee about this trouble. He couldn't handle his outrage, most of which would be directed at Dewey for letting his jacket be desecrated. To Travis, the yellow UGLI jacket was more sacred than the American flag.

"So where are we going?" Dewey asked.

"Our brothers are standing up against the oppressors at Rich Creamery. We are going to help them."

Dewey thought about that for a minute.

"I didn't know we could strike a different place."

Travis Tee turned his head and looked at Dewey. "What?"

"You said our brothers are going to do a strike against the creamery place. I didn't know we could do that." Dewey knew he was entering dangerous territory with his question. Travis Tee got mad when he didn't understand things like he did.

"Oh man, not our union. We are helping another union. Damn, Dewey, what's the matter with you? We are all together in this fight." Travis shook his head.

"Oh yeah." Dewey decided it would be a good idea to not say anything for a while.

CHAPTER 44

Travis Tee and Dewey turned onto Eighth Avenue and could see the throng of people a block away. Travis started to feel his heart pump with excitement and his hands start to shake on the steering wheel. He pulled the car to an open space by the curb and they got out.

Across the street from the creamery building they saw a large red-and-white Winnebago with Federated Food Workers emblazoned on its side. On the roof of the vehicle three people stood, and one of them was yelling into a megaphone. A table was set up near the front door of the vehicle with a pile of picket signs next to it.

Travis started off in a hurry toward the table while Dewey tried to keep up behind him. A man wearing a letterman's jacket with the union's logo stitched over his heart was sitting at the table.

"Do you need help here, brother?" Travis Tee asked in a voice filled with energy and resolve. "We're here to help if you need it."

"We can always use help. Are you with this union?" the man asked.

"No. We're with another one, but we support all of labor," Travis Tee said.

"Great. Help yourself to a placard," the man said. "So what union are you with?"

"The United General Laborers International," answered Travis Tee.

"Yeah, we're UGLI!" added Dewey.

"O-kay," the man said, looking around at the others by the table. "Well, thanks for helping. Just jump into the picket line over there."

Travis Tee took off toward the line, and Dewey trotted after him, barely keeping up. They blended into the mass of bodies and bobbing signs and joined their voices to the others as they chanted: "No contract! No work!"

Travis Tee and Dewey were at the other end of the picket line and didn't notice the news van pull up. By the time they worked their way to the other end of the line, they could see the bright lights and cameras recording the activities.

Travis Tee's eyes gleamed when he saw them and immediately walked over to the camera. He shook his sign at the camera and tugged on his yellow jacket.

A reporter saw Travis Tee and walked over to where he was demonstrating.

"Excuse me, sir. Can I talk to you on camera?"

"Fuck yeah!" Travis yelled into the camera.

"Ah, we'll cut that part out. Can you tell me what you hope to gain from this strike?"

"We're fighting for the rights of workers everywhere. We want justice and fairness. We want to strangle corporate greed and bring the bosses to their knees." The veins in Travis Tee's neck stuck out.

"Isn't this more about wages and working conditions?" the reporter asked then pointed the microphone back to Travis Tee.

"You can't translate the real purpose of unions into dollar and cents. Workers want respect. We want to be recognized as part of the company and not like some shitty piece of furniture."

The reporter quickly pulled the microphone away and thanked Travis Tee as he moved toward another striker. Dewey managed to yell "Fuck corporations" and make longhorn hand signs at the camera before it turned away.

Twilight started intruding into the light of day when after-work commuters started parading by the picket line. The strikers increased the level of their fervor upon the arrival of their mobile audience. Some of the cars honked and waved while others stared indifferently at the boisterous crowd that was delaying their trip home.

One by one the vehicles passed until the parade seemed to trickle to a stop. Horns started blaring at the delay, which angered the edgy strikers. The stoppage was caused by a car that stopped to confront a striker who allegedly struck the vehicle with his picket sign. The driver of the stopped car got out of his car and began yelling at the striker, his arms waving around his head.

The crowd of strikers mistook this incident as a confrontation between the strikers and an adversary to the union cause. The strikers turned into an unruly mob and circled the car. The driver, seeing himself in danger, managed to get back into his car but couldn't leave unless he was willing to run over the people that blocked his way. Soon he could feel his car start to violently rock back and forth.

Travis Tee stood on the passenger side of the car as he helped the crowd push the vehicle up and down. Dewey, fueled by the image of his shredded jacked, pushed his way to the rear of the crowd. He looked frantically around the ground until he found what he was hoping to find. He picked up a mud-encrusted brick and pushed his way back to the front of the screaming throng of strikers.

The car had started moving, taking care not to run over any of the strikers that were holding him in siege. Dewey, seeing this escape in process, reared his arm back and threw the brick toward the car with everything he had.

Only the person standing right next to Travis Tee saw blood spray out of his head before he fell to his knees then tipped over on his side on the ground. Blood quickly spread around his head as he lay motionless among the moving boots and shoes.

CHAPTER 45

Dewey was back in his apartment lying in his bed with the covers pulled over his head. His head started to pound and nausea poured itself over the walls of his insides. He replayed the events of the evening in his head hoping to reprogram them in a way that made sense to him. He had watched as the mass of people turned inward toward the spot where Travis had been standing moments earlier. He heard the world become silent as if someone had muted a TV and watched people's mouths open and close wordlessly as they thrust picket signs into the night sky. He remembered frantically looking around to see if anybody had identified him as the brick thrower. He saw the crowd was an oblivious mass of cacophony and chaos, reinvigorated by the violence directed at one of their own. Becoming as small as possible, he edged away from the scene and left.

Even if he wanted to drive home in Travis's car, he couldn't because the keys were in Travis's pocket. So he started walking the three or so miles back to his apartment. As he walked, he heard sirens getting louder as they came down the street toward the creamery. He turned onto a side street moments before he saw two police cars and an ambulance zoom by, their sirens crying out to the world what he had done.

He only vaguely recalled walking and running his way back to his apartment. It was only after he was standing inside the door of his apartment that he became aware that his heart was pounding through his ribcage, his body covered with cold sweat. The only one that could help him was loaded up in an ambulance and headed, dead or alive for all he knew, to the hospital.

His cell phone intruded into his safety underneath the blanket, playing a shrill version of "Back in Black" by AC/DC. From then on, he would hate that song whenever he heard it. In a moment it stopped ringing, and the silence became a shiny wet anaconda squeezing the air out of his chest. "Back in Black" returned; Dewey picked up the cell phone.

"Yeah," he croaked.

"Dewey!" He recognized the excited voice as belonging to Travis Tee's wife, Barbara.

"Yeah . . . Hi," he said, his voice low and tentative.

"Dewey, where the hell are you? Travis is in the hospital here. They say he's in bad shape," she said. "Weren't you with him tonight?"

"Yeah."

"Yeah? So what happened? The police are here asking questions."

Dewey felt his stomach clench into a large knot. "What are they asking?"

"What are they—shit, Dewey, Travis got hurt and now they don't know if he will live."

Dewey heard the tears in her voice and felt shame and sympathy add themselves to his pile of emotions.

"I . . . I don't know, Barbara. I . . . I wasn't by him when it happened. I was afraid, so I went home." Dewey noticed his hands were shaking.

"How could you?" Barbara sobbed. "I thought he was your best friend. He always talks about you and how you will be great someday."

Dewey was shocked at what he just heard her say. *Great someday?* The words echoed in his head over and over. His shame grew as he came to understand that Travis Tee had positive things to say about him. All he had ever heard were the criticisms and admonishments, and now, now he discovered that he wasn't the loser he felt he was in Travis Tee's eyes.

"He is my best friend! I didn't know what to do. I just got scared," Dewey said.

"Dewey, a policeman wants to talk to you." Barbara's voice disappeared, and a new one came out of Dewey's phone.

"Mr. Dumphrey, this is Officer Wallin. I understand you were on the scene when Travis was injured. I would like to talk to you. Are you home now?" The voice was firm and matter-of-fact. The lack of warmth frightened Dewey, who felt his guilt throbbing like a neon strobe light through his apartment door into the night sky.

"Yeah . . . I am," Dewey muttered.

"We'll be over right away." The phone went dead. Dewey closed his cell phone, but AC/DC sang out again causing Dewey to jump and drop the phone. He watched it lie on the floor singing out heavy metal at him. He picked it up and opened it but paused before pressing the send button. "Back in Black" barked at him until he finally hit the button. The voice he heard was female and unfamiliar.

"Mr. Dumfee?"

"What?" Dewey asked in a voice that said "Now what."

"Mr. Dumfee, I'm Trisha Gabrielson from Fox News. I wonder if I could ask you a couple of questions?"

"Dumphrey," Dewey said into the phone.

"Excuse me?" the voice named Trisha asked.

"My name is Dumphrey, not Dumfee."

"I'm sorry, Mr., ah, Dumphrey. I must have heard the name wrong," Trisha said without remorse. "I understand you were at the scene of the strike when the assault on Mr. Travis, ah, Tee occurred? Did you see what happened? We've been informed that someone injured him with a brick. Did you see that happen?"

Dewey listened, but the flurry of questions sounded like garbled static in his ears. He snapped his cell phone shut and fell backward onto his bed. A moment later, he heard a solid knock on his door. He wearily rose from his bed and walked to the door and opened it.

*   *   *

Two policemen loomed in his doorway staring into his eyes.

"May we come in?" said the shorter, older-looking officer. The other officer was large and strongly built and looked like he needed to hurt someone soon. Dewey decided to comply with whatever they wanted.

"Sure, come in," Dewey said, stepping aside as the men strode in glancing around his apartment. The apartment became suddenly crowded with their presence, and Dewey started feeling claustrophobic.

"We need to ask some questions," the shorter officer said while he flipped a small notebook open. He looked at Dewey with steady eyes that didn't waver. They seemed to penetrate right into his mind. "Do you mind if Officer Moore looks around while we talk?"

"Yeah . . . sure. I don't have any drugs or anything," Dewey said, watching the large policeman move away from him and the older man.

"We just want to know what happened tonight at Rich Creamery. I understand you were with the victim tonight." Dewey was speechless upon hearing Travis Tee referred to as a victim.

"I-is he okay?" Dewey asked.

"He's suffered from a head injury," the older officer said, looking down at his notebook. "Why don't you tell me everything you know that happened tonight?"

"I didn't see much. I-I didn't see Travis get hurt or anything," Dewey said, trying to stay calm under the officer's unbelieving glare.

"Just tell me what you do know. You went to the strike together, is that correct?"

"Yeah, he picked me up and we drove over there," Dewey said, making a vague gesture with his hand indicating a direction.

"So you both drove over there in his car?"

"Yeah. In his car. Yeah."

"I understand neither of you were a member of that union. Why did you participate in the strike?"

"Travis wanted to because . . . because he thought we should support the union because . . . because they are fighting for rights for, ah, workers." Dewey found himself struggling to defend unions without Travis by his side. He glanced around trying to locate the other officer. He heard him moving around in his bedroom. "What's he lookin' for?"

The interrogating officer glanced up at Dewey then glanced toward the bedroom. He returned his gaze to Dewey and continued as if no question was asked.

"So you joined the strike to support the strikers. When did you arrive there?"

"Around three, I guess—no, it was after four," Dewey said.

The officer sat studying Dewey with his pen poised above the notebook. "So is it three or four?"

"Yeah, it was after four because I was watching SpongeBob SquarePants and it just got over," Dewey said, his voice expressing confidence for the first time this night. "It was the show when Gary told—"

"Yeah, yeah, okay," the officer interrupted, "so it was after four when you got there. What did you do after you got there?"

"Well, we started striking," said Dewey, looking at the police officer as if he were retarded. Dewey noticed for the first time the name on the officer's name engraved on a gold nameplate. "Mr. Wallin, why are you asking me these questions? You already know I was there."

"Let me ask the questions, Mr. Dumphrey. I'm the police officer here," Wallin said, pointing at his badge. "So I ask again, what did you do when you got to the strike scene?"

"We, ah, went to a table where a couple of guys from their union were sitting." Wallin jotted notes. "Then we got some picket signs and started striking."

"Were you with Mr."—Wallin flipped pages—"Tee? Were you with him the whole time?"

"Yeah."

"So you saw him get hit."

"No, I guess I wasn't with him then."

Wallin's eyebrows arched up waiting for Dewey to go on. When he didn't, Wallin shrugged his shoulders and stretched both hands outward, palms up.

"So where were you if you weren't with him?"

"I was still walking on the, ah, picket line and, and he took off toward the street." Dewey's face blushed noticeably.

"He took off toward the street," Wallin repeated, noting Dewey's blushing face. "Then what happened?"

Dewey's head began to throb, and he felt nauseous. He wished the cops would leave so he could hide under his covers. He was tired of the night—the strike, the frightening march home, and the interrogation—and wanted it to end, to turn itself off like a light switch and hide himself in the darkness.

"I don't feel good. When is this going to be done?"

The other officer had returned and was sitting on a kitchen chair near where Dewey and Wallin sat. Wallin glanced at his hulking partner then flipped his notebook shut.

"I think we have enough," Wallin said as he pulled a small white card out of his breast pocket. "If you think of anything that will help us in our investigation, give me a call. My number's on the card." Dewey took the card and studied it, admiring the embossed replica of a police badge printed on it.

"Yeah, okay. Thanks." The police officers stood up to leave while Dewey sat looking at the card. Dewey's eyes suddenly brightened as Wallin pulled the door open to leave.

"Do you have any openings there?" Dewey said with giddy excitement.

"Do we have what openings where?" Wallin said, looking at Moore with a confused look.

"At the police station—do you have any openings for new cops?" Dewey said, his breath now panting with excitement. "I would like to be a cop."

Wallin stood regarding Dewey for a moment. "Have a good evening, Mr. Dumphrey."

The police officers smiled at each other as they walked out the apartment.

CHAPTER 46

It had been seven months since her accident in the Kmart parking lot. She was still jobless; her unemployment benefits had recently run out and her meager resources were running on fumes. It had never occurred to her to sue Kmart where she, for the first time, may have had a valid claim.

Today, she checked her mailbox not expecting anything and was surprised to find an official-looking envelope. She quick-tore the envelope open and pulled the letter out, allowing the envelope to fall to the entryway floor. She hoped it was a job offer. Anita knew she had given good interviews and was surprised she hadn't gotten any offers.

After a few moments scanning the letter, she was shaken to discover that she was holding an eviction notice. The letter stated that she was three months in arrears on her rental payments and was required to move out by the end of the week.

She emitted a stifled howl and crumpled the paper. Didn't they know she was trying to find a job? She was recently injured-crippled practically—and they were going to throw her out on the street! How could they do that? This was discrimination, pure and simple.

Ex-UGLI steward Anita Kloo bounded up the stairway and rushed into her apartment. She straightened the wrinkled paper to find the phone number of the rental office and started punching numbers on her phone. It took her a few seconds before she realized her phone line was dead. She tapped the cutoff button several times before slamming the receiver down.

"Fuck!" She looked around as if looking for something or someone responsible for her current problems. "Fuck!"

She remained standing, her whole body shaking until she finally fell onto her couch. She buried her head in her hands and began sobbing. After a few moments, she shuffled quickly into her bathroom and opened her medicine cabinet. She reached for her Oxys and saw that the container was empty. She had meant to get it refilled and forgot. Now her frustration was at a boiling point, and she started running through her apartment: first the bedroom, then the living room, then the kitchen, and back to the bedroom; and then grabbing her purse, she ran out the door.

Kloo, panting and pouring sweat, lumbered the ten blocks to the clinic and fell through the front doors and staggered up to the reception desk.

"I need to see the doctor now!" she shouted to a startled young lady behind the counter.

"Do you have an appointment?" the receptionist asked.

"This is an emergency! I need to see him now, goddammit!"

"Ma'am, please lower your voice. You need an appoint—"

"It's an emergency! I need to see a doctor now!" Anita screamed as she stood there shaking with her arms wrapped around her chest.

"The emergency room is only two blocks down the street. They should be able to help you," said the patient receptionist.

"Fuck!" Anita shouted then turned and dashed toward the door. She sideswiped an elderly lady who was pushing her walker as she entered the clinic. The lady was able to recover as she grumbled under her breath.

*   *   *

The emergency room, though two blocks from the clinic, was considered part of the same medical complex that spanned a three-block area. After frantically asking several startled pedestrians the directions, she finally barged through the doors and charged up to the admittance desk. She repeated the drama of her earlier visit to the clinic but was once again delayed with questions.

"What is your condition?"

"I need more pain meds. I'm in pain, dammit!"

"Who is your insurance carrier?"

"Who shit—I'm on medical assistance. When can I see the doctor?" Anita answered, trying a calmer tact.

"Have you tried to visit the Community Health Center?" The CHC handled people who couldn't afford health coverage.

"No. They aren't open now."

"Okay," the receptionist said and handed Anita a clipboard with paper attached to it. "Please fill out your information below this line and we'll get you in to see a doctor as soon as we can."

"How long will it take? I need to see him right away," ex-UGLI steward Anita Kloo whimpered.

"It should only be a few moments. Please have a seat and fill out the form. Bring it back to me when you get done." The receptionist gave Anita a forced smile then looked at the person standing next in line.

Anita found a chair in the waiting area and looked down at the form. The hand holding the pen was shaking, and she had a difficult time writing in the spaces. Someone sat down in the chair next to hers even though there were many empty ones in the large room. She looked up with annoyance and noticed it was the person that was behind her in line.

"Hi," he said. He was a medium-built man who wore his long hair tied back into a tight ponytail. He sported a necklace made with small white seashells over a plain white T-shirt. His long black jacket was hanging open, and she noticed he was wearing sandals.

"Yeah," she answered and returned her attention to her form.

"Why did you wait?" the man asked.

"What?" Anita said with a scowl. "Wait for what?"

"Why didn't you get a refill before you ran out of your painkillers," he said as he turned in his chair toward her with his left arm hanging over the backrest.

"Why don't you mind your business?" she said then turned away from him.

"I'm just wondering because maybe they won't be able to refill them, you know," he said. "That happened to me once. I had a 'no-refill' prescription. They wouldn't give me any more."

Anita stopped writing but continued looking down at the form as she thought through his comments. She didn't know whether she had a no-refill prescription or not. She only ever had the one bottle, and that lasted a long time until recently when she started taking more of them each day. Before that they had her using ibuprofen, but that wasn't helping much, so they issued her a prescription for OxyContin.

"What did you do then?" Anita asked without making eye contact with the man.

"When I couldn't get anymore? I found someone who sold them to people like us."

"What the fuck do you mean 'people like us'? I'm not like you," Anita snapped.

"Yeah, I'm sure they'll refill your prescription no problem," the man said as he picked up a magazine and started flipping through it. She stared at the side of his head thinking about what he said. It never occurred to her that the prescription might not be filled. What would she do then? Even in the short time she had been without them, she was ready to jump out of her skin.

"Anita Kloo!"

Anita jumped upon hearing her name called, and she quickly got up and walked over to the nurse who was waiting for her. She handed over her clipboard and followed the nurse down the narrow carpeted hallway. She was taken into a small room where she was asked to have a seat, and the nurse took her blood pressure and pulse.

"Your BP is a little high. What can we do for you today, Ms. Kloo?" the nurse asked as she looked over the form Anita had filled out. The form asked for her and her family's history of medical problems.

"I need more Oxys. I ran out and I'm still in pain," Anita said, thinking about what the man in the waiting area had told her.

"What were your meds for?" the nurse asked, looking hard at Anita, who found herself fidgeting in her chair.

"I had an accident and broke both my legs and hurt my back," Anita said while trying to read the nurse's expressions. She had to give her the drugs, she thought. She needed them.

The nurse tapped on the keyboards of a terminal on the small desk for a few moments then rose from her chair.

"The doctor will be in shortly," she said then left the room.

Shortly turned out to be ten minutes, and Anita began sweating and feeling nauseous. She stood up and paced around the small room until there was a knock at the door and the doctor walked in.

*   *   *

The man Anita met earlier was still in the waiting area when she arrived in tears. She found the man sitting and casually flipping through the same magazine, appearing to not notice her trauma. She flopped down next to him.

"Okay, goddamn it. How can I get some Oxys? I need them. Now!" She had her hand tightly on his arm, and he looked down at her hand and then at her.

"So you are now like us?" he said with a sneer. "How much money do you have?"

"I don't have any. Shit, I'm broke," she wept. He stared at her as she cried then jumped up out of his chair.

"Let's go then." He started walking quickly toward the exit. Surprised at his abrupt actions, she quickly gathered herself and followed him out the door.

CHAPTER 47

Scott Carlson smiled when he heard her steps behind him as he walked quickly to his '93 Arctic White Corvette parked on the second level of the parking ramp. She was an easy mark, jonesing like she was right there in the waiting area—the shaking, the darting eyes, the hysteria—it was all there. And now he had her. Too bad she didn't have it going on in the looks department. She was ugly as shit and wore too much make up, her ass and thighs were over the top, and what was with her tits? One was big and the other was damn near missing.

"Hey, where are we going?" Anita asked as she tried to keep up with Scott. She was almost out of breath with the effort.

"To my car."

"I mean, where are we going in your goddamn car?" Anita's face was flushed, and she was panting. "Shit, slow the fuck down."

Soon Scott Carlson slowed his pace as he neared his car then unlocked his doors with his remote, causing an echoing tweet throughout the dark-enclosed parking structure lit by intermittent underachieving lamps.

"Get in. I'll get you hooked up." Scott was already sitting on the driver's side and reaching over the passenger seat popped the other door before Anita arrived. She settled in her seat with an audible exhalation of breath then slammed the door shut.

"Easy on the door, sweetheart. This ride cost me a shit load of money."

He backed out of the parking space and started driving slowly through the turns inside the structure, and soon they were back into the light of day. Kloo looked at Carlson and studied him for the first time since meeting him in the clinic. He was good looking in a slick way, with his long blond hair pulled back into a neat ponytail. His long jacket was clean and looked expensive.

"What's your name?" she asked.

"Scott," he said and reached out his hand to shake. She took it and noticed right away his firm grip. He went back to quietly focusing on the road in front of him.

"Aren't you going to ask my name?" ex-UGLI steward Kloo asked.

"You are Anita Kloo. I saw it on the form you were filling out at the clinic."

"Do you always snoop in other people's business?"

"Not always. Sometimes."

Anita pondered her situation for a moment, and soon she felt the jitters coming back. She felt a bead of sweat start working its way down her forehead. She wiped it away with her hand.

"Are you taking me to get some Oxys? I really need one soon. I don't think I can make it much longer before I blow up inside your nice car," Anita said in a rare attempt at levity.

"I don't know about Oxys, but I can fix you up with something better. It'll get you right," Scott said as he gave Kloo a quick glance.

"What are you talking about?"

"Have you ever tried meth? That shit will send you to heaven."

"All I want is my Oxys. I don't know this crap you're talking about."

"Just try it, and if you still want Oxys after, I'll ask around and see if I can find some."

"Find some now. I don't want your fucking meth. I don't do drugs," Anita said with a huff.

"You don't do drugs," Scott said with a smirk. "What do you call OxyContin? Flintstone Vitamins?

"No, smartass. They're for my pain I got in my fall," said Kloo.

"Two a day right?" Scott's smirk held.

"Maybe more because I'm in a lot of pain. So just get me Oxys and forget the meth shit."

"Yeah, well, maybe I should just take you back to the clinic. I don't think I'll be able to help you."

Both were quiet for a minute before Anita finally spoke. "Fuck. I'll try one shot or hit or whatever of that meth stuff, but if I don't like it you said you'd get me Oxys, right?

"Right. I'll get you Oxys. But you'll dig this shit, I promise," Scott said as he tapped on his cell phone. She heard him telling someone that he was bringing a visitor by.

*   *   *

They arrived at a ratty-looking house with a sagging partially enclosed porch. It looked like it hadn't been painted since it was built seventy-five years ago. Various broken down objects that belonged in a junkyard were scattered around the house. The bushes looked feral, and weeds comprised what space would otherwise accommodate a lawn. The surrounding neighborhood blended forlornly with the house with sheets and blankets acting as curtains in most of the other homes. Every house seemed to be guarded by barking dogs securely chained to pegs stuck into the ground.

"You live here?" said a puzzled Kloo.

"Nah, I don't live in this shithole. My connection lives here," Scott said as he pulled into the dirt driveway. He opened his door to get out, looking over at Kloo. "Let's bounce."

"Can't I just wait out here?" she said as she glanced around nervously.

"Follow me," Scott said and started walking toward the side of the house.

Reluctantly, Anita got out and ambled in the direction of Scott, who was already tapping on the side door. She was just arriving when a black face poked through the partially opened door.

"Goddamn, Scottie. What up, player?" the man said, his toothy smile a radiant white against his black skin. He grabbed up Scott's hand and pumped it in acrobatic motions. He looked at Anita, who was trying to hide behind Scott. "And who be this frightened bird?"

"Hey, Trevon. How is going? I brought a customer for you," Scott said, tipping his head toward Kloo. "Her name is Anita Kloo."

"Anita, Anita she is so bonita," Trevon sang then produced a bellowing laugh. "Enter, my Kmart shoppers. I have some blue light specials for you." Kloo flinched at the reference to Kmart, and her pains returned as if on cue.

Anita looked around in amazement. The inside of the house was the total opposite of the outside. The walls were painted a subdued shade of brown and covered with tasteful artwork. The furniture came right out of an IKEA catalog, with lush plants placed tastefully around the main living room.

"She needs some get-go bad, Trev. I don't think she has a lot of money, though."

"I want Oxys," Anita said.

"She want Oxys," Trevon said to Kevin and busted out laughing. "She do want them Oxys."

Trevon continued chortling and watching Anita, his stale eyes belying his mirth. Anita glanced over to Scott, who had made himself at home, taking a seat at the kitchen table and occupying himself with a newspaper.

"I ain't got no Oxys, little sister, but I got other products. I have a new batch of crank I can provide for you. That shit's tight, yo."

"You don't have Oxys?" Anita barked. "What kind of drug dealer are you? And what kind of name is Trevon? You got a last name?"

"Last name! You writing a phone book, bitch? Who you bringing me here, Scottie? She be five-o, nigger?"

"Nah, it ain't like that," Scott said without taking his eyes off the newspaper. "She's crashing."

"She better be learning to watch her mouth, dawg," Trevon said, his eyebrows furrowed. "So what? We be parlaying or you be leaving. What."

Anita remembered she promised to try meth and Scott Carlson promised to get her Oxys if she didn't like it and she needed to score soon.

"I've never had meth before," Anita said. "I don't even know how to take it."

Anita counted on her inexperience to bail her out of doing the meth.

"No problem, little sister. We is also a training center," Trevon said with a heavy chuckle.

"Yessa, we is a tek-nical college." Scott smiled without taking his eyes off his reading.

"Here's what you can do. Injecting the shit is the bomb. It sends you up like the space shuttle," Trevon said as he rose from his chair to prepare the hit.

"I hate needles," Anita whined. "I hate them."

Trevon froze and turned on his heels. He looked down at Anita and smiled.

"That's cool. It ain't nothing." He stood scratching his chin then said, "Do you smoke? You can smoke this shit."

"Smoking makes me choke," Anita said. Sweat had started draining down her forehead and cheeks. She was wringing her hands, and her legs were bouncing off the balls of her feet as she sat in the chair. "Can't I just get Oxys? Can't you see I don't have any experience with drugs?"

"You is a difficult customer. But you is a customer and the customer is always right, right?" Trevon said. He strolled out of the room and returned a minute later holding up a little vial between his thumb and forefinger. He uncapped it and sprinkled it on a saucer. Using the edge of a sugar packet, he shaped the powder into a straight line on the saucer. He opened a nearby drawer and produced a short straw and held it out to Anita.

"What you do is close one nostril and inhale this here powder into the other one." Trevon mimed, placing the straw to his nostril, lowering his head toward the table, and inhaling loudly.

"Goes right to the head. You'll feel a'ight in a second."

Her hand visibly shaking, Anita took the straw and lowered her head toward the powder. She glanced up toward Trevon, who was smiling at her in encouragement. Her eyes shot over to Scott, who was still engaged in his newspaper. She looked down at the powder then, with the straw in her nostril, inhaled. Her head popped up.

"Oh my god," Anita said. She paused a moment feeling the drug take hold. "Oh, wow." She smiled.

CHAPTER 48

Abi Deng had his back to the television, but he heard it and turned around, his eyes wide and white like an actor in a minstrel show. Across town, Joe King was sitting in front of the TV and working on a crossword puzzle when his head snapped up. Toivo had one elbow on the bar in the Broken Saddle and was leaning into a gorgeous brunette when he looked up and saw the picture on the tube above the mirror behind the bar.

"Hey, Jason, turn that up, man," Toivo said to the young bartender. Jason was an architecture student at the university. Not only was this bartending gig extra money for him, it was a wide departure from the activities involved in the exacting calculations and other mental concentration required in the designing of buildings and other projects. There wasn't a whole lot of brain power needed to pour drinks, and listening to the assortment of conversations taking place around him was entertaining. He grabbed the remote control and pulled the volume up.

Travis Tee was speaking on the screen. His fist was shaking next to his enormous head.

"Justice and fairness. We want to strangle corporate greed and bring the bosses to their knees," Travis said. The camera flipped over to the throng of picketers, and a voiceover continued.

"A short time later, this same striker was severely wounded during an incident involving a confrontation with a passing vehicle. He was rushed to the hospital, where his condition is considered serious. The name of the injured striker is not known at this time, but the head of the striking Federated Food Workers stated that the injured striker wasn't a member of the union, but rather a member of the United General Laborers union who was present to show support for their cause.

"The cause of the injury is undetermined at this time, but he appears to have suffered a severe blow to his head. The police state that they are investigating the incident."

The head of a police officer came up on the screen. He had a serious but calm voice as he spoke to the reporter.

"We have no information on the cause of the individual's injury, but we believe it is related to a confrontation with a passing motorist. We are currently interviewing anybody that might have been in the area at the time of this occurrence."

The reporter held his microphone as he spoke in earnest into the camera. "The driver of the car involved in the confrontation with the strikers has been identified as William McDonald, a local businessman. He has expressed anger and says that he intends to file a lawsuit against the union and possibly Rich Creamery. John Richards with News Time Nine. In other news, the state legislature . . ."

Toivo continued to stare at the screen, with his mouth wide open but no longer listening. The brunette was talking to him.

"What are you looking at? Do you know that guy?" she asked, barely interested as she glanced down to visually admonish her full cleavage, which she felt wasn't properly doing its job of holding Toivo's attention.

Toivo's head was still pointed toward the TV after the news bit was over, but his eyes floated downward, eventually finding a spot on the bar to focus on. A slow chuckle began to exit his mouth building in tempo like cooking popcorn.

The brunette watched him in confusion and growing disdain as Toivo found heartless amusement over the injury of another person. She snatched up her small black purse and huffed away. She was soon in the company of another man, who she was sure would maintain an appropriate level of attention to her.

Back at the bar, Toivo had expended the bulk of his amusement that was now evaporating in occasional hiccups. He picked up his glass of beer and gulped down a cheek-puffing quaff of the amber drink. He wiped his mouth with the back of his hand then realized his bar mate went missing. He glanced around and noticed her talking to a youthful college man wearing a sleeveless T-shirt, his rippling muscles proudly exposed. Toivo took another swig of beer and watched with a smirk on his face as the brunette pushed one large breast against his arm in an apparent acknowledgement of a shared celebration of body part pride. He raised his glass in a silent toast toward them.

He pivoted back around to face the bartender, who glanced at Toivo and raised his eyebrows in question. Toivo drained his glass and held it up toward him, who nodded and started filling another glass from the tap. Toivo looked to his left as a young blonde-haired woman smiled and climbed up on the stool next to him. She glanced shyly at Toivo and smiled. He smiled back.

CHAPTER 49

"Yo, bitch. Get yo ass outta bed!" Trevon barked as he walked by Anita's room on the second floor of the old house.

"Shit. I can't. I'm too tired," Anita whined, her eyes still closed as she pulled the covers up over her head. It was going on two o'clock in the afternoon, and she had been sleeping since ten the night before.

Trevon wandered back and entered her messy bedroom. He looked down at the sleeping form then grabbed her by both ankles and hauled her out of the bed and on to the floor. Anita let out a plaintive howl and attempted to climb back into bed.

"Oh no, you don't. You get yo ass up and get to workin' around here, yo."

"Why can't you leave me alone? Shit," Anita whined.

"Goddamn, bitch. You ain't livin' here for free. You think you the motherfuckin' Queen of England?"

Kloo managed to slither under the blanket, whining and moaning.

"You need to get yo ass correct," Trevon said as he pulled the blanket off her body bent in a fetal position.

"Leave. Me. Alone!" ex-UGLI steward Anita Kloo yelled, her hands chasing the pulled blanket.

"That's it. I'm rid of yo ass, you hippo bitch," Trevon said as he punched numbers on his Blackberry.

"Hey, who are you calling, Trevon?" Anita said, her eyes opening wide with worry.

"Yo, Scottie. I needs you to come and take out some trash for me," Trevon said with anger in his voice. After pausing to listen, he said, "Goddam Anita. She won't do nothin' around here. She been here two months and all she do is gets high, sleep all day, eat all the food, and foul up the john, man. An' she always keep her legs clamp shut. I wants her gone, man. You brought her here, you get her outta here."

Trevon lowered the phone and walked out of the room, returning with a brown grocery bag and started picking her clothes up from the floor and violently shoving them into it. The deal was simple: She got free room and board and, of course, her goddamn meth and all she had to do was keep the house clean and be available for male satisfaction. But she barely did any of that, and when she did manage to perform her duties, she did it lethargically and half-assed. Hell, even his friends and associates wouldn't come into his house anymore, opting instead to conduct quick business at his door. Door business is risky, but a nigger's got to eat.

By now, Anita was sitting at the edge of the bed whimpering. She could barely hold her head up as she scratched vigorously on her upper arm. Her unkempt hair stuck to her sweaty face, and the skin under her eyes was baggy and dark. She had started to show sores and blotches on her face and body.

"Trevon, please," she sobbed. "I'll get up and work. Let me stay. I'll do better."

Trevon was done filling the bag and was scanning the room looking for anything he forgot. Satisfied he had everything, he looked down at Anita, who was getting into a good cry. He grabbed her by the arm and hauled her out of her room. Soon he pushed her out the door and slammed it on her. She immediately started banging on the door and begging Trevon to let her in. Begging soon turned to anger and threats.

"I'll call the police, you bastard! I'll tell them you raped me! I'll tell them you have drugs!" She yelled loud enough for the neighbors to hear.

Trevon opened the door again and grabbed her, yanking her back into the house. Blood vessels throbbed on his temple as he stood before her quivering with rage.

"Bitch, you done fucked yourself," Trevon said with clenched teeth. He dragged her back to her room and slammed the door on her. Soon he returned with a needle filled with clear liquid. Without pausing, he grabbed her arm and poked the needle in hard. Her reaction was instantaneous as she gasped for air, and her face went slack. Trevon heard the doorbell sound, and he jogged over to the door and peeked out.

"Scottie, damn, get yo ass up in here! You need to get her to the doctor. She got wild and took an overdose," Trevon said, pushing Scott toward Anita's room, where he found her rolling on the floor gasping for air.

"Shit. Help me get her up," Scott said as he reached down to grasp her arm. Trevon took the other arm, and they both got her to her feet and carried her to the door with her feet dragging behind. Soon they had her loaded in Scott's Corvette, and he squealed tires as he headed to the hospital.

As Scott neared the emergency services entrance, he saw that there were no people in the area. Pulling up to the entrance, Scott put the car in park and ran around to the passenger door and pulled Anita out, manhandling her to a nearby bench by the entry. He ran back to his car and tore off in a cloud of smoldering rubber. About a block away, he called 911 on a payphone to report Anita's overdose and where she could be found.

*   *   *

Back at the house, Trevon was boxing up drugs and paraphernalia to transfer to a rental storage unit for the time being until he saw how this situation played out. In a couple of hours, his place was swept clean and, for all intents and purposes, looked like a nice bachelor's pad.

He put "Kind of Blue" into his CD player and settled into his easy chair with headphones over his ears. Miles Davis always relaxed him at times like these.

He had done this before.

CHAPTER 50

Physically, Travis Tee was healing at a lightning pace; his head wound showed a light scarring that wasn't noticeable to anyone that didn't have previous knowledge of his big adventure. His wound would soon disappear as his shaved head would gradually be reclaimed by his natural curly brown locks.

Curiously, he was putting on additional weight under his controlled dietary plan. The doctors wrote it off as a side effect of his medication and restricted physical activity. His facial expression had also changed from its prior glare of hateful challenge to one of open-eyed wonderment. This last change, the doctors said, was a manifestation of his brain damage.

Mentally, the doctors had determined that he had acquired permanent brain damage from the impact of the brick against his skull. At first, the medical team held out hope that his disorientation and speech loss was a temporary condition that would abate as time passed. After a couple of weeks, they saw no improvement and feared that he would be stuck at his current level permanently. The medical team decided that Travis Tee would be better off remaining in the hospital for further tests and moved him to a low care wing for observation. It would soon become apparent that other arrangements would need to be considered.

Travis Tee had not regained his ability to control his bowels, which required him to wear adult disposable diapers. Much to the consternation of the floor nurses, the large man-child would run giggling down the hall wearing only his diapers until some nurse's aides could corner him and return him to his room. On at least two occasions, Travis Tee barreled over two tottering patients causing them additional injuries and time in the hospital. After two more days of this, the hospital assigned husky aides to ride herd on him in order to mitigate the danger of his excursions through the ward. Not only was his presence causing a physical threat to others on his ward, there was also a problem with an introduction of infection resulting from excrement falling out of Travis's diapers during his runs.

Other patients were getting annoyed by the all too common sight of Travis Tee sprinting down the halls with golf ball-sized poop rolling along beside him, stopping only when they collided with someone's slippers or gowns and bounced off a nearby wall finally coming to a reeking rest. When this happened, the roaming patients would be herded back into their rooms until the housekeeping department could mop and disinfect the floor.

Keeping Travis Tee in the hospital was not only a stressor on the staff and patients; it was becoming a legal risk with the physical and sanitary issues he introduced to the facility. It became very obvious, now, that plans needed to be made to outsource his care to a facility that was better equipped to handle his special needs. A social worker was tasked to make it a priority to locate a new home for Travis Tee; and she contacted the Agassiz Mental Health and Retardation Center, which was found to be the most appropriate choice and, to their great fortune, had a bed available.

Within a week, Travis Tee was escorted giggling to a waiting van and transported to his new home at the center. Along the way he gaily chanted, "Going for a ride, going for a ride," again and again until the driver was ready to throw himself out of the moving vehicle into following traffic. But they finally arrived, and after Travis Tee and his escort were off-loaded, the driver squealed away leaving a confused and stranded attendant calculating how he would get back.

Travis Tee was already trotting off toward the front doors of the center as his escort picked up the two large bags of clothing and staggered after him. The escort soon caught up with Travis, who was becoming agitated as he tried to push the glass door open. The escort set one bag down and reached around the excited Travis to pull the door open.

Travis Tee squeezed through the opening door, which pushed the escort backward. He tumbled over the parked bag and hit the ground hard knocking him unconscious. Meanwhile, Travis was running through the center, crashing into everybody that fate brought into his path. It didn't take long for a group of residential trainers to join in pursuit of the unidentified intruder.

At times one of the pursuers would get close enough to get a hand on him, only to have it shaken off by the bounding behemoth. The chase moved through the many hallways and sections, with several near misses as startled residents and aides dove out of the way. The pursuers started tiring as the chase hit the fifteen-minute mark when suddenly Travis Tee skidded to a stop near a nurse's station.

The panting pursuers slowed and approached the intruder who was reaching over the counter on his tiptoes. They noticed that he showed no signs of the recent race; no heavy breathing, no sweat, nothing. As they crept up behind him, they noticed the object of his quest. Travis Tee was stopped by a decorative cut glass bowl of Hershey's Kisses.

With hand signals given back and forth, the aides positioned themselves in a semicircle behind Travis Tee. After a quick nod, the four men pounced on Travis, who arched his back and fell backward taking two of the aides down with him. Travis's mouth was stuffed with Kisses, most of which were still wrapped in foil.

Travis offered little resistance as he was coaxed back to his feet and escorted back toward the entrance on the other side of the building. When they arrived, they found his attendant being administered first aid by a nurse. Travis spit out a couple of saliva-drenched Kisses into his hand and scampered over to the attendant. He offered them to the woozy escort. "Please? Candy?"

The escort carefully pushed his hand away, careful not to get any saliva on him. "No thanks." He looked at the nurse. "I think I'm okay. Can you just call me a cab?"

The nurse dabbed a swab of cotton delicately on the reddened mark on the attendant's head. "I think you should go into the hospital and get an x-ray. You took a hard shot. You might have a concussion." She waved a nearby aide over. "I'll have Frank take you there."

"Nah. I just want to go home and rest. I feel tired." The attendant struggled to his feet and swayed as he stood in place.

Frank was by his side holding his arm. "Let's go, dude. You'll be okay as soon as we get you checked out." The attendant allowed himself to be walked toward the entrance and to a van parked nearby. Within minutes he was on his way back to the hospital, but as a patient this time.

At the center, the nurse quickly briefed the loitering staff members on Travis Tee's arrangement, which she confirmed from the dazed attendant. The center had expected his arrival but wasn't prepared for the dramatic entrance.

Travis Tee was escorted to his waiting room, where he sank down on the edge of his bed bouncing as an aide tried to orient him to the furniture and bathroom while he unpacked his suitcases. After his clothes were organized in drawers and hung in the closet, the aide accompanied him on a tour of the facility even though Travis had already taken the running visit moments before.

The aide, accustomed to the short attention span of the residents, patiently walked the excited Travis through the dining area, the library, the gymnasium, the nurse stations, and finally the social area outside his room. Travis giggled and tugged at the aide's firm grip on his arm like an eager dog on his daily walk. The new environment was a curious and exciting new adventure for him, and he wanted to take it all in at once.

The aide introduced Travis to his fellow residents who were lounging in the sofas and easy chairs in the social area. He greeted each person with a husky "huh-eye" and tried to shake their hands, but either the residents would recoil away from his hand or the aide would intercept his hand. The staff didn't have any history on his physical interactions with others and so took great pains to keep him in check until they could observe him in more controlled environments. Until then, touching, innocently intended or not, was forbidden.

Travis Tee wasn't one to sit still and watch TV or play games with the other residents. He was continuously on the move, walking around clapping his hands together and giggling. The residents were annoyed by his nonstop displays of nervous energy that often resulted in them being jostled in their seats as he bumped into them. TV watching became impossible even with the volume turned up to dangerous decibels.

Over time, the residents gradually kept to their rooms rather than deal with their over-stimulated co-resident, who they could hear howling and crashing into furniture in the social area. No amount of encouragement from the center staff could coax the residents out of their safe havens to interact with each other. The interaction was a necessary component of their education and therapy. It hadn't yet occurred to the staff that Travis Tee was the root cause of this demonstration of self-imposed exile.

Travis Tee, on the other hand, was sociable and craved the attention that he instinctively felt was declining.

CHAPTER 51

"Huh-eye!" Travis Tee yelled to each car as they passed. The white cotton dribble bib around his neck was already soaked with saliva as another stream of thick drool oozed its way down over his chin. As part of his vocational rehabilitation, Travis was provided with a job as a sign walker for Circus Pizza. He and his job coach would stand on a busy street while Travis bobbled the colorful sign over his head. Sometimes he would hammer at the sidewalk with the sign until his job coach got him refocused.

"Keep the sign up straight, Travis," the job coach said. "People have to see what it says."

"It says pizza!" Travis screeched out as he hopped up and down. "Huh-eye."

"That's right. Soon we'll go back and maybe we can get some on the way."

"Yes. Me and Janelle can have pizza!" Travis stepped forward a little too far toward the road causing a car to honk its horn.

"Careful, Travis. You don't want to get hit, do you?" the aide said as she gently pulled him back.

"Nooo. I would go boom." Travis laughed, making a rapid haha sound.

* * *

The light blue minibus, emblazoned with the Valley Recovery Center logo, sped along on the interstate for a short time then took the Exit 6 ramp onto Fiftieth Street. It slowed down before coming to a full stop at the signal light. Ex-UGLI steward Anita Kloo's head rested on her chest as her eyes rolled around in an uncertain scan of the images outside her window. She saw many colorful sights, mostly restaurants that she barely remembered going to once in a great while when she had enough money to spend on such extravagances.

Cars filled with people on the move passed by underneath her window. Most drivers appeared focused on the traffic ahead. Others were filled with talking and laughing people. All of the cars were oblivious to her condition, her pain and loss. They were on their way somewhere else. She was on her way for a group trip to McDonald's. She could spend five dollars they said. She would have the Big Mac combo, but not super size. She would barely be able to finish her food as it was. What teeth she had left hurt like hell, and chewing was a chore.

Prior to her addiction to crystal meth, Kloo could tip the scale at 215 pounds. Now she could only manage 120 pounds of displacement. Her face, haggard and drawn, peaked through a shaggy mop of thinning hair. Her arms bore scars from incessant picking and countless needles.

Her eyes were drawn to a large man holding a sign from a pizza place standing on a busy street corner. Next to him was a young lady who looked like she was trying to talk to him. The man wore a wide smile and waved at the passing cars with his free hand. He reminded her of someone.

*   *   *

Janelle Gordon walked to her car with Travis alongside, the Circus Pizza sign bobbing above his head. Travis was chanting "pizza" over and over again causing her to develop a throbbing headache. He seemed very happy and eager to brandish the sign, and she had to wrest the placard from his strong grip. After getting Travis and the sign into the car, she started off toward the Agassiz Mental Health and Retardation School. She drove while managing to block out Travis's nonstop chanting as she thought about signing out and going home to an early bedtime. She didn't realize that she passed Circus Pizza until he let out with a yelp. She pulled the car over to the side of the busy street, and before she could find out what happened, Travis opened the door and jumped out into traffic. He started running back from where they had just driven, yelling "pizza" over and over.

Surprised drivers veered around him while laying on their horns. Janelle turned in her seat and watched as Travis kept running straight at the oncoming traffic. She jumped out of the car nearly having her car door taken off by a FedEx truck. She ran to the curb and sprinted down the side of the street in the direction of Travis. Honking cars and squealing tires told her that he was still on the run and, therefore, still alive.

Janelle was about fifty yards away from her car when she heard a loud screech of tires and a hideous crash of metal behind her. She stopped, panting and out of breath, and looked back. There was her car shoved up over the curb and another car sitting sideways on the street, with smoke billowing out the front of the car's smashed front end. She started to run back but remembered Travis and continued running in his direction again, this time holding her cramped side.

A block away, she saw the Circus Pizza sign with the red-nosed clown holding a slice of pizza up to its mouth. And she saw Travis running toward it but now off the street at least. With the sound of sirens behind her, she pressed onward toward the pizza restaurant. When she finally reached the door, she saw through the window what appeared to be a riot inside. With her headache now grown into a throbbing migraine and the cramp in her side holding fast, she pulled the door open and went inside.

People were yelling and standing by their tables as a manic Travis scrambled among them helping himself to their pizza. He was trying to say "pizza" over and over, but it came out muffled with flecks of pepperoni and crust flying out of his puffy mouth. One table was tipped on its side, and two nearby children were clinging to their mother's leg wailing. Janelle sidled over toward Travis, but then she heard sirens again, but this time coming closer. In the next moment, two cars rolled up in front. Two police officers jumped out and burst through the door.

*　　*　　*

The Valley Recovery Center van angled into a parking space and came to a stop. The passengers opened the doors and the passengers exited, milling around the van until everybody was out. Except for the logo on the side of the van, to anybody looking at them they looked like a regular group of people traveling to or from some official function. The driver nodded and the group moved toward the entrance of the restaurant. Kloo lagged behind, walking slowly.

"Not in a hurry today, are we, Anita?" asked the driver/escort. She didn't answer but ambled on toward the door. The driver turned his attention back to the rest of the group, which was now entering through the door. Kloo finally made it into the restaurant while the rest of the group was already spread out into the lines.

Kloo filtered through the crowd toward the counter in time to bump into a lady holding a full tray of food. The lady gave out a scream as the contents of her tray fell off and onto the floor.

"Goddamn it! What's the matter with you?" the lady said. She looked at Kloo and noticed her dazed look. "Are you on drugs or something?"

Kloo ignored her and told the skinny teenager behind the counter that she wanted a Big Mac combo.

"Hey! Are you going to pay for this?" the lady said.

A man who appeared to be the manager came through a side door holding a mop. "It's okay, we'll take care of it. We'll get you a new order," he said, hoping to get this incident behind them. The angry woman stood silently glaring at ex-UGLI steward Anita Kloo, who was looking at the skinny order taker behind the counter through her hollow eyes.

The driver/escort squeezed his way toward Kloo and placed his hand around her arm.

"Anita, we got—"

"Let me go!" she screamed. "He's trying to rape me! Help!" Kloo twisted sideways to break his light hold and tumbled to the floor into the food mess. The restaurant became completely silent as they watched her writhing on the floor. A couple of the people in the crowd pulled out their cell phone and made calls. Some held their cell phone up to film the scene, hoping it would get play on YouTube.

The manager stood helplessly by as the driver/escort tried to calm Kloo down. He spoke in a hushed tone to her that seemed to help, but she would let out a scream each time he tried to help her stand. Within minutes, a couple of police officers quickly entered the restaurant and rushed to where Kloo was lying.

"He's trying to rape me!" she yelled in a hoarse voice to the nearest police officer. The officer looked up at the manager, who quietly shook his head. He looked over at the driver/escort.

"Do you know this lady?" he asked.

"Yes, she's a patient of ours," he said.

"A patient of whose?"

"Valley Recovery Center," the driver/escort answered as he checked on the others in the group, which was huddled nervously by the door.

"Oh, that explains. Okay, let's get her out of here," he said as he reached down to help her up.

"No! Don't touch me! Help!" By now the other officer had moved near the scene. They each grabbed an arm and moved her toward the door, she kicking and screaming all the way.

*   *   *

The two officers quickly confronted the wild-eyed Travis Tee, who was focused on his pursuit of pizza. They each tried to grab an arm, but the hungry man-child fought them off. After a few more frustrated attempts, one of the policemen pushed a Taser into his side causing him to scream and fight even harder. The second Taser shock caused Travis Tee to issue a large amount of vomitus in the officer's face and down the front of his uniform. A whole slice of pepperoni slowly slid down the slimy nose of the stunned policeman.

The vomit-free officer called for backup on his shoulder mic as he moved in to help his partner. His partner was now on the floor, pinned underneath the bulky Travis Tee. The free officer leaned over to pull Travis off when he slipped on the spew and landed atop both men. By now, the crowd began seeing the levity in this slapstick comedy being played out in front of them and began laughing.

Soon two more cars pulled up near the entrance of the pizza place. Four more police officers ran into the store and quickly saw the real circus occurring in Circus Pizza. They were faced with bewildering scene of tangled bodies writhing on the floor like a low budget Jell-O wrestling contest. The laughing crowd added to the inability of the newly arrived officers to make a risk assessment of this incident.

After a moment, they saw Travis Tee rolling around on the floor babbling and laughing, his face streaked red with pizza sauce. One of the officers noticed a young lady standing nearby the fray with a panicked look on her face. He went over to find out what she knew about the chaos in the family pizza parlor.

"Ma'am, do you know this person?"

"Yes, he's a patient of mine. We're from the Agassiz Mental Health and Retardation Center," she said with worried tears forming in the corner of her eyes.

"Can you tell me your name?" he asked more as a way to calm her than for information. He looked at her as she gave her name. He found himself attracted to this beautiful woman, and her overt display of vulnerability pulled at his heart in a personal way. He felt a strong need to become her protector.

"Okay, Ms. Gordon, just tell me what happened. How did this get started?"

Janelle then broke down crying as she remembered her now wrecked car and the foot chase down the busy street leading to this devastation. She knew she was finished as a caregiver for the school. She had no car. She had no job. It was all too much for her to bear at this moment.

"Please, calm down, Ms. Gordon. Take your time and tell me how it all happened." the officer asked as he made a sweeping gesture around the room. He noticed that the other officers managed to get control of the individual.

"Janelle," she said.

"Excuse me?"

"Call me Janelle."

"Okay, Janelle. My name is Lt. Todd Franks. You can call me Todd."

"Thanks, Todd," Janelle said. "Everything just happened so fast. Travis jumped out of the car when I was taking him back to the center from his job. He just started running down the street toward this place."

"Why did he do that?" Franks asked.

"I guess I might have told him that we might stop here after he was done working, and I forgot to," Janelle said. "I guess I had a lot on my mind, and he yelled out when I passed the place, so I pulled over. That's when he jumped out."

Franks looked over toward the other officers who had calmed Travis Tee with a Diet Pepsi and started taking statements from the giggling witnesses. He returned his attention to Janelle, who was looking over at Travis Tee. Travis noticed Janelle looking at him.

"I've got a Pep-seee!" he sang out.

"Good for you, Travis," she answered with a weary smile. He turned his concentration back on his soda.

"After he left your car, what happened next?" Franks asked.

"Well, then he started running down the middle of the roads and I thought he was going to get run over," she sobbed. "I thought for sure that he would get killed or something."

"Then what did you do?"

"I chased him down the street."

"You got out of your car and chased him?"

"Well, yeah. I had to. He could have been run over," Janelle said.

Franks remembered hearing a radio communication concerning a car abandoned on the busy Fourteenth Avenue causing an accident. He correctly figured it was her car but decided not to pursue that line of questioning right now.

"So you chased him here. How soon after he got here did you arrive?"

"I guess it was about one or two minutes later." Janelle looked around. "Not soon enough," she intoned.

*   *   *

"Where are you taking me? Let me out! Help!"

"Baker six twenty-one, we have a four fifteen at Circus Pizza on Twelfth. Person is subdued and in custody," the radio squawked.

"Full moon," said the driver of the patrol car. They were transporting ex-UGLI steward Anita Kloo to Valley Recovery Center, where they called ahead to meet the medical officer who would take custody of her. They listened as another unit responded to the call. The officer riding shotgun glanced back at their passenger, who was now lying down on the backseat sobbing. He glanced up at his partner, who held his finger up to his lips to signal him to let this sleeping dog lie. He chuckled at his metaphorical thought.

"What?" shotgun asked.

"Shh . . . nothing." The driver, Officer Remming, had made many of these pickups before and knew what he had to do. In this case, he would pass the basket case over to the care center with harsh warnings to keep a leash on her next time she's in public. No problem there. The follow-up with the restaurant and the paperwork were the killers. His partner managed to contain the crowd and ascertain whether any injuries occurred, which none had. But they would go back there later and pick up any information missed the first time. He glanced in the backseat to check on the passenger, who was very quiet now. Almost too quiet.

"Hey, is she okay?" he said to his partner. His partner had recently fallen in love, and lately his mind was with his sweetheart. His head popped over toward him, then to the backseat.

"She looks okay—wait! Stop the car," shotgun said in a voice marked with sudden urgency. Remming jerked the unit over to the roadside and braked to a stop. He engaged the overhead light bar. "She's bleeding."

Both drivers exited the car and were at each rear door in seconds. They saw that she was gushing blood from her left wrist. Her eyes were rolled back, and saliva crept from the corners of her mouth. Remming noticed the plastic knife resting in her limp right hand; blood and skin were lodged in its serrations.

"Call it in," Remming ordered. He moved around the open back door to the front seat and grabbed the first aid kit. Most of its contents fell out when he jerked it open. He found a roll of gauze and returned to the woozy woman bleeding all over the backseat of the squad car. He heard his partner calling in the situation with the location as he commenced wrapping the gauze around her wrist. After he had exhausted the roll into a fat wrap around her wrist, he positioned her so that her legs were higher than her head, careful not to get blood on her face. Soon he heard the siren approaching.

CHAPTER 52

The ambulance pulled to a quick stop behind the patrol car in a flourish of flashing lights and siren sounds. The two EMTs calmly but deliberately stepped out of their vehicle and rushed over to the patrol car carrying their large first aid kits. They went to work on Kloo, who was barely conscious, expertly redressing the wound and hooking her up to a saline drip. One of the technicians returned to the ambulance and pulled out a collapsible gurney.

Thankfully, the EMTs didn't have to fight with ex-UGLI steward Anita Kloo when they hoisted her small body onto the gurney. She was immediately wheeled away and loaded up into the ambulance. Within minutes, she was en route to the Prairie Central Hospital.

Kloo remained in stable condition for two days and then was released to a Valley Recovery Center employee who drove her back to the center. Later that day, a sergeant from the police department visited her to charge her for disturbing the peace at the McDonald's drive-in. She informed the police officer that she was being molested and was trying to protect herself. She was told that she would be able to make that defense in front of the judge. She told him to bet his fucking ass she would. The officer made a quick note and left.

Officer William Lund had returned to his patrol car and was finishing his notes when he received a radio call for him to return to the station. He clicked his mic.

"Ten-four. On my way." Lund wondered what would be the cause of his need to return to the station. He flipped his cell phone open and hit the speed dial for the dispatcher.

"Joan, Bill here. What's up?"

"I don't know, Bill. The chief just told me to call you back," said Joan. Then in a lower voice she said, "He sounded upset so watch your step."

Bill Lund's mind went into a quick scan of recent events, trying to peg on something that he did. Nothing came to mind. To the best of his knowledge, he had no open or unresolved business with the chief. Nor did he have any beefs pending with other officers. He calmed a little with this mental inventory, but the curiosity was eating at him. Soon he had arrived back at the station and was walking down the hallway toward the chief of police's office. Chief Erik Erickson was a former marine who had served in Vietnam and considered his job an extension of that war. He expected the best from himself and those under his command. If you screwed up, he wasn't shy about letting you know how he felt about it. But if you did your job and kept your nose clean, the chief left you alone. He was old school in his approach when it came to doling out kudos. In other words, he expected you to achieve as part of your job. No commendations were necessary in his book.

Now Officer Lund found himself seated in front of his desk in a stiff posture of attention. Chief Erickson finished making notes while Lund sat waiting, his mind racing. Finally, the chief set his pen down and rested his clasped hands on the desk. He quietly regarded Lund, which served to increase the building tension within the clueless officer. Finally, he cleared his throat to speak.

"I have received a disturbing report on your recent behavior toward one Anita Kloo," Chief Erickson said. "She reported that you made sexual advances on her a short while ago."

"What!" Lund couldn't believe what he was hearing. "You've got to be joking!"

"I don't joke, Sergeant. And I hope you have an explanation for this report."

"All I did was issue her a summons for disturbing the peace. I was in and out of there in five minutes." Lund's face was red.

"Do you have any witnesses that can speak for your actions while you were in her presence?"

"I, uh, well, the door to her room was open and I believe an attendant from the center was at the door. Jesus, this is unbelievable. I would never—what did she say I did or said?"

"She said you touched her breasts."

Lund's jaw dropped as he stared at the chief of police, who gave him a cold steady glare. How could he think he would ever do anything like that? He knew the chief was a perfectionist and expected perfection from everybody from his captain on down to the patrol officer. So particular was he that Lund recalled once somebody spelling his first name with a c instead of a k and he went ballistic. Many considered the chief neurotic, if not fundamentally odd.

"That is just not true, sir. I would never do such a thing."

"Fill out a report then go home. This department will not stand for that kind of behavior," Erickson said then swiveled in his chair signaling the end of the conversation.

CHAPTER 53

William Lund spent a painful evening trying to calm his wife, who took the news badly; she had heard the news of the accusation on the six o'clock news along with everybody else in the tri-state area. And she, along with everybody else in the tri-state area, believed it really did happen. He had molested a vulnerable young lady.

She spent her rage pounding on his chest when he tried to convince her that it never happened. She hurled several of her treasured antique china dishes at him, which he was able to bat away with his hands but leaving the expensive plates in pieces on the hardwood floor. She eventually broke down in hard tears and ran up the stairs and into their bedroom with a violent slam of the door.

William Lund collapsed onto the sofa and spent the rest of the night in panicked horror, unable to sort through all that had happened to him that day. He tried to reconstruct the visit to the Valley Recovery Center and figure out what he did that would have caused the woman to accuse him of that heinous act.

He recalled arriving at the center and locating the reception desk. He requested to speak to Anita Kloo. The receptionist paged an attendant who escorted him to her room.

He recalled that she was sitting on her bed with her arms wrapped around her legs rocking back and forth. She was very quiet and distant and didn't acknowledge his presence in her room. He remembered that the attendant was standing nearby when he stood in front of her and read the summons to her. He handed her the document, which she took without looking at them. He had asked her if she had any questions, but she only shook her head no. As he walked out her room, he recalled that she became very agitated and claimed that she was trying to defend herself and she would tell the judge.

He found the attendant standing right outside her door and told him he was done. He nodded his head and gave Lund a smile of understanding. Lund thanked the attendant and left. He didn't take her into custody due to the fact that she was under care and assumed that her charges would be dropped due to her circumstances.

All this he had written down in the statement before they told him he would be placed on administrative leave until the investigation was completed. He walked out of the station under the furtive looks of his fellow policemen.

Nothing made sense. Why him? Life had been going well for him and his wife. They were planning to have a baby and start a family. But now he was a pariah to the city, his wife, and the countless friends and acquaintances he had in his life. His stomach tightened as he took an inventory of everybody he knew that now think he was a pervert. How would he ever be able to face people on the street? It was all so unfair.

He was still awake and slouched tiredly on the sofa when the telephone rang by his elbow. He wondered who would be calling. A news reporter? One of his acquaintances wanting to reproach him? An angry citizen who would threaten his life? It rang again.

"Hello," Lund said in a thick voice.

"Lund, this Ed Grayson from the Inspectorate General Office calling about your molestation case."

"Yes, sir," Lund said with the phone cradled under his chin as both hands covered his face.

"I wish to inform you that you have been cleared of the allegations made against you. It appears the lady in question frequently accuses people of molesting her and you are just one of her victims."

Lund was speechless. Relief mixed with confusion mixed with anger.

"Sergeant Lund?"

"Yes. I hear you," Lund said. "Is . . . is something going to be reported about his? I mean, it was on the news and everything. People think I'm a sick pervert. My wife won't talk to me."

"I'll see what I can do. I'm sure everything will be straightened out. You can return to work tomorrow."

"Yeah, okay," Lund said then hung up the phone. He was relieved that he was exonerated, but the whole thing left a sour taste in his mouth. Would people believe that he was innocent, or would they think the police was able to cover up the crimes of one of their own? Would he always be the man that was once accused of molestation? Would it ever matter to anyone that he was found innocent?

He heard his bedroom door open and heard his wife's soft steps come down the stairs. He stood up to face her as she stood at the bottom of the landing looking at him.

"I was cleared—"

"I know. I heard you talking on the phone," she said. She walked over to Lund and put her arms around him and started crying. "I'm sorry I didn't believe you, honey."

Lund felt the knot unclench inside. Her words were all that mattered.

CHAPTER 54

The U.S. Labor Department's Office of Labor-Management Standards out of Minneapolis began to get bits of information concerning a potential issue of embezzlement in a local union working out of Fargo, North Dakota. The investigation was handed down to Michael Slater, who began a file starting with a letter from the Union Fidelity State Bank in Fargo reporting overdrafts on a union checking account.

Slater accessed the list of criminal actions made public on the OMLS site and found an earlier case of embezzlement at the local in question. He subpoenaed the United General Laborers International records from the bank and the local. He received a prompt response from the bank but was still waiting on a response from the local treasurer: Dewey Dumphrey.

After a two-week wait, Slater phoned the treasurer several times at his phone but was never able to make contact with him. He attempted to contact the union hall, but that was to no avail as well.

Michael Slater was left with no other options but to swear out an arrest warrant and have the U.S. Marshal Service pick him up.

*   *   *

Dewey was returning to his work area from his morning break when he saw his supervisor standing there waiting for him. The supervisor started walking toward Dewey and intercepted him in the aisle.

"You have to go to HR," the supervisor said.

"They know where I work. They can come to my area if they want to talk to me," Dewey said.

The supervisor shrugged and left the area walking toward the office area. Shortly after, the supervisor returned with Joe King and two stone-faced marshals. Dewey's eyes got wide, and he quickly started walking in the other direction. The marshals took chase, causing all work to come to a halt to watch the drama unfolding before their eyes.

Dewey, not knowing why the marshals were coming for him, ran down the main aisle. He assumed it was about the can of Orange Crush he stole from the employees' refrigerator. The marshals were closing in on him, but Dewey cut through a cluttered assembly bay and ran into a side aisle. He didn't see a forklift carrying a pallet of parts that slammed into him causing him to fall hard against the cement floor.

The marshals and Joe King caught up with the injured union steward, who was wailing in pain on the floor. Joe contacted a first responder to the area as the marshals carefully placed handcuffs on Dewey.

The first responders checked Dewey's injuries but didn't find any broken bones. An ambulance was called to transport him to the hospital for a more thorough checkup. One marshal rode along with Dewey in the ambulance, and the other followed in their car.

After Dewey was released, he was taken into custody and read his rights. Dewey complained that he hadn't done anything wrong since his last arrest.

"Why are you arresting me? What did I do?" Dewey asked as he squirmed in his handcuffs.

"Mr. Dumphrey, you are being arrested on charges of embezzlement."

"Embez-what?" Dewey said, confused. "What is that?"

"Do you have an attorney, Mr. Dumphrey?" The passenger-side marshal asked. "These are serious charges."

"Can I call my union steward?"

"I think you'll need more than a steward, sir."

"Are you taking me to jail?" Dewey said as tears started to fill his eyes. Life was so confusing these days. He was a good person. He was a union man.

"Yes. You are being taken into custody until your hearing."

"But I'm a good person. I fight for the rights of workers. I—"

"Mr. Dumphrey, you were read your rights. I suggest you remain silent," the somber agent said. Dewey started crying as the car continued down the street.

Dewey was kept in custody until his hearing where he was indicted for several counts of embezzlement totaling $36,000 in checks written for personal use. He contacted the UGLI Grand Lodge, but they refused to offer legal help and so Dewey had to find his own attorney.

Travis Tee was also named in the indictment, but he was deemed unfit for trial due to his permanent head injuries. He was remanded to continued professional care at his current facility.

*   *   *

Dewey's trial for his several counts of embezzlement lasted one day, and he was found guilty on all charges. He was subsequently sentenced to twenty months in prison to be followed by thirty-six months of supervised release and restitution.

CHAPTER 55

Kevin didn't care with whom or with what. She could be a skinny, fat, pretty, or ugly woman. It could be a dog or uncooked chicken. Kevin had a sex drive that was as unquenchable as a sandy beach on a scorching day in August. He was a sexual predator and rapist.

Kevin was forty-five years old with a head getting used to the idea of hair loss. He was of average build; and, other than being a sexual predator, nothing about him seemed to indicate any sign of deviance.

And Kevin was a residential trainer at Valley Recovery Center.

Residential trainer is a glorified term, meaning someone who watches over the residents of the center. *Resident* is a euphemistic term that sounds better than patient or even prisoner. In a nation obsessed with covering up its nasty parts, politically correct terms such as *resident* appeal to society's need to assure some form of dignity to the less fortunate. Most of the residents of Valley Recovery Center didn't give a damn what they were called. They fell into their individual snake pits and now had fang scars all over them.

Kevin looked at his job as a source of income, of course; but more importantly, it provided a steady supply of names to add to his dance card. He volunteered for the overnight shift because he would be one of the few people on duty then. The center didn't believe there was any need to have a full staff watch over its sleeping residents. So Kevin was like a homeless child locked overnight in a bakery.

Ex-UGLI steward Anita Kloo shared a room with another addict named Sophia, who may or may not have been considered beautiful in her premeth days. Anita always suspected she was beautiful based on her pretty sisters and mother who came to visit her. They would gather with her in the homey lounge, which was furnished with comfortable leather chairs and sofas that faced a faux fireplace that shimmered and glowed in the subdued lighting.

Sophia would sink into one of the soft chairs as her mother and sisters stood and kneeled around her giving her words of encouragement and pats on her shoulders and arm. Sophia's depression was deep and infinite, and her family expressed great concern to the center's onsite psychologist that she was not recovering and, in fact, was heading in the wrong direction.

The young psychologist harbored concerns himself but tried to extend hope to the worried family members. He had tried to penetrate the silent world that was Sophia but could barely get her to acknowledge even his presence. She would sit in a slightly upright position in a chair huddled behind her knees and her face hidden underneath her long black hair.

He had ordered blood tests and found nothing abnormal. She was drug tested at random but frequent intervals and was always found to be clean from drugs of any kind. While she didn't have much of an appetite, her diet was adequate to sustain her health. Whatever was going on was taking place inside her brain, which the psychologist found to be as impenetrable as a state-of-the-art security vault. He had to admit to himself that he was stymied as to what had happened to her.

*　　*　　*

Tonight, Anita was lying in bed when she saw Kevin's shadowy figure creep into their room. He stood over Sophia's bed looking down at her. He looked over at the bed where Anita was pretending to be asleep.

Sophia wasn't pretending, as evidenced by her steady breathing and one arm lying above her head as if she knew the answer to a teacher's question. Kevin reached down and gently pushed a lock of hair away from her face. She stirred slightly but continued her sound sleep.

Kevin pulled her bed cover away enough to reveal the top of her light green pajama top. Carefully, he opened two buttons and pushed the garment away exposing her left breast, which was piled to the side of her ribcage. "Nice tits," he whispered.

He took another glance toward Anita's bed and one toward the door then returned his attention to Sophia's sleeping form. He held an open hand hovering over her face as the other hand pulled the cord on his navy blue scrubs causing his trousers to float down his legs.

When he placed his first knee onto the bed, Sophia gasped awake. Kevin covered her mouth with his hand, her eyes wide and frightened over the top of his fingers. She tried to scream, but his hand was able to muffle her enough to reduce any risk of drawing attention their way. He put his face right next to her head as if he was telling her a secret. What he was telling her was to shut up or he would fucking kill her.

To demonstrate the seriousness of his threat, he pinched her nipple causing a sharp sting of pain to shoot through Sophia's body—the toes on her bare feet convulsing up and back. She emitted a muffled squeal, and tears filled her dark eyes before they ran down her face toward her ears.

* * *

In less than two minutes, Kevin was done but kept his hand pushed tight over Sophia's mouth as he panted and gasped for breath atop her now still body. Coming out of his postcoital euphoria, he looked at Sophia lying beneath him as if he hadn't noticed her before. He looked over at Anita Kloo, who continued her pretend sleeping role.

He brought his face close to Sophia's. He whispered in her ear. "You say anything about this and I will cut you to pieces. Do you hear me?" he hissed. She kept her eyes close as she nodded her head. He glared down at the small woman then hopped off her as if dismounting a horse. He tugged his trousers back up and tightened the cord around his waist.

Anita's eyes opened as she watched him steal out of their room. She looked over at the motionless lump of person covered by a blanket that was silently whimpering in the dark. Anita felt a warm feeling begin to waft through her, and her thoughts went back to a night many years ago when she was nine years old.

* * *

Anita Kloo had just climbed into her bed for the night; the chill under the covers would soon change as her body heat created comfortable warmth there. She snuggled under her covers as she listened to her parents prepare for bed in the room next to hers. Soon they, too, were settled into their bed, their voices whispering indistinctly in the quiet house.

The young Anita was just falling off to sleep when she heard the noises coming from her parents' room. She came awake and focused her attention. She listened and heard heavy breathing and the smacking sound of kissing. She heard her mom let out a loud moan bookended by grunts emitted in steady cadence.

Quietly, she crept into the hallway and slowly tiptoed toward her parents' room. Their door was slightly ajar, so she peeked into the dark room but couldn't see what was happening from her angle. Carefully, she pushed on the door, which opened without a sound. It never occurred to her that it might have emitted a squeak resulting in her reconnaissance mission being discovered.

The curious nine-year-old girl poked her head through the door, and what she saw both frightened and confused her. She saw her dad perched on top of her mom, and they were both naked. He held her hands out to the side and was pushing down hard on her mom while she tried to push back. Both were tired and breathing hard, and their groaning was quickening.

Anita stood frozen in place not knowing what to do; her parents were trying to kill each other. Who would take care of her? What would Grandma and Grandpa say? They might say she killed them. The police would come and put her in jail.

She started to weep when all of the sudden they both stopped. She watched as her dad was gently touching her mom's face and telling her that he loved her. Her mom's eyes were closed as she smiled while wiping her hair away from her face that glistened with sweat. They both kissed for a little while longer then her dad rolled off her mom, who quickly pulled the sheet over her bare body. Anita backed away from the door and snuck back to her room and got back into her bed.

She lay in the darkness trying to process what she just saw. It didn't make any sense to her young mind that had nothing to reference it to. The image of their lovemaking played over and over in her mind until she drifted to sleep.

But what she saw that first night between Kevin and Sophia was drastically different. They both made the same painful noises, and at least Kevin was breathing hard when he was done. Sophia was quiet and didn't say anything. She didn't smile afterward. This had happened on previous nights as Anita had lain quietly listening. But tonight as she listened to Sophia's silent anguish, something took hold in Anita's heart.

Anita's eyes drifted to the window where a full moon sat glowing in the night sky. She wondered at it—her life, Sophia's life . . . everybody's life. A sudden epiphany washed warmly over her body causing goose bumps as a realization overtook her for the first time. Her past became unreal to her as scenes flashed before her in perfect color. What had happened to cause her anger? Why was she so out of control of her whole life?

For most, there is no knowledge that life is a road taken among a choice of others. For the lucky few, realization comes that the chosen path is rocky, brush filled, narrow, and steep and, worse, leads to nowhere. To those few, a new choice emerges and you achieve that sense of renewal—a rebirth.

For Anita Kloo, something in the evil of this night and the beckoning moon in the window triggered her awakening. Her cluttered and angry past dropped away like a load of bricks from her back. She never knew a higher purpose that felt as strong as it did at this moment of her life. She felt invigorated and new, as if drained of all pain and hollowness and refilled with love and meaning. This was a new sensation that possessed her. It was confusing and disorientating but easily acceptable and desirable.

Anita heard the quiet whimpering in the nearby bed. She felt Sophia's despair and loneliness pouring out of her in heavy waves, washing over Anita as she lie in her bed. She pulled the covers off and rose beside her own bed. She walked over and sat on the edge of Sophia's bed and began gently stroking her hair.

"It's going to be all right, Sophia. I won't let it happen to you again," Anita said in a soothing voice. After a few moments, Sophia's hand crept from under her covers and found Anita's hand and squeezed it tight.

"I'm so scared, Anita," Sophia said in hushed voice.

"I know you are, dear," Anita said while a single tear appeared in her eye. "You'll be okay from now on. I promise."

*　　*　　*

Though Anita had made a history of false accusations in her past—including her recent past—she was able to report on Sophia's rape in a calm voice to the shift nurse, even going so far as to suggest they check her that night for evidence of semen.

A middle-of-the-night call was made to the director of the center, who gave her approval to transport Sophia to the emergency room at the hospital and submit her to a rape kit. The police were notified when the test proved positive for semen. Anita was allowed to sit with Sophia holding her hand throughout the examination.

Anita returned to the Valley Recovery Center in time to see Kevin being charged and taken into custody by two uniformed police officers. She recognized Officer Lund, who had visited her a few months ago concerning her incident at McDonald's. She walked over to where he was standing while the other officer was cuffing the sullen prisoner. Lund looked nervously at her as she approached him.

"Sir, I just want to say that I'm sorry for what I said about you. It was a horrible lie," Anita said. She paused a moment, looking into his eyes. "I'm sorry." Anita turned and walked away as the two officers left the center with their prisoner.

CHAPTER 56

Travis Tee was a 320-pound toddler to the resident attendants at the Agassiz Mental Health and Retardation Center. He alone accounted for the large turnover of employees at the center, with his constant need for attention and amusement. If Travis saw something he wanted, he would take it whether it was another resident's lunch or a whole tray of meds being delivered by one of the unlucky nurses. Too often the nurses would have their tray sent flying, leaving the floor littered with multicolored pills. Eventually, the nurses wouldn't go into that section of the center without a large attendant running interference for them.

As with the hospital, he posed a medical and legal risk for the center, with his bulky exuberance requiring a special training module to the new employee orientation process that supplemented the normal physical restraint techniques. The accepted techniques involved approved physical holds, the administration of psychotropic medication, and/or mechanical devices—all used to protect himself or other residents. Those that are assigned to work in close proximity to Travis Tee were required to learn additional techniques that included avoiding prolonged eye contact and being prepared to dart out of his way when he made sudden moves toward the caregiver. Another strategy involved carrying a squeaky toy that could be thrown away from the endangered employee, which often, but not always, sent him running to retrieve it like a hunting dog. After such a class, many new hires were too frightened to return the next day. New residents required a 24/7 chaperone until they got used to the potential threat to their wellbeing.

Yesterday was a bad day for the center. Travis Tee had just finished a struggling bowel movement and was on his celebration romp when he leaped into a group of ladies trying to learn how to play Uno. His landing caused the card table to crumble underneath an avalanche of red, blue, yellow, and green cards. He and a corner of the table crushed against the knee of one of the players. No one could be sure if it was the loud snap of the hyperextended leg or the piercing scream that caused at least two residents to wet themselves. What happen when didn't matter to the frightened groups of people who ran screaming and wailing to their rooms. Even Travis Tee stood stock still in front of the thin woman writhing on the floor. Travis glanced around muttering then collapsed to the floor himself as he too began to sob in barking gulps.

"Travis bad, Travis bad, Travis bad," he repeated over and over.

In an instant, nurses and resident attendants encircled both adults on the floor performing a quick triage and administering first aid. The injured woman was carefully transported to the medical room leaving Travis Tee alone on the floor bawling and muttering his mantra of self-loathing.

After a long period of time, the attendants were able to calm the despondent Travis Tee and escort him to his room. Travis stayed sitting at the head of his bed hugging his legs and muttering to himself the rest of the day and into the evening.

*   *   *

Outside the windows of the center, fluffy snowflakes could be seen churning in the gale as the wind chill factor dropped the temperature to minus 39 degrees. The radio reported whiteout conditions on the roadways, and a no-travel advisory was issued by the North Dakota State Highway Department.

Area schools and businesses closed allowing people to stay in bed and enjoy a day off courtesy of Mother Nature. Certain groups of people missed out on this entitlement, including the police, hospital employees, and snow plow operators. The center was included in this exemption; but several employees, especially those living outside the city, couldn't make it into work. Those that did were rewarded with extra duties as the needs of the residents didn't abate for their benefit.

In fact, weather of the kind they were in today seemed to cause an uncontained excitement among the center population. The frazzled workers found themselves trying desperately to divert the attention of the residents to activities that would bring some calm to the center. Attempts were made to engage them in sing-alongs or storytelling, but the attendants found that the usual short attention spans had decreased even more. After many creative ideas were tried and tested and failed, the attendants resigned themselves to riding herd on them.

Adding to the chaos were the door alarms that were constantly being triggered as the gusting wind battered against them. Whenever the constant warbling siren sounded, the residents would laugh, clap their hands, and squeal their delight.

Travis Tee remained quietly withdrawn in his room, much to the relief of the attendants who postponed their concern for him as they struggled through the day. Every so often, someone would stick their head into his room to make sure he was okay, only to rush back out into the commons to react to another emergency.

The weather continued its assault on the region into the evening. With the novelty of the blizzard wearing off, the residents seem to calm down as they gathered around the television to watch cartoons or gab among themselves. The weary dayshift attendants broke away to brief their nightshift counterparts and thankfully plunged themselves into the inclement weather to escape to their homes.

Adequately briefed, the night attendants loitered in the office area sharing their storm stories, which always turned into a contest of one-upmanship as each detailed how they suffered deeper snow conditions or worse travel conditions than the others on their way to work. After it became apparent that there would be no winner declared on this day, they each strolled to their assigned areas.

Ed Smithwick and Josh Cook entered the adult wing to a hail of loud and hearty hellos from the residents. The residents enjoyed both of the young attendants, who were always willing to spend time talking and laughing with them. Ed and Josh greeted each resident personally and joked with them about the army of snowmen that were having a fight outside earlier in the day. Ed was chuckling as he looked around noticing that Travis Tee wasn't around.

"Where's Travis?" he said out loud.

"He's hiding in his room," answered one of the residents. "He was being bad yesterday."

"Ah, he didn't mean to do anything bad," he told the giggling resident. "He was just a little excited."

"Well, he hurt Cindy really bad. Now she has to wear a cass."

"I'm sure he feels bad about that," Ed said as he arose.

He headed over to Travis's room and walked in finding the room totally dark. He flipped on the light and saw that Travis wasn't anywhere to be found. He walked around the room and opened the closet knowing that he wouldn't be in there. He looked into the small bathroom and found it empty. He walked back out to the commons.

He saw Josh swaying back and forth in his chair singing to a group of female residents as they clapped and cheered.

"Hey, Sinatra. Have you seen Travis around?" Ed asked as he walked over to the kitchenette.

"No. He's not in his room?" Josh rose out of his chair with a look of concern on his face. He had been on his day off yesterday but had heard about incident from the dayshift report. He and Ed were told he was sticking to his room. Both he and Ed walked toward the restroom in the hallway and went inside. No Travis.

"I'll check the desk to see if they know anything," Ed said as he walked toward the nurse's station. Josh walked back toward the group of residents. "Have any of you seen Travis?" he asked matter-of-factly so as to not cause a stir among the weather-addled residents.

* * *

Travis Tee was two blocks away from the center when Ed and Josh first noticed his absence. He was trudging through the snow in the ditch, which ran along the road that would eventually find it bookended by farmland as it left town toward the north.

He soon ambled up the slight incline as he exited the ditch and headed into a flat snow-covered farm field. He felt himself shivering violently, and the feeling in his fingers and toes were disappearing. He continued on seemingly unaware that even if he was wearing shoes and a coat, he only had a few more minutes to find safety in a warm place.

But he moved forward with great difficulty as he soon found himself in waist-deep snow requiring him to lift his heavy legs high in order to step forward. He was into the field about fifty feet when he stepped down into the fluffy snow and stumbled on a plowed ridge of frozen ground underneath sending him falling face forward into the deep snow.

Travis lay panting on his stomach spitting snow. He rolled over onto his back causing snow on the walls of his hole to fall over him. He slowly moved his near frozen arm to brush away the snow. He looked up at the hypnotic display of swirling snow in the dark sky at the top of the hole. The falling snowflakes tickled his eyes making him blink. He opened his mouth and let the snow sprinkle unto his tongue.

His eyes remained open as he gazed unblinking into the frozen night.

Chapter 57

Dewey stared vacantly into the darkness, his thoughts rooted in confusion and bitterness. His hair had grown long and tattoos covered his arms. He finally achieved the badass look he always wanted, but it brought him no joy. Everybody wore tattoos here. Everybody was a badass here. He was nothing special unless you count everybody treating him like he was a lame bitch. Which he was, he mulled in sadness.

He gave up from day one—there was no point trying to prove that he was better, fitter, more savvy than the rest. They were stronger, meaner, and nastier than anybody he had ever known in his life.

Tonight he remembered his time in the union; the freedom and the status of being a union steward and doing whatever he wanted. He recalled the power he had over the weak ass supervisors at AgMotiv. They couldn't tell him what to do because he had the power of the United General Laborers International backing him up.

But the union let him down when he needed it the most. He gave so much of himself to the union and never said no when asked to help. He never wanted the treasurer job, but he agreed to take it because Travis Tee asked him to. Now Travis Tee was gone. Where is the loyalty, the brotherhood?

"Baby, I'm waiting."

Dewey slowly turned, releasing his grip on the bars. He looked down at his cellmate who smiled sweetly at him. The smile didn't fit his face, a long scar running diagonally and covered in tattoos. He hated him. He was only nice to Dewey when he wanted sex; then afterward he got mean again, slapping him around the small cell. He would never think of refusing his advances because the slapping would become hitting with a closed fist. Nobody seemed to notice when he returned to the general population with new marks or eyes swelled shut. Not his fellow prisoners. Not the guards.

Nobody.

CHAPTER 58

The day's work had been long and hard at AgMotiv because of the rush of new orders coming in. The economy was flying high and sales were at record levels. This was due in large part to the excellent dairy and beef cattle markets. Spreaders were flying off the lots at all the dealerships carrying the AgMotiv line.

Toivo went to his refrigerator and retrieved a cold can of beer and popped it open as he walked toward his easy chair in the living room. He dropped into it and held the can to his forehead before taking a long draw from it. He was worn out.

Toivo was getting on in age, and it was getting harder every day jumping on and off the forklift. He had been offered supervisory positions in the last few years, but the thought of having to take responsibility over employees' actions didn't sit well with him. Most of the employees were good workers and people who took great pride in their work. But it's the handful of employees who brought their troubles to work that would cause him the most headaches.

Then there was the union to deal with. It had gotten better since Travis and his drama club left the company a few years ago, but a union is a union and managing with one of those on site is like trying to run a 100-yard sprint wearing a backpack full of canned peaches.

His thoughts drifted to Travis Tee.

Toivo recalled attending his funeral a few years ago. He was found frozen to death underneath a snowdrift five days after he went missing. It was a small funeral, if funeral is the right word. His wife, Barbara, who had remarried barely a year after his accident, did have a big enough heart to see to his burial. She arranged a service right in the funeral home and purchased a casket using money from a life insurance policy provided to all employees at AgMotiv. A young lady from human resources contacted Barbara to inform her that she was the beneficiary of his life insurance policy. The total funeral bill including the casket came to just under $3,000. She pocketed the rest, and she and her new husband purchased tickets to the Daytona 500 race in Florida.

But she didn't show up for the actual funeral service. In fact, Toivo was the only visitor that day. For that reason, tears welled up in his eyes at the thought of the loneliness that fills some people's lives and it's never more sadly apparent than at someone's funeral. Toivo could take a measure of consolation that Travis was gone and likely didn't care wherever he was now.Clyde would hold that there is a vibrant life after death and Travis would be aware of his funeral and many other truths now revealed to him in the afterlife. Even after all these years after his adopted father's death, he still struggled with the idea of an all-powerful God or higher power or whatever. With so much horror in this world, he had to question the idea of a god that would sit by idly watching innocent people suffer.

Toivo's thoughts drifted to that cabin in northern Minnesota. He wondered if the new tenants appreciated all the handiwork that went into making that cabin the beautiful place it was. But as wonderful living in the cabin was, it was nothing without Clyde since the day he passed away. That day rested in the back of his mind where he kept it locked up for all these years. He still had his ashes stored in his bedroom closet. He was stuck in denial after all these years. That's what it was. He couldn't bring himself to let go.

Toivo's eyes focused on the bookshelf across the room. It was filled with a large number of books he had read over the years. He scanned them book by book until they fell upon the Huckleberry Finn book Clyde had purchased for him one Christmas. He recalled all the conversations they had about the book back when Toivo was in high school. He came away knowing more about that story than anyone since. But he never read that particular volume, but rather kept it as a memento of those good times.

As tired as he was, Toivo pushed himself out of his chair and walked over to the bookcase. He pulled the book from the shelf and returned to his chair. He held it in his hand as he pondered the cover. Even though he had never read this particular copy, it was starting to look aged. He opened the book and to his surprise found a notation on the inside of the cover. In Clyde's neat handwriting was written:

> *Toivo,*
> *I will always cherish our talks in the shop.*
> *Don't forget the lessons you learned from Huck.*
> *You are a great man and I love you.*
>
> *Your friend,*
> *Clyde*

Toivo sat staring at the words with a quiet smile on his face.

"I love you too," Toivo mumbled to himself as tears welled up in his eyes.

After some time, Toivo closed and lifted the book from his lap to return it to the bookshelf. The book flipped open exposing the inside of the back cover, where he found a small envelope taped to it. He looked at the envelope with a puzzled look, gently touching it as if it might explode in his face. In Clyde's handwriting was written "Northland Bank."

Gently, he pulled the envelope off the cover and held it up level to his eyes. He turned it in his hands feeling something hard inside. Toivo opened the envelope flap and peeked inside, seeing a card, a handwritten note, and a small key, which he took out and held between his right thumb and forefinger. He then perused the card with the name of the bank printed along the top with "Authorization of Duly Appointed Agent." Clyde Gray Eagle's signature was there along with a statement making Toivo Jurva the duly appointed agent.

He then opened the folded note and recognized Clyde's handwriting again. In neat block letters the note said:

> Toivo,
>
> I hope it didn't take long for you to find this envelope. I would recommend you reread Huckleberry Finn. It is one of those classics that bear several readings. Anyway, the key you have goes to a safe deposit box at Northland Bank in Duluth. The authorization card gives you ownership of the contents. I had almost everything, and then you came along and completed all I needed and wanted in life. I saved a fair amount of savings bonds during my early years. I hope you are able to put it to good use.
>
> Clyde

Toivo reread the note then looked at the key again. He smiled at the thought of Clyde hiding the key in the book. Somehow he knew Toivo would discover the key inside, but Toivo was thinking that it was just happenstance that he would look at the book again. Toivo was an avid reader, but the thought of rereading a book was an unlikely possibility. But he found it, and that meant he needed to plan a trip to Duluth in the near future if for nothing else to satisfy his curiosity.

*   *   *

Toivo put in for a day off the following Monday to take a drive to Duluth. He liked that town and enjoyed sitting on a bench by the harbor and watching the big boats float in. He planned to stop by Clyde's shop on the return trip to see if it was still being used as they did.

Toivo arrived in Duluth around one in the afternoon and quickly located the Northland Bank, which was northwest of the city, huddled among franchise retailers and restaurants. He found a parking spot and went inside the bank.

An attractive young receptionist smiled brightly at him as he walked up to her desk.

"Good afternoon. How can I help you?" she said.

"I need to access a safe deposit box," he answered as he pulled the envelope with the card and note from the back pocket of his jeans. "My name is Toivo Jurva."

"I'll get someone to help you, Mr. Jurva. One moment, please," she said, maintaining her friendly disposition. "Why don't you have a seat? There's coffee and cookies right over there."

"Thanks," Toivo said. He poured himself a Styrofoam cup of coffee and sat in one of the swank easy chairs. In a few moments, a middle-aged man with hints of graying hair starting around his temple walked up to Toivo with his hand extended.

"Mr. Jurva, how are you? My name is James Pittman." They shook hands. "Follow me, please."

They were soon seated in a medium-sized office appropriately decorated with bland but tasteful wall art. A family photo was framed on the credenza behind him next to a gold decorative putter head and golf ball mounted on a mahogany base. Toivo presumed it to be some sort of trophy.

"I understand you have a safety deposit box in our bank," Pittman said with a polite smile.

"Yeah. I just found out about it last week. Clyde Gray Eagle left me a key and some sort of authorization card so I can get into it." Toivo handed both to Pittman.

"Does he live around here, Mr. Jurva?"

"He died a few years ago."

"I'm sorry to hear that," Pittman said absently as he read the card then turned to his computer screen. "Yes, I see that you are the deputy of the account."

"I'm the deputy?" Toivo said with a chuckle.

"Yes. I'll show you the vault where we keep the boxes," said Pittman as he notified the bank guard to meet him at the vault with the key. Toivo was escorted into the room and was shown Clyde's box. The guard placed his key into one of the locks and motioned for Toivo to place his in the other. They removed the box and Toivo was given a small room to go through its contents in private.

Toivo lifted the long lid and looked at the neat bundles of bond certificates lying inside. He saw right away that the bonds on the tops of the stacks were in denominations of $1,000. His head swam as he rifled through the stacks, noting that they were all in that denomination. He had no idea of the amount he was looking at but suspected it was a large sum of money. He sat for several minutes in confusion wondering what this meant and what he needed to do next.

He decided to call Pittman and have him bring a calculator in the room. He soon arrived with calculator in hand, and his eyes widened when he saw the stacks of bonds. They both got to work counting the bonds, noting that they were all well past maturity. They concluded that the matured bonds were valued in excess of $420,000.

"That's a lot of money, Mr. Jurva. Maybe it would be a good idea for you to visit with one of our financial advisors to get set up in some good investments. This money has been sitting dormant for too long, in my opinion," Pittman said, trying his hardest to keep this money in his bank.

Toivo remained in a state of shocked disbelief at the amount of money Clyde had left him. He felt a little guilt that he didn't really deserve all this bounty. He wondered if Clyde's family would object and fight it. But then he reasoned that there really wouldn't be any way that they would know about this. He relaxed at this thought.

"Can you just wire a check to my bank in Fargo?" Toivo said after thinking it through. He could hear Pittman talking in the background as he tried to figure out what he should do to safeguard the money. He had no idea when he left for Duluth this morning that he would end the day as a man of some wealth. Not a millionaire, but definitely well-off enough to end his career as a forklift driver. Those days were soon to become history.

CPSIA information can be obtained at www.ICGtesting.com
Printed in the USA
LVOW061306070113

314676LV00001B/6/P

9 781479 753857